W9-BPN-104

"Ruby Murphy, the Coney Island drifter whose free spirit accounts for the ravishing originality of this idiosyncratic first mystery, falls for a perfect stranger's sob story and goes undercover as a stablehand at Belmont Park to keep tabs on a stable groom with sexy eyes and a mysterious past."
—*New York Times* "Notable Book" Selection

for *Diary of an Emotional Idiot*

"*Diary of an Emotional Idiot* is a coming-of-age novel, as it might be trod by steel-toed shoes and stippled by hypodermics; it's a roman à clef featuring sex and chains, same-sex sex, sex in rehabs, and ridiculously compulsive abuse of multiple partners; it's a primitive, joyous mess of a cartoon book about the way some people live now, and it should infuriate nine out of ten lovers of heartfelt, carefully wrought novels about rural life. Be in on the controversy." —Rick Moody, author of *Right Livelihoods*

for *Soft Maniacs*

"*Soft Maniacs* is a beautifully written book, simple and direct."
—Hubert Selby, Jr., author of *Last Exit to Brooklyn*

"There is about Maggie Estep's work a directness, a clear determination—a drive to cut through, to break through, to claw through—that is impressive."
—A.M. Homes, author of *The Mistress's Daughter*

"The stories in *Soft Maniacs* and the characters who inhabit them are alternately dark, funny, sad, sweet, and twisted—right up my alley."
—Steve Buscemi, actor

for *Love Dance of the Mechanical Animals*

"Maggie Estep is the bastard daughter of Raymond Chandler and Anaïs Nin. Her prose is hard-boiled and sexy; she turns a good phrase and shows some leg. *Love Dance of the Mechanical Animals* is one hell of a great book!" —Jonathan Ames, author of *The Alcoholic*

ALICE
FANTASTIC

ALICE FANTASTIC

by MAGGIE ESTEP

AKASHIC BOOKS
NEW YORK

Published by Akashic Books
©2009 Maggie Estep

ISBN-13: 978-1-933354-81-1
Library of Congress Control Number: 2008937348

First printing

Akashic Books
PO Box 1456
New York, NY 10009
info@akashicbooks.com
www.akashicbooks.com

Acknowledgments

Much appreciation to the Atlantic Center for the Arts, the Virginia Center for the Creative Arts, and Yaddo, where portions of this book were written.

Thanks to many others, including: Dr. Andrew Stewart for rescuing my shoulder, Jim Gaarder, DVM, for saving Mickey, Avrom Robin for vetting legal matters, and Ira Jaffe for many kindnesses.

My brother, Chris Murray, for merciless questioning of everything.

My family, Jon, Maman, Neil, Ellen, Lion, and Myrna.

Jenny Meyer for glorious enthusiasm about everything.

Alex Glass, a girl couldn't ask for a more valiant agent.

Steven Crist, reader, editor, ogre.

And . . . Matt Hegarty, Tess Kelly, Paul Pagnozzi, Amy Lonas, Stuart Matthewman, John Rauchenberger, Andy Sterling, Annie Yohe, and Gerard Hurley.

1. ALICE

I'd been trying to get rid of the big oaf for seventeen weeks but he just kept coming around. He'd ring the bell and I'd look out the window and see him standing down there on the stoop looking like a kicked puppy. What I needed with another kicked puppy I couldn't tell you since I'd taken in a little white mutt with tan spots that my cousin Jeremy had found knocked-up and wandering a trailer park in Kentucky. Cousin Jeremy couldn't keep the dog so he called me up and somehow got me to agree to give the animal a home. After making the vet give her an abortion and a rabies shot, Jeremy found the dog a ride up from Kentucky with some freak friend of his who routinely drives between Kentucky and Queens transporting cheap cigarettes. The freak friend pulled his van up outside my building one night just before midnight and the dog came out of it reeking of cigarettes and blinking up at me, completely confused and kicked-looking. Not that I think the freak actually kicked her. But my point is, I already had a kicked puppy. What did I need with a guy looking like one?

I didn't need him. But he'd ring the bell and I'd let him in and, even if I was wearing my dead father's filthy bathrobe and hadn't showered in five days, he'd tell me, "You look fantastic, Alice." I knew he actually meant it, that he saw something fantastic in my limp brown hair and puffy face and the zits I'd started getting suddenly at age thirty-six. It was embarrassing. The zits, the fact that I was letting a big oaf come over to nuzzle at my unbathed flesh, the little dog who'd sit at the edge of the bed watching as me and Clayton, the big oaf, went at it.

My life was a shambles.

So I vowed to end it with Clayton. I vowed it on a Tuesday at 7 a.m. after waking up with an unusual sense of clarity. I opened my eyes to find thin winter sunlight sifting in the windows of the house my dead father left me. Candy, the trailer trash dog, was sitting at the edge of the bed, politely waiting for me to wake up because that's the thing with strays, they're so grateful to have been taken in that they defer to your schedule and needs. So Candy was at the edge of the bed and sun was coming in the windows of my dead father's house on 47th Road in the borough of Queens in New York City. And I felt clear-headed. Who knows why. I just did. And I felt I needed to get my act together. Shower more frequently. Stop smoking so much. Get back to yoga and kickboxing. Stop burning through my modest profits as a modest gambler. Revitalize myself. And the first order of business was to get rid of the big oaf, Clayton. Who ever heard of a guy named Clayton who isn't ninety-seven years old anyway?

I got into the shower and scrubbed myself then shampooed my thick curtain of oily hair. I got clean clothes out of the closet instead of foraging through the huge pile in the hamper the way I'd been doing for weeks. I put on black jeans and a fuzzy green sweater. I glanced at myself in the mirror. My semi-dry hair looked okay and my facial puffiness had gone done. Even my zits weren't so visible. I looked vaguely alive.

I took my coat off the hook, put Candy's leash on, and headed out to walk her by the East River, near the condo high-rises that look over into Manhattan. My dead father loved Long Island City. He moved here the 1970s, when it was almost entirely industrial, to shack up with some drunken harlot right after my mother broke up with him so she could take up with the rock musician who fathered my half-sister. Long after the harlot had dumped my father—all women dumped my father all the time—he'd stayed on in the neighborhood, eventually buying a tiny two-story wood frame house that he left to me, his lone child, when the cancer got him last year at age fifty-five. I like Long Island City just fine. It's quiet and there are places to buy tacos.

"Looking good, *mami*," said some guy as Candy and I walked past the gas station.

I glowered at the guy.

As Candy sniffed and pissed and tried to eat garbage off the pavement, I smoked a few Marlboros and stared across at midtown Manhattan. It looked graceful from this distance.

The air was so cold it almost seemed clean and I started thinking on how I would rid myself of Clayton. I'd tried so many times. Had gotten him to agree not to call me anymore. But then, not two days would go by before he'd ring the bell. And I'd let him in. He'd look at me with those enormous brown eyes and tell me how great I looked. "Alice, you're fantastic," he told me so many times I started thinking of myself as Alice Fantastic, only there really wouldn't be anything fantastic about me until I got rid of Clayton.

I'd start in on the *This isn't going to work for me anymore, Clayton* refrain I had been trotting out for seventeen weeks. At which, he would look wounded and his arms would hang so long at his sides that I'd have to touch him, and once I touched him, we'd make a beeline for the bed; the sex was pretty good the way it can be with someone you are physically attracted to in spite of, or because of, a lack of anything at all in common, and the sex being good would make me entertain the idea of instating Clayton on some sort of permanent basis, and I guess that was my mistake. He'd see that little idea in my eye and latch onto it and have *feelings* and his *feelings* would make him a prodigious lover and I'd become so strung out on sex chemicals I would dopily say *Sure* when he'd ask to spend the night and then again dopily say *Sure* the next morning when he'd ask if he could call me later.

But enough is enough. I don't want Clayton convincing himself we're going to be an everlasting item growing old together in a trailer park in Florida.

Right now Clayton lives in a parking lot. In his van. This I discovered when, that first night, after I picked him up in the taco place and strolled with him near the water, enjoying his simplicity and his long, loping gait, I brought him home and went down on him in the entrance hall and asked him to fuck me from behind in the kitchen and then led him to the bedroom where we lay quiet for a little while until he was hard again at which point I put on a pair of tights and asked him to rip out the crotch—after all that, just when I was thinking of a polite way of asking him to leave, he propped himself up on one elbow and told me how much he liked me. "I really like you, I mean, I *really* like you," looking at me with those eyes big as moons and, even though I just wanted to read a book and go to sleep, I didn't have the heart to kick him out.

All that night he babbled at me, telling me his woes. His mother has Alzheimer's and his father is in prison for forgery. His wife left him for a plumber and he's been fired from his job at a cabinet-making shop and is living in his van in a parking lot and showering at the Y.

"I've got to get out of Queens soon," he said.

"And go where?"

"Florida. I don't like the cold much. Gets in my bones."

"Yeah. Florida," I said. I'd been there. To Gulfstream Park, Calder Race Course, and Tampa Bay Downs. I didn't tell him that though. I just said, *Yeah, Florida,* like I wasn't opposed to Florida, though why I would let him think I have any fondness for Florida, this leading him to possibly speculate that I'd want to go live there with him, I don't know. I suppose I wanted to be kind to him.

"Just a trailer is fine. I like trailers," Clayton said.

"Right," I said. And then I feigned sleep.

That was seventeen weeks ago. And I still haven't gotten rid of him.

Candy and I walked for the better part of an hour before heading home, passing back by the gas station where the moron felt the need to repeat, "Looking good, *mamí*." I actually stopped walking, stared at him, and tried to think of words to explain exactly how repulsive it is to be called *mamí* because I just hear it as *mommy*, which makes me picture the guy having sex with his own mother who is doubtless a matronly woman with endless folds of ancient flesh and cobwebs between her legs, but I couldn't find the words, and the guy was starting to grin, possibly thinking I was actually turned on by him, so I kept walking.

Once back inside my place, I gave Candy the leftovers from my previous night's dinner and sat down at the kitchen table with my computer, my Daily Racing Form, and my notebooks. I got to work on the next day's races at Aqueduct. No matter how much I planned to change my life in the coming weeks, I still had to work. It wasn't much of a card, even for a Wednesday in February, so I figured I wouldn't be pushing much money through the windows. But I would watch. I would take notes. I would listen. I would enjoy my work. I always do. No matter how bad a losing streak I might endure, no matter how many times common sense tried to dictate that I find stable employment and a life devoid of risk-generated heart arrhythmias. I am a gambler.

Several hours passed and I felt stirrings of hunger and glanced inside my fridge. Some lifeless lettuce, a few ounces of orange juice, and one egg. I considered boiling the egg, as there are days when there's nothing I love more than a hardboiled egg, but I decided this wasn't one of those days. I would have to go to the taco place for takeout. I attached Candy's leash to her collar and threw my coat on and was heading to the door when the phone rang. I picked it up.

"Hi, Alice," came Clayton's low voice.

I groaned.

"What's the matter? You in pain?"

"Sort of."

"What do you mean? What hurts? I'll be right there."

"No, no, Clayton, don't. My pain is that you won't take no for an answer."

"No about what?"

"No about our continuing on like this."

There was silence.

"Where are you?" I asked.

"In the parking lot."

"Ah," I said. "Clayton, I know you think you're a nice guy but there's nothing nice about coming around when I've repeatedly asked you not to. It's borderline stalking."

More silence.

"I need my peace and quiet."

More silence. Then, after several minutes: "You don't like the way I touch you anymore?"

"There's more to life than touching."

"Uh," said Clayton. "I wouldn't know since you won't ever let me do anything with you other than come over and fuck you."

Clayton had never said *fuck* before. Clayton had been raised in some sort of religious household.

"My life is nothing, Clayton, I go to the racetrack. I make my bets and take my notes and chain-smoke to keep from vomiting out of fear. I talk to some of the other horse-players. I go home and cook dinner or I go to the taco place. I walk my dog. That's it. There's nothing to my life, Clayton, nothing to see."

"So let me come with you."

"Come with me where?"

"To the racetrack."

"I'm asking you to never call me again and get out of my life. Why would I want to take you to the racetrack?"

"Just let me see a little piece of your life. I deserve it. Think of it as alimony."

I couldn't see why I should do anything for him. But I agreed anyway. At least it got him off the phone.

I took Candy with me to the taco place. Came home and ate my dinner, giving half to the dog.

I'd told Clayton to meet me the next morning at 11:00 and we'd take the subway. He offered to drive but I didn't trust that monstrous van of his not to break down en route. He rang the bell and I came downstairs to find him looking full of hope. Like seeing each other in daylight hours meant marriage and babies were imminent. Not that he'd asked for anything like that but he was that kind of guy, the kind of guy I seem to attract all too often, the want-to-snuggle-up-and-breed kind of guy. There are allegedly millions of women out there looking for these guys so I'm not sure why they all come knocking on my door. I guess they like a challenge. That's why they're men.

"Hi, Alice," he beamed, "you look fantastic."

"Thanks," I said. I *had* pulled myself together, was wearing a tight black knee-length skirt and a soft black sweater that showed some shoulder—if I ever took my coat off, which I wasn't planning to do as I figured any glimpse of my flesh might give Clayton ideas.

"I'm just doing this cause you asked," I said as we started walking to the G train, "but you have to realize this is my job and you can't interfere or ask a lot of questions." I was staring straight forward so I didn't have to see any indications of hurt in his eyes because this was one of his ruses, the hurt look, the kicked-puppy look, and I was damn well sick of it.

"Right," said Clayton.

We went down into the station and waited forever as

one invariably does for the G train and all the while Clayton stared at me so hard I was pretty sure he would turn me to stone.

Eventually, the train came and got us to the Hoyt-Schermerhorn stop in Brooklyn where we switched to the far more efficient A train. I felt relief at being on my way to Aqueduct. Not many people truly love Aqueduct, but I do. Belmont is gorgeous and spacious and Saratoga is grand if you can stand the crowds, but I love Aqueduct. Aqueduct is where you see down-on-their-luck trainers slumping on benches, degenerates, droolcases, and drunks swapping tips, and a few seasoned pro gamblers stoically going about their business. My kind of place.

Thirty minutes later, the train sighed into the stop at Aqueduct and we got off. It was me and Clayton, a bunch of hunched middle-aged white men, a few slightly younger Rasta guys, and one well-dressed man who was an owner or wanted to pretend to be one.

"Oh, it's nice," Clayton lied as we emerged from the little tunnel under the train tracks.

The structure looks like the set for a 1970s zombie movie, with its faded pastels tinged with that ubiquitous New York City gray and airplanes headed for JFK flying so low you're sure they're going to land on a horse.

"We'll go up to the restaurant, have some omelets," I told Clayton once we were inside the clubhouse. "The coffee sucks but the omelets are fine."

"Okay," said Clayton.

We rode the escalator to the top and, at the big glass doors to the Equestris Restaurant, Manny, the maître d', greeted me and gave us a table with a great view of the finish line.

Then Clayton started in with the questions. He'd never been a big question guy, wasn't a very verbal guy period, but suddenly he wanted to know the history of Aqueduct and my history with Aqueduct and what else I'd ever done for a living and what my family thought of my being a professional gambler, etc.

"I told you, I have to work. No twenty questions. Here's a Racing Form," I said, handing him the extra copy I'd printed out, "now study that and let me think."

The poor guy stared at the Form but obviously had no idea how to read it. Sometimes I forget that people don't know these things. It seems like I always knew, what with coming here when I was a kid when Cousin Jeremy still lived in Queens and babysat me on days when my father was off on a construction job. I'd been betting since the age of nine and had been reasonably crafty about money management and risk-taking since day one. I had turned a profit that first day when Jeremy had placed bets for me, and though I'd had plenty of painful streaks since, the vertiginous highs still outnumbered the lows. I scraped by. I'd briefly had a job as a substitute high school teacher after graduating from Hunter College but I found it achingly dull. So I gambled. Not many people last more than a few years doing it for a living but I have. Mostly because the thought of doing anything else is unbearable. I would feel like a citizen.

I was just about to take pity on Clayton and show him how to read the Form when Arthur appeared and sat down at one of the extra chairs at our table.

"You see this piece of shit Pletcher's running in the fifth race?" Arthur wanted to know. Arthur, who weighs 125 pounds tops, isn't one for pleasantries. He had no interest in being introduced to Clayton and probably hadn't even noticed I was with someone. He just wanted confirmation that the Todd Pletcher–trained colt in the fifth race was a piece of shit in spite of having cost 2.4 million at the Keeneland yearling sale.

"Yeah," I said, nodding gravely. "He'll be 1-9."

"He's a flea," said Arthur.

"Yeah. Well. I wouldn't throw him out on a Pick 6 ticket."

"I'm throwing him out."

"Okay," I said.

"He hasn't faced shit and he's never gone two turns. And there's that nice little horse of Nick's that's a closer."

"Right," I said.

"I'm using Nick's horse. Singling him."

"I wouldn't throw out the Pletcher horse."

"Fuck him," said Arthur, getting up and storming off to the other end of the place where I saw him take a seat with some guys from the Daily Racing Form.

"Friend of yours?" asked Clayton.

I nodded. "Arthur. He's a good guy."

"He is?"

"Sure."

I could tell Clayton wanted to go somewhere with that one. Wanted to ask why I thought some strange little guy who just sat down and started cursing out horses was a good guy. Another reason Clayton had to be gotten rid of.

One of the waiters came and took our omelet order. Since I'd mapped out most of my bets, I took ten minutes to give Clayton a cursory introduction to reading horses' past performances. I was leaning in close, my finger tracing one of the horse's running lines, when Clayton kissed my ear.

"I love you, Alice," he said.

"Jesus, Clayton. What the fuck?"

He looked like a kicked puppy.

"I brought you here because I thought it'd be a nice way to spend our last day together but, fuck me, why do you have to get ridiculous?" I asked.

"I don't want it to end. You're all I've got."

"You don't have me."

"What do you mean?"

"Clayton, there's no future. *No más*," I said.

"No who?"

"*No más*," I repeated. "No more. Spanish."

"Are you Spanish?"

"No, Clayton, I'm not Spanish. Shit, will you let me fucking work?"

"Everything okay over here?"

I looked up and saw Vito looming over the table. Vito is a stocky, hairy man who is some kind of low-level mob or mob wannabe who owns a few cheap horses. He fancies himself a gifted horseplayer but is, I'm sure, one of the many who flat out lies about his profits.

"Everything's fine," I said, scowling at Vito. Much as Clayton was pissing me off, it wasn't any of Vito's business. But that's the thing with these Vito-type guys at the track, what with my being a presentable woman under the age of eighty, a real rarity at Aqueduct—these guys get all protective of me. It might have been vaguely heartwarming if Vito wasn't so smarmy.

Vito furrowed his monobrow. He was sweating profusely even though it was cool inside the restaurant.

"I'm Vito," he said, aggressively extending his hand to Clayton, "and you are . . . ?"

"Clayton," said my soon-to-be-ex-paramour, tentatively shaking Vito's pudgy, oily paw.

"We all look out for Alice around here," Vito said.

Go fuck yourself, Vito, I thought, but didn't say. There might be a time when I needed Vito for something.

"Oh," said Clayton, confused, "that's good. I look out for her too."

Vito narrowed his already small eyes, looked from me to Clayton and back, then turned on his heels.

"See ya, Vito," I said as the tub of a man headed out of the restaurant, presumably going down to the paddock-viewing area to volubly express his opinions about the contestants in the first race.

A few races passed. I made a nice little score on a mare shipping in from Philadelphia Park. She was trained by an obscure woman trainer, ridden by some obscure apprentice jockey, and had only ever raced at Philadelphia Park, so in spite of a nice batch of past performances, she was being ignored on the tote board and went off at 14-1. I had $200 on her to win and wheeled her on top of all the logical horses in an exacta. I made out nicely and that put me slightly at ease and reduced some of the Clayton-induced aggravation that had gotten so severe I hadn't been able to eat my omelet and had started fantasizing about asking Vito to take Clayton out. Not *Take Him Out* take him out, I didn't want the guy dead or anything, but just put a scare into him. Only that would have entailed asking a favor of Vito and I had no interest in establishing that kind of dynamic with that kind of guy.

The fifth race came and I watched with interest to see how the colt Arthur liked fared. The Todd Pletcher–trained colt Arthur hated, who did in fact go off at 1-9, broke alertly from the six hole and tucked nicely just off the pace that was being set by a longshot with early speed. Gang of Seven, the horse Arthur liked, was at the back of the pack, biding his time. With a quarter of a mile to go, Gang of Seven started making his move four wide, picking off his opponents until he was within spitting distance of the Pletcher horse. Gang of Seven and the Pletcher trainee dueled to the wire and they appeared to get their noses there at the same time.

"Too close to call!" the track announcer exclaimed.

A few minutes later, the photo was posted and the Pletcher horse had beat Big Arthur's horse by a whisker.

"I'm a fucking idiot!" I heard Arthur cry out from four tables away. I saw him get up and storm out of the restaurant, presumably to go to the back patio to chain-smoke and make phone calls to twenty of his closest horseplaying friends proclaiming his own idiocy.

"Guy's got a problem," Clayton said.

"No he doesn't," I replied. While it was true that Arthur had a little trouble with anger management, he was, at heart, a very decent human being.

I got up and walked away, leaving Clayton to stare after me with those dinner plate–sized eyes.

I went down to the paddock, hoping that Clayton wouldn't follow me. I saw Vito there, staring out the big glass window, his huge belly pressing against it. Searching for a spot as far away as possible from Vito, I craned my neck just to check that Clayton hadn't followed me. He had. I saw him lumbering around near the betting windows, looking left and right. He'd find me at any minute. And then I'd never get rid of him. Another seventeen weeks would follow.

I needed to give him a clear message, so I did something a little crazy.

"Vito," I said, coming up behind him.

"Huh?" He turned around.

"Favor?" I asked.

His tiny black eyes glittered.

"Anything, baby," he purred.

I already regretted what I was doing.

"Can you scare that guy I was sitting with? Just make him a little nervous? Make him go home?"

Vito's tiny eyes got bigger, like someone had just dangled a bleeding hunk of meat in front of him.

"You serious?" He stood closer to me.

I had a moment's hesitation. Then thought of Clayton's love pronouncements.

"Yeah," I said.

"Sure. Where is he?"

I glanced back but didn't see Clayton.

"Somewhere around here, let's look."

Vito followed at my side. We looked all around the betting windows of the ground floor, but no Clayton. Then I glanced outside and saw him standing near an empty bench, hunched and cold and lost-looking under the dove-gray sky.

"There," I said.

"You got it, baby."

Without another word, Vito marched outside. I saw him accost Clayton. I saw Clayton tilt his head left and right like a confused dog would. I thought of Candy. Later this afternoon I'd go home to her and just maybe, thanks to Vito, I wouldn't have to worry about the big oaf turning up with his big eyes and his inane declarations. Candy and I would have some peace and quiet.

Now Clayton and Vito had come back inside and were walking together. They passed not far from where I was standing. Where was Vito taking him? I'd figured on his just saying a few choice words to Clayton and that would be that. But Vito seemed to be taking him somewhere.

I followed them at a slight distance. They went down the escalator and out the front door. Vito was only wearing a thin button-down shirt but he didn't seem to register the bite of the February air. Clayton pulled his coat up around his ears.

They headed over to the subway platform. I saw Clayton take out his MetroCard and go through the turnstile. Then he handed his card back to Vito who went through after him.

What the fuck?

I stopped walking and stayed where I was in the middle of the ramp leading to the turnstiles. The two men were about a hundred yards in front of me but they had their backs to me. There wasn't anyone else on the platform.

They started raising their voices. I couldn't hear what was being said. There was wind and a big airplane with its belly low against the sky.

Then the sound of an oncoming train and a blur of movement.

A body falling down into the tracks just as the train came. I braced myself for the screeching of brakes. There wasn't any. The train charged into the station. The doors opened then closed. No one got on or off. The train pulled away. There was just one guy left standing on the platform. He was looking down at the tracks.

My fingers were numb and I was getting a headache.

I slowly walked up the platform. Found my Metro-Card in my coat. Slid it in and went through the turnstile. I walked to the edge and looked down at the tracks. There was an arm separated from the rest of the body. Blood pouring out the shoulder. The head twisted at an angle you never saw in life. I wasn't sure how the train conductor had failed to notice. The MTA has been very proud of its new One-Person Train Operation system that requires just one human to operate the entire train. Maybe that's not enough to keep an eye out for falling bodies.

I felt nauseous. I started to black out and then he steadied me, putting his hand at the small of my back

"He was talking about you," said Clayton, staring down at Vito's big mangled body, "said you were going to blow him in exchange for him getting rid of me. He was just trying to upset me but it was disrespectful of you. I just wanted to scare him but I pushed him too hard and he fell onto the tracks." Clayton spoke so calmly. "He was talking shit about you, Alice," he added, raising his voice a little.

"Well," I said, "that wasn't very nice of him, was it?"

Clayton smiled.

He really wasn't a bad-looking guy.

2. ELOISE

The phone woke me.

"Yeah?" I said, after reaching blindly toward the nightstand, knocking the lamp off, and finally grabbing the phone.

"Eloise Hunter?"

"Yes?" It sounded like very bad news.

It was.

Indio, my lover, a Brazilian trapeze instructor, had plunged to his death while scrambling up the side of the Queensboro Bridge.

His family had been contacted in Brazil but could not come up. They had given the medical examiner my name. Would I identify the body?

"The body," I said.

"Yes," said the voice. "If you could."

Could I?

I said I would.

I hung the phone up. Looked at the clock. It was just after 8 a.m. I picked the bedside lamp off the floor. I went into the bathroom. I banged my shin into the toilet. I tried to vomit but could not. I threw water on my face. I looked around the bathroom. The tiny, blue-tiled bathroom of my tiny apartment on Riverside Drive and 101st Street. I don't know what I was looking for. There was nothing to find.

Indio and I had broken up. Seven times. He wanted to be around me constantly. I wanted to be around him occasionally. I didn't love him but he was always there. Now he was a body that needed identifying.

He had told me about it. How he was going to practice,

in the middle of the night, an illegal stunt he planned to do later in daylight, for a few dozen invited friends. Swinging from one part to another of the Queensboro Bridge. When he'd told me about this plan, I had just shrugged. It wasn't any stranger or more dangerous than other stunts he had performed. At least, I hadn't thought so.

I went into my small kitchen. My cat, Hammie, was on the counter, clamoring for breakfast. I fed her then knelt down and ran my hand over the gray fur on her spine. I hunkered over her and sniffed at the back of her neck, taking in the soothing creature smell there.

I stared around at my little kitchen. I got the can of Café Bustelo out from the cupboard. Scooped some into a filter and started the coffee brewing. I watched the thick brown liquid drip down into the glass carafe.

It was long done brewing by the time I was able to make my body move in order to pour myself a cup.

I went to sit at the edge of my bed. I picked up my book. A Harry Crews novel I was just starting. I'd planned to have a lazy morning, reading in bed. I tried to read a sentence but it blurred.

As I sipped my coffee, I watched Hammie bathing herself. I pictured Indio's beautiful body.

I took my pajamas off and stood naked, staring into my closet.

My bad leg, which had been shattered when I'd fallen in a manhole three years earlier, was aching.

I didn't have to wait long. A woman in a white coat brought me to a window. I looked through and saw Indio on a stretcher. Only his head was visible, the rest covered in a sheet. His face looked fine. There was some bruising on the right side but he just looked tired. Like he was napping after a nasty spill and would wake up, thrilled to find me there.

I truly expected him to sit up, bang on the glass, and

maybe ask me, in his singsongy voice, if I'd like to go have an adventure.

"Yes," I said. "That's him."

I wondered what the rest of him looked like. The parts covered by the sheet. I'd been told he'd broken his spine. But it didn't show on his face.

"Goodbye," I said to him through the glass. The woman standing next to me, some sort of morgue worker, said nothing.

I walked out into the cool spring morning. Traffic was bustling up First Avenue. The sky was a pale blue.

I came home and sat heavily on the bed that took up most of the small living area. Hammie rubbed her gray head against my calves. I stared at my boots. They were sexy, knee-high boots. Indio had loved them.

As I sat considering whether or not to go back to bed, the doorbell rang. I went to the window to look down and saw my mother standing on my stoop with a massive brown pit bull at her side.

"Mom," I called down through the window. "What is it?"

My mother lives a hundred miles north of New York City, in Woodstock, where she has a little wooden house and two acres on which she keeps rescued dogs that she tries to find homes for. Whenever she encounters a dog she doesn't have room for, she turns up on my doorstep, unannounced, expecting me to foster the dog in question.

"I have a present for you, sweetheart." My mother was craning her neck and her still-youngish face looked exuberant, like a little kid who has just played a prank on her elders.

"Indio is dead," I said.

"What?" My mother screwed her face up.

"Indio fell off a bridge and died."

As my mother struggled with this information, one of

my downstairs neighbors, Jeff, opened his window and looked up at me.

"Eloise, you're not taking that monstrous dog into your apartment. It will kill you and eat your flesh."

"Yes, Jeff, I know," I said.

Jeff likes to think about things like my being devoured by wild dogs. Maybe this is why I find him attractive.

"Just come on up, Mom," I said. I pulled my head back out of the window and hit the buzzer, opening the downstairs door.

"You're not serious about Indio," my mother said as she came into my apartment, gently tugging on the massive brown dog's leash. The pit bull seemed hesitant to cross my threshold. Looked timidly from my mother to me and, after much encouragement, finally came in.

"Yes. He's dead. I had to identify his body," I said without emotion.

"Oh Eloise." My mother dropped the beast's leash and threw her arms around me. I felt myself stiffen.

My mother gave up on trying to get me to surrender to the hug and sat down on the bed. The pit bull looked around nervously, waiting for a cue from Mom, who patted the bed, indicating the dog should jump up there.

"Mom, I don't even like dogs."

"Eloise, tell me about Indio," my mother said, willfully ignoring my statement. "How did this happen, when did you find out?"

I gave her the facts.

"I don't like dogs, Mom," I reiterated when I'd finished telling her about Indio. "I appreciate what you do to save them but I'm tired of taking dogs in."

"Eloise, you're shut down. You've just experienced something incredibly painful. You need to talk about it."

My mother's face was so earnest. So lovely. Her olive skin clear and free of wrinkles. Her wild, curly black hair flying all around. At fifty-three, she is twenty-four years older than me but could pass for my older sister. She has led an unconventional life and it has agreed with her.

"Oh, Mom," I said. "I can't talk about it. Do you want some coffee?"

"Yes, please."

I trudged over to the kitchen area where Hammie was perched on the counter, looking extremely upset about the presence of a dog.

"Did you tell Alice?" my mother called out.

"This just happened this morning."

"I wish you two were closer," my mother said.

"It's not a lack of closeness. I haven't had time to call my sister. I literally just got back from the morgue when you turned up on my doorstep with a pit bull." I motioned at the beast tentatively wagging its tail.

"Having experienced death today, surely you can understand why I could not leave Turbo to die. She was scheduled for the gas chamber tomorrow."

"Mom, you're guilt tripping me when my lover has just died?"

"I'm sorry." My mother actually hung her head.

It took forty-five minutes to convince my mother I was all right and get her to leave me in peace. Of course, I had to agree to foster Turbo. And now, Turbo and I were staring at each other. I hadn't wanted to admit it in front of my mother, but I thought that this solid brown dog with a shady past might help keep the ghosts at bay.

"Hello, Turbo," I said as I sat at the kitchen table, sipping another cup of coffee. She tilted her big, square head and appeared to smile. She couldn't have actually known her name since it had just been assigned to her at the shelter. She was simply responding to the sound of my voice. She seemed to like me, but then again, she would have probably liked anyone who showed her kindness.

A week after Indio's death, I tried getting back to work.

Not that I have to work. I'm rich, or at least rich by my standards, having gone from dirt poor to 1.2 million just about overnight when I fell in that manhole, crushed my pelvis, stayed in a coma for two weeks, and came out of it to find an ambulance-chaser lawyer with a comb-over sitting vigil at my bedside. It was a big case for him, actually winning and getting all that money out of the city. And, as I mourned the fact that the city I love had literally tried to devour me by sucking me down into its entrails and crushing my pelvis, the doctors and surgeons pieced me back together. I can walk, but I have a hitch in my step from one leg being shorter than the other. And I'm extremely wary of movable *things* in the streets and sidewalks.

But as a result of that money, I don't have to work. Yet I do. I've had my own small business since the age of sixteen when I started making unconventional stuffed animals. Mythical beasts with enormous heads, tiny bodies, and long, snaking tails. Sometimes they have the heads of dogs and the bodies of rats. Other times they are part giraffe. Still others are entirely unrecognizable except as things I've seen in my dreams. I love my beasts and it's a heartbreak each time I finish one and have to put it into the closet where I store all the finished animals that I'll eventually distribute to the toy stores that carry my work. Now that I have money, I could just hoard them all until I've spent every last dime. But that wouldn't be right either. I make my beasts so they can go out into the world.

I had just started making drawings for a giant cockroach with a dog's head. But my heart wasn't in it. In fact, I wasn't sure I had a heart. Since Indio's death, I had felt nothing other than swells of affection for Turbo, whose sweetness and willingness were hard to ignore.

"Do you want to walk?" I asked Turbo.

Her language skills were improving. She now understood "Walk," "Food," "No Kitty," and "Sit." "Walk" was her favorite. She got up off her dog bed, spun around in two quick circles, then sat and grinned up at me, exposing her pink gums and the tip of her tongue.

Turbo bounded down the stairs and out onto the side-walk. She trotted proudly at my side. The first week she'd been with me, she'd alternated between pulling wildly and stopping dead in her tracks, staring all around at this world that by turns amazed and frightened her. Now she had some confidence. She was a dog who believed in some-thing.

We walked then walked some more. Turbo was enthu-siastic about each new block, each garbage can that needed sniffing, each person or dog we passed, most of them ignor-ing her grinning face and wagging tail, some going so far as to cross the street. I liked this about her. That she looked like a monster but was filled with love for everything.

We wandered all the way to Central Park and, since Turbo was still full of beans, we entered. Darkness was falling, the budding trees throwing shadows, but it's not like I was worried with the powerful brown beast at my side. I doubted she would actually attack someone com-ing after me, but her looks alone would give any would-be thugs pause.

We had ambled all the way down to the boathouse and were following a nice, well-lit path, when I somehow tripped over a tree root, went sprawling, and landed face first.

I wanted to wail. I'm ridiculously accident-prone but I hadn't actually banged into anything or fallen off a side-walk in well over a week and thought maybe this was due to the death of Indio, that this was a big enough dose of emotional pain to ward off any physical stumbles.

As I lay there, feeling my face stinging and my lip throb-bing, Turbo put her muzzle next to my mouth and tried to lick the blood pouring out of my lip.

I gently pushed her back.

"That looks awful," a voice said.

I glanced up to find a lanky, fair-haired guy standing there. As I blinked up at him, he squatted down and reached over to touch my face. I stared at him, transfixed. Turbo looked from the guy to me and back, waiting for a signal in case I needed protection.

"It's okay, Turbo," I said, though I wasn't sure that it was.

"You're going to need stitches. Your lip is bleeding. Here."

The stranger produced a handkerchief from a pocket. A genuine handkerchief. I hadn't seen one since my Grandpa Edgar had died in 1987.

"You have a handkerchief?" I asked as I held said handkerchief to my lip, soaking it with blood.

"A gentleman always has a handkerchief," he replied. "What happened to you?"

"I tripped on a branch. I'm very clumsy," I said. "And unlucky. My half-sister earns a living as a professional gambler. She got all the luck in our family. My mother and I are clumsy losers." I was babbling, as I often do right after an accident. The day I came to after my manhole coma, they couldn't shut me up.

"Oh?" the guy tilted his head.

He was big and attractive. Or maybe I was just dazed and susceptible.

"Can I help you to the hospital?" he asked.

"I'd prefer not to."

"Prefer not to what?"

"Prefer not to go to the hospital. They're all crazy."

"Hospitals or the medical profession?"

"Both," I said.

He smiled. He was missing a front tooth. It was incongruous. He was well-dressed, apparently solvent and healthy, yet missing a front tooth. I stared at the space in his mouth as he helped me to my feet.

"As much as it may pain you to put yourself at the mercy of the medical profession, I do believe you should let me take you to the emergency room. My car is right on Fifth Avenue. I'll run you down to NYU Medical Center. It's arguably less offensive than other ERs."

I nodded dumbly, tugged on Turbo's leash, and followed the man with the missing tooth to his car.

He helped me usher Turbo into the backseat where she plopped down, pleased at our adventure's unusual turn.

"I'm Billy, by the way," he said as he simultaneously maneuvered the car into traffic and gave me another handkerchief, this one plucked from the glove compartment of his Saab.

"Eloise," I said.

"Nice to meet you."

Billy kept Turbo entertained outside the hospital the entire two and a half hours it took for me to get taken care of. As I got my lip numbed then sewn up by a young and enthusiastic resident, I thought of Billy. It made no sense. I am not impulsive with men. That's my sister Alice's department. I prefer getting to know them, building up tension, making sure the attraction is solid and that the individual in question is not married or mentally ill.

When I finally emerged from the ER, I found Billy and Turbo standing out front. Turbo was gazing up at him, obviously communicating something. Billy in turn was looking at Turbo as if she were the most beautiful creature on the face of the earth.

"She's an incredible dog," he said.

"Yes," I agreed, coming closer. I looked up at him with what I hoped was less obvious longing than Turbo's. I stood on tiptoes and kissed his mouth.

He was surprised at first. He pulled back fractionally, then returned the kiss, trying to be gentle on my injured lip, wrapping me in his long arms, crushing me to him as if he'd been waiting for me for years.

"This is unusual," he said, when he pulled back from me.

"What is?"

"This affinity I feel for you."

"Do you usually dislike people?"

"Mostly, yes."

"Oh," I said. "Well, that's sad."

"How can you possibly say that?"

"Isn't life more interesting when you can look forward to chance affinities?"

"I hadn't considered that," he answered. "Can I take you home with me?"

"Yes. Please."

We put Turbo in the backseat then got into his car, driving to his place way down on the Lower East Side where, Billy told me, he's been living since the days when boys with sawed-off shotguns stood on the corners guarding the street drug trade.

"I used to get knifed and mugged a few times a month back in the day," Billy said, in that wistful way people in their forties speak of New York as a very different place, a place where anything was permitted and the rich were confined Uptown.

Billy's apartment was on the top floor of an old four-story building that had once been some sort of factory. The apartment was airy with high ceilings, old rusted steel beams, and a wall of windows.

"Is your dog a cat chaser? I have cats," Billy said.

"No, she's fine with my cat. How many cats do you have?"

"Three," he said, "but I guess they're all hiding."

Three? I thought. But before I could thoroughly examine the red flags raised by the fact of multiple cats, Billy threw me down on the bed. He pinned my arms back and stared at me so deeply I thought he was going to paint my portrait. I was surprised by his intensity. Then surrendered to it in a way I couldn't remember surrendering before.

He explored every inch of my body with his large hands and his soft mouth. He penetrated me with his fingers and then his very thick cock. I had a fleeting thought of condoms and with it AIDS, herpes, gonorrhea, and syphilis, but some part of my mind whispered, *Don't worry, Eloise, let it go.* And I did.

"Do you run dog fights?" Billy asked at some point, maybe 4 a.m., after we had exhausted each other and were laying in the darkness, flat on our backs, shoulders touching.

"What?"

"Turbo's ears are cropped."

"Do I look like I run dog fights?"

"Yes," he said, putting his hand between my legs.

"She was that way when my mom rescued her. Someone probably tried to get her to fight but she's about the least aggressive dog I've ever met."

"Are you a paratrooper?" he asked then.

"Where'd you get that one?"

"The hitch in your giddyup. The scars on your thighs. I thought you'd jumped from a plane and landed awkwardly."

"Oh," I said. "No. No plane jumping. Though I flew one once when I was eighteen."

"And the hitch will remain a mystery?"

"Yes," I said for reasons I failed to understand. I usually love telling all about the manhole crushing my pelvis and, if I trust and like the person, I even hint at the money the city gave me in exchange for swallowing me. But I didn't want to discuss such things with Billy.

I fell back to sleep, my head in the crook of Billy's neck, and woke as dawn was breaking through the wall of windows. Turbo was licking my face.

"You need to go out?" I asked the brown dog.

She looked at me meaningfully and wagged her tail.

"Okay," I said softly, not wanting to wake Billy.

As I searched the floor for my pants, Billy suddenly

sprang from the bed and ran into the bathroom. I put on my clothes and was looking for Turbo's leash when he came back out, fully dressed.

"Oh," I said, "you're dressed. You want to come walk with us?"

"Walk?" He looked confused. "No, I have a lot of things to do. You're going home now, yes?"

"Excuse me?" I said, shocked. It wasn't even 6 a.m.

"Don't take it personally. I just have things to do."

I stared at him without blinking. He stared right back. There was nothing on his face. His eyes were a washy blue.

Turbo looked from me to Billy and back, sensing that something had gone wrong.

He offered me cab fare. I considered seeing if Turbo understood the command *Kill*.

"No, thank you," I said.

"Is something wrong?" he asked, his eyes wide and innocent-looking.

"What could possibly be wrong?" I spat.

"Eloise, don't be upset, I have things to do. You were awake. I figured you have things to do too."

"Millions of things," I said. "Come on, Turbo."

I marched to the door, yanked it open, then slammed it behind me and went down the stairs as fast as my hitched giddyup would permit. Turbo bounded at my side, like we were heading for an exciting adventure.

I stood outside Billy's building half expecting him to come to his senses, call out to me, etc. . . . But he didn't. A rat scampered toward a garbage can.

I walked to Houston Street where, after hailing four cabs, I found one who was willing to take Turbo and me.

I got home, fed Hammie, and got into bed.

The phone woke me.

I grabbed it without checking the caller ID. "Yeah?"

"Are you sleeping in the middle of the day, you little slut?"

"Hi, Amy," I said. "Rough night."

Amy is my money manager and confidante. I met her on the subway one day when I dropped my keys and she picked them up and handed them to me. We'd gotten to talking and I'd trotted out my story of the manhole incident and even told her about the money. She was appalled when I'd confessed I had it all sitting in a savings account.

"Your money should be working so you don't have to," she'd said.

I don't like money enough to send it to work. But Amy convinced me to let her tend to my modest vat of cash. This she does at a greatly reduced fee as she keeps hoping I'll sleep with her even though I've always made it clear that that's not on the horizon.

"What was rough about it?" Amy asked brightly.

"I had phenomenal sex."

"With a woman, I hope."

"Of course not."

"What do you mean, of course not? You'll see the beauty of my ways someday. There's a big dyke inside you just waiting to get out."

"Un huh."

"So?" said Amy.

"So what?"

"Who was the lucky stud?"

"Some rotten piece of crap."

"Nice."

"No, he wasn't very nice."

"That's what I meant. Nice that he's not nice. Who wants nice?"

I could tell Amy wanted to go on and on like this, but her endless appetite for sex talk had actually started to get tiresome. She never wants to discuss the things I am genuinely curious about, like her bicycle racing career, her mountain climbing expeditions, or even her high-powered job. To Amy, that stuff is all too personal. Yet she'll gladly go into graphic detail about, say, a corpulent virgin she deflowered with her fist.

"Was there a reason for calling, Amy?"

"Yes," Amy sighed, "I made you some more money."

"Oh, thanks." I felt slightly embarrassed. If the money grew enough, I'd have to do something with it. Have an extravagant spending spree. Give it all away. Something.

"Are you okay, Eloise? I know the Indio thing was awful for you. And it doesn't seem like you've acknowledged that."

"I've acknowledged it," I said curtly.

"Okay. I'll leave that one alone."

"Thanks."

"I suppose I will release you from the bondage of this call now."

"Thank you," I said.

I put the phone back in its cradle and it rang again. This time my sister, Alice.

"El, do you know any cops?" she asked after a cursory greeting and a brief inquiry into my emotional state.

"Cops? What for?"

"Do you know any?" Alice asked insistently.

"Not that I'm aware of, Alice, no."

"Shit," she said.

"What is it? What did you do now?"

"Nothing," Alice lied.

Alice liked playing this game. Getting me to extract information from her. In fact, she'd get downright furious if I didn't. It was even more exhausting than detailing my sexual exploits for Amy. Why was everyone in my life so tiring?

"Alice, why do you want to know if I know any cops?"

"Clayton got into trouble."

"The big oaf?" I asked. I was pretty sure the guy who'd

been borderline stalking my sister for several months was named Clayton, but I'd never heard her call him anything but The Big Oaf.

"Let's call him Clayton for now."

"Okay. What did Clayton do?"

"I can't tell you that. I was just wondering if you knew any homicide cops you could talk to."

"Homicide? Shit, Alice, did he kill someone?"

"It was an accident. I'm just trying to find out if anyone's pursuing the case. There was a little mention of it in the papers right after it happened, then nothing."

"Jesus."

"Don't say *Jesus*, Eloise. Religion is too incendiary. I get angry just at the thought of it."

"Alice," I said, "what happened exactly?"

"I like Clayton a little."

"That's not what I meant."

"I know. We shouldn't talk on the phone. The line might not be secure."

"Ah," I said.

Alice had had a crystal methedrine phase in her early twenties. She and Mom had gone on a few speed jags together, Alice coming back to stay at the old apartment on Charles Street, before Mom moved to Woodstock and went into Narcotics Anonymous. The two of them would gnash their teeth and overzealously clean the house. Mom, of course, didn't know when or how to stop and got so skinny she nearly died. Alice one day decided speed was unhealthy and stopped doing it. But she has a touch of residual paranoia.

"He pushed someone," Alice said after a pause, during which she presumably wrestled with herself about her need to tell me what happened versus her paranoia about the phone line. Her need won out. "It was an accident. Guy fell on the train tracks and got run over by a train."

"Oh my god."

"Don't say *God*, please."

"Alice, I'll say what I want. And I don't need to hear about any more bodies right now."

"I'm sorry, El."

"Your oaf is a homicidal maniac."

"You know that's not true."

"How do I know that?" I demanded. "The guy lives in a parking lot."

"He's living with me now. And it was an accident."

"I don't know what to tell you, Alice. I don't know any homicide cops. Or any cops at all."

"What about your friend Dennis?"

"He's a fireman, Alice, not a cop."

"Oh yeah. Well. Shit."

"How's work going?" I asked even though I could never quite get used to the idea of gambling being my sister's work.

"Fine. Holding steady."

"Right," I said. "Well . . ." I added to coax her toward hanging up.

"Okay then."

Alice hung up. I knew I should have pressed her a little more about the Clayton thing. Tried to see exactly how worried she was, if she really cared for that big oaf. But I didn't have the strength.

I crawled back under the covers.

The next few days blurred the way they do sometimes when I've gotten new fabric and am drawing up various trolls and beasts to render in felt and buttons and big awkward stitching. I drew, then I cut fabric and started experimenting. I had failed with my first dog-headed cockroach. The head was so enormous the animal couldn't stand, even on the eight legs I'd given it. The new model was a slightly smaller-headed version and I was giving it thicker legs.

Between bouts of work, I walked Turbo. Some days, I

talked to Amy Ross or to Mom or to my friend Jane who has four kids by four different fathers and lives in New Jersey.

One morning, I was in the bathtub with a Lyle Lovett CD playing as loud as Jeff from downstairs will tolerate. I was soaking in Epsom salts after taking Turbo for a six-mile run the previous day.

The landline rang, and for some reason, I decided to answer it even though it was probably a telemarketer. I scampered out of the tub, grabbed the cordless phone, then jumped back into the bath before answering.

"Good afternoon," I said.

"It is, isn't it?" the voice said.

"Yes," I agreed. "How did you get my phone number?"

"You're listed."

"But I never told you my last name."

"I looked in your wallet while you were sleeping."

"That's an invasion of privacy."

"Yes. It's even a little psycho. But you like that."

"How do you know what I like?"

"Just guessing."

"I'm going to hang up now," I told Billy.

"Why? And why were you so pissed off at me the other morning?"

"You kicked me out. And it was 6 in the morning."

"I'm an early riser. I had a lot of things to do. Besides, it was a quarter to 7 by the time you left."

"You should have been savoring me."

"I savored you all right."

"Don't be cocky."

"That you don't like?"

"Stop thinking you know anything about me."

"Is your lip still fat? Those stitches were sexy."

"I have to go now," I said. I hung up without giving him a chance to protest.

I couldn't do it. Could not open myself up to a man who

had kicked me out of his apartment at 6 a.m. The kicking out, the willingness to potentially hurt my feelings, signaled to me that I could not trust him.

My lip, which hadn't bothered me one bit since the day after I'd smashed it, started throbbing. Turbo had come into the bathroom and was licking up the puddles of bathwater I'd left on the floor when I'd gone to get the phone.

I got out of the tub, threw clothes on, and attached Turbo's lead to her collar. My hair was wet and the air was cold. I didn't care. I needed to walk. I suddenly longed for my mother. My dead father. My lunatic sister.

I took Turbo to the dog run in Riverside Park. There were many well-dressed people with tiny designer dogs. They all stared at Turbo.

"She's a very friendly dog," I announced.

Within five minutes, all the designer-dog people had left and it was just Turbo and me and a thin old white man with an even older black Lab. Turbo went over to politely introduce herself to the Lab. The dog showed Turbo his teeth and she came running back to me and glued herself to my legs.

We left the park and headed toward Broadway where I decided to stop in at Irene and Sue's, an upscale toy store that carries my animals. I'd see if any had sold and if the store wanted to order more.

The toy store buyer wasn't in and the store's cat kept giving Turbo dirty looks. We wandered back outside, into the unseasonably brisk day. I hadn't dressed warmly enough and I was cold to the bone. Now, no doubt, I would get consumption.

I didn't contract actual consumption but did get a severe cold accompanied by a bone-wracking cough. I spent three days under the covers hacking and sneezing and falling into a pit of depression. I turned the phone ringer off. I shut the blinds on the window facing the street. I didn't watch TV or listen to Lyle Lovett. I didn't drop in on my neighbor Jeff. I coughed and slept and, twice a day, took Turbo out for her business.

Several days into all this, the doorbell rang. I ignored it. It rang and rang and rang again. Then, after a while, someone knocked at the front door. I tiptoed to my peephole and looked out. It was my sister, Alice, standing there with her big oaf and Jeff from downstairs. I opened the door.

Turbo, who wasn't getting nearly enough exercise, bounded into the hall, licked everyone, and tried to jump into Alice's arms.

"Come in," I begrudgingly waved them in.

"Not you," I said as Jeff started coming in too, "I'm sick. I'll give you germs."

Jeff, a germaphobe, turned on his heels.

"I've been trying to call," Alice said. "What's wrong? You look awful."

"I'm sick."

"I'll say."

"There," I said, motioning at my beautiful and expensive red love seat that no one ever seemed to identify as one of the few extravagances I'd allowed myself, "sit."

Alice sat down, tucking her skirt under her, very lady-like. She was dolled up, especially for Alice. My sister is attractive but she tends to be a bit unkempt. Now, though, her long mouse-brown hair was actually combed and she was wearing a skirt and a tight sweater. Her skin looked nice, like she'd actually been outside somewhere other than at a racetrack.

"You look nice," I said.

"Thank you." She seemed like she felt guilty over looking decent.

The big oaf just sat there taking up a lot of space on the couch next to Alice. He wasn't overweight but he had to be at least 6'4" with big bones and a big face and longish hair hanging in two curtains over his cheeks. He didn't know what to do with his hands. He put the palms flat on his knees, then two seconds later folded his hands together, then tented them, then put them back on his knees. They were huge hands.

No one said anything. I looked at Alice and Alice looked at the big oaf.

"I can't offer you a beverage cause I don't have any," I said after a while.

"How are you doing with the Indio thing?" Alice asked.

"Fine," I shrugged.

"You getting the dog out okay?" Alice looked at Turbo, trying to gauge her wellness.

We all have the animal sickness. Mom and Alice and me. We could be at death's door and not give a shit for our own welfare, but if anything is slightly off with an animal, we're frantic. Which is why I'd tried not to have any animals and just make stuffed animals instead. But then Hammie came in the window. Then Mom started making me take in her foster dogs. I surrendered to being an animal person.

"Yeah, she's getting out twice a day. When I'm better I'll take her hiking at Bear Mountain or something."

"Oh." Alice nodded, then asked, "Should I take her?"

"To Bear Mountain?" I'd never known my sister to go hiking.

"Home. To my place. Adopt her. I think my dog is lonely."

I was aghast that Alice would consider taking Turbo from me. Turbo *was* up for adoption. Mom had her listed on Petfinder.com, and now and then someone would call making inquiries. None of these would-be suitors had passed the initial screening, though, since a massive pit bull with cropped ears often attracts exactly the type of human the dog shouldn't go live with.

"But Candy is so small," I said. This was true. Alice's

dog weighed about fifteen pounds. She wasn't an offensive yapper, but she was small. Turbo might crush her by accident.

"She's not that small," Alice said defensively.

It was ridiculous, I knew, but I was wounded that Alice was trying to take Turbo.

"I don't think Turbo is the right dog for you," I told her. "But if you really want a second dog, tell Mom. She never got over how you rescued a dog through someone other than her."

"It was through Mom's own damn nephew. And it wasn't my idea. The animal was foisted upon me."

"Right," I said. I'd never heard my sister say *upon* before. Where was she getting this? Surely not from the big oaf. Maybe she had another boyfriend. A guy who said *upon*. We would refer to him, in our sporadic sisterly chat sessions, as Upon Guy. If we ever had a private conversation again.

"So I can't have the dog?"

"Not right now." I wasn't going to tell my sister that it had suddenly dawned on me that I was really partial to this dog. It would just make her want Turbo that much more. Alice is competitive. I don't mind when this competitiveness is tuned toward outsmarting her fellow horseplayers at the racetrack, but I can't bear when it's pointed in my direction.

Alice stared at me. The oaf stared. I thought of the body he had generated. I thought of Indio's body.

"So what's with the murder case?" I asked.

Alice and the oaf both looked at me like I'd cattle prodded them. They glanced at each other, then Alice shrugged. "Nothing has happened. We're in the clear. We think," she answered.

"Well, that's nice," I said even though it wasn't nice at all. They were two people with a murder hanging over their heads and Alice has been many things, but she's never been someone who had to worry about *murder*.

I glanced at the oaf. This was all his fault. He was so oafish he'd murdered someone by accident. He was a nuisance and I wished he would go, leaving Alice and me to pick on each other for a while and, when we were done with that, talk about Mom and her dogs and her girlfriend who I imagined to have hairy legs because she's German.

"Do you think Mom's girlfriend has hairy legs?" I asked then, since I refused to listen to them speaking lightly of murder and couldn't think of any other topic to bring up.

"What kind of a question is that? I don't need to think about that," said Alice. "And what if she does? There's nothing wrong with hairy legs, Eloise, you've always been a little OCD about the hair-removal thing."

"You're the one who made me shave my armpits when I was like three years old."

Alice rolled her eyes. Clayton looked like he wished the couch would devour him.

After a few more fits and starts of conversation, Alice said she'd just wanted to check up on me and that, since I wasn't dead, she was leaving.

"You sure I can't have that dog?" she asked.

"I'm sure you can't have that dog," I said.

I walked them to the door. Some part of me, the part that wanted to be unconditionally supportive, wished I'd been able to make conversation with the oaf. The only thing he had volunteered was that he was thinking of renting a trailer in Florida. His eyes had gotten shiny when he said it, like the wished-for Floridian trailer was an exotic, hard-to-attain thing. It broke my heart slightly. That this guy's dreams were so small. That my sister was keeping time with a guy with small dreams.

I locked the door behind them then tried putting my sister, the oaf, and the murder rap out of my mind. Turbo looked at me so forlornly I decided to pull myself together and take her out for more than three minutes. I put on lay-ers of clothing and could barely get her collar on she was squiggling so much.

My body felt atrophied and limp and I went into some sort of shock once I exceeded the three-minute mark of being outside. I got lightheaded and had to sit down on a bench. The cool air singed my lungs; the brightness of the sky hurt my eyes. Turbo waited patiently until my spell passed. I got to my feet and we walked east to Central Park, climbed up Harlem Hill, and crossed over the roadway. I took off Turbo's lead to let her run ahead a bit.

I started taking extra care, watching where I put my feet as night was falling rapidly now. Which is when something very heavy hit me on the head. I stumbled and fell.

"What are the odds?" a voice said.

I looked up and there was Billy Rotten.

"With me, the odds are even money," I replied, looking from Billy to what appeared to be a gallon jug of maple syrup that had fallen from the sky and hit me on the head.

"I meant, what are the odds that I'd find you here again. On the ground again."

"That's what I meant," I said, rubbing the spot where the thing had hit me, waiting to feel a giant bump begin to rise there. "I am accident-prone and I frequent the same spots. New York is a very small town."

Billy peered at me. The washy blue eyes searching for something. "But this," Billy said, "seems unlikely even by your small-world-accident-prone standards."

He picked up the jug of maple syrup and examined it. I stayed on the ground, dazed. I didn't want to look at him. I had erased from my being any sense memory, any emotional memory, of that night. Looking at him threatened to waken it all.

Billy gazed up above my head. There was a tall tree there, and as I followed his gaze, I saw other gallon jugs suspended from branches by slender ropes.

"Did that fall?" A small, dirty-looking guy suddenly materialized and pointed at the maple syrup jug.

"Yeah, on my head," I said.

"Sorry sorry," he said, picking up the jug. "But you're fine, right?" He examined his maple syrup, clearly more concerned about it than about me. He stared up at the other containers dangling from the tree, as though wondering if I'd somehow disturbed them too.

"I guess I'm fine," I said reluctantly. "But you ought to secure your jugs."

He burst out laughing, clutched his maple syrup to his chest, and walked away.

Neither Billy nor Turbo was paying attention to me. Billy was squatting down next to the dog, scratching her formidable chest. She was licking his ear and cheek.

"What are you doing here anyway?" I asked, irritated.

"It's a bit illegal," said Billy.

"What is?"

"My reason for coming here."

"Oh?" I said carefully. I instantly pictured the many illegal activities one could engage in at Central Park after dark, from putting tacks out along the roadway for giving cyclists flat tires, to anonymous gay sex, to mugging people. I pictured Billy mugging old women or blowing businessmen. It didn't quite fit.

"I'll show you," Billy said. He offered his hand and pulled me to my feet. "You okay?"

"Fine."

He led me to the other side of the lake and pointed at a big flat stone partially buried in the earth. "There," he said.

"What's that?"

"Dingo's grave."

"Who?"

"My dog. Dingo. I buried her there. This was her favorite place. But it's not a pet cemetery. I could be fined or worse."

"You put her whole body in there? Didn't varmints dig it up?"

"I had her cremated first."

"Then it's probably not illegal."

"I'm sure it is," Billy insisted.

He seemed to want his burying of Dingo's ashes to be illegal so I tried to humor him. "I think you should take Turbo," I said, after we'd been staring at Billy's dead dog's unmarked grave for several minutes.

"What?"

"You're a man who needs a dog."

"What are you proposing? To give me your dog?"

"She's not my dog. I told you. My mom dropped her on my doorstep while she awaits a home."

"But she seems like your dog."

"I like her, but I'm going through some things. I might move." I waited for him to protest this concept. He didn't. "Turbo likes you. And you like her."

He stared at me. I felt transparent, flimsy, like he might take hold of me, fold me into pieces, and take me with him. And he couldn't be trusted to transport me with care.

So I gave him the dog.

"This is it?" he asked when I handed him Turbo's lead.

"Yes." I turned my back to them and started walking away. After going fifty feet, I turned to look. Turbo was staring up at Billy, declaring her love. Billy was staring down at Turbo. Neither man nor beast was watching me.

I slept and woke up wondering where Turbo was. *She wasn't your dog*, I told myself. I knew it was true. But I always miss what I've just given up.

I made coffee. Fed Hammie. Looked out the window at a bright blue day. The phone and doorbell rang simultaneously. I vowed to move. Soon.

I looked at the caller ID. Amy Ross. I let the machine

pick up. I went to the front window and tried peering though the blinds without actually moving them. Mom was standing there with another giant beast at her side. This one bigger than Turbo. Caramel-colored with a black nose.

"I can see you!" she shouted up from the street. "And I brought Turbo a friend."

I buzzed her in. I didn't want to, but she's my mother.

"Where's Turbo?" my mother asked after looking all around my small apartment.

"She found a home."

"She what?" my mother's head swiveled on her neck and her eyes popped out of her head.

"It was the right thing to do, Mom, you have to trust me."

I told her about giving Turbo to Billy. About why I had given Turbo to Billy and how I was sure that dog and that man belonged together.

"But he's a creep who kicked you out of his apartment in the middle of the night."

"Actually, it was 6:45 in the morning and certain men who are unwilling to give their love to women give it freely to dogs."

My mother couldn't be appeased that easily. Her voice went into a high register and she cursed me out. Though she has softened as she's gotten older, my mother still has a foul mouth. It's a generational thing. Her generation fucked indiscriminately, did lots of drugs, and cursed a lot. Mine carries huge handbags that give them neck pain.

My mother wouldn't calm down.

"Mom, I'm going to have to sedate you," I said.

"Sedate me how?"

"I'll get Valium from Jeff downstairs."

"Really?" My mother grew calm at just the mention of it.

"No," I said.

Mom has been in Narcotics Anonymous for fifteen

years. But she keeps hoping someone will accidentally stab her in the arm with a syringe full of heroin. Or force Valium down her gullet.

By now I was examining Otis, the dog Mom had brought. He was beautiful. Even I had to admit that. A huge Rhodesian ridgeback. His shoulders were massive, his hind end muscular, the fur on his back stood up permanently along his ridge. His humans had been killed in a plane crash. It looked like he was keenly aware of this. His eyes were the saddest eyes ever.

"If you give this dog to some one-night stand, I will disown you."

"Don't make promises you can't keep."

My mother finally calmed down and left, off to Queens to counsel Alice about Clayton's murder problem.

I got down on my haunches and looked Otis in the eyes, my face just inches from his. He stared back for a very long time, then gave my nose one solemn lick.

3. ALICE

"Your sister gave a dog away without my approval." My mother had shown up on my doorstep, unannounced, apparently not long after showing up on Eloise's doorstep unannounced. My mother is an old hippie. She believes in spontaneity. I hate spontaneity.

"Mom, Eloise wouldn't give a dog to an unworthy human. And please sit." I motioned at the kitchen table. She had been standing, hovering in the kitchen doorway, since arriving thirty minutes earlier. She seemed to think that if she didn't actually sit down during one of these unscheduled visits, it wouldn't count as an unscheduled visit.

My mother screwed up her face and stared at me.

"Sit and drink your coffee," I told her.

"Where is that nice boyfriend of yours?" she asked, finally sitting down.

"I *hope* he's looking for a job. And he's really not my boyfriend. I have to end it."

"You're always trying to end things. Why not start something for once?

"Do you really want me to start something with an imbecile who accidentally murdered someone and was living in a parking lot until I let him move in with me?"

"How can you talk that way about someone you make love with?" Mom said, stretching out the word *love*.

"Mother," I said, "your generation may have made *love*, but mine fucks."

My mother is a mass of contradictions. Though she curses and peppers regular conversations with profanity, she refers to sex as *making love* and probably did so even in her heyday, when she screwed indiscriminately and injected heroin into every vein of her body, shortly after giving birth to me at the age of seventeen.

"I don't know how I had such heartless bitches for daughters." My mother tried to look stern but eventually cracked a smile and then laughed.

"I do feel affection for the big oaf," I admitted as my mother got up and opened the fridge door to stare in at the slim pickings. "For Clayton, I mean. I even refer to him by his actual name most of the time. I'm humanizing him. He's not just a *thing* anymore."

My mother sighed and shook her head. Though she pretends to be appalled by my black heart, I know she is secretly pleased that I'm so hard on my paramours. She was easy on her men and it screwed up her life and forever turned her against that gender.

"Can I eat those?" she asked, motioning at two peeled hard-boiled eggs in a bowl.

"Can I really stop you?"

"No. But I swear, after this I'll leave."

She put the bowl on the kitchen table, bit into one of the eggs, then gave a piece of it to Candy, who was diligently begging at her feet.

I was about to yell at her for feeding the dog from the table when we heard a key in the door and Clayton came trundling in.

"Clayton!" my mother shouted, jumping out of her chair, throwing her arms around him and hugging him fiercely.

She'd only met him twice before, but since I rarely kept a man around long enough for her to inspect, she practically considered Clayton her son-in-law. It didn't matter that he had accidentally murdered someone, that, for all we knew, this was the beginning of a life of crime. My mother didn't care about any of that.

"Kimberly," Clayton said, with as much buoyancy as he ever musters.

My mother hugged him for an unreasonable amount of time, probably getting some sort of sexual charge out of it because my mother is proudly oversexed. Clayton didn't seem to mind her pressing up against him like that. I suppose most people wouldn't. My mother is a very young fifty-three with masses of curly dark hair and a well-proportioned, compact body. Her eyes are wide-set and slanted making her look slightly Asian. By fifty-three, I will probably be hideous as I favor my dead father's side of the family with my long limbs, sick-looking pale skin, and mouse-brown hair that gets limp and greasy within three hours of washing.

"Goodbye, Mom," I said, when she finally released her grip on my paramour and walked to the door. "Call next time, would you?"

My mother laughed, like my wishing for advance notice of her next visit was a frivolous and ridiculous request.

"Your mom is great," said Clayton once my mother left.

"Yeah," I said. "Any luck with the job search?"

"No." He shrugged.

He went to sprawl on the couch with a newspaper, ostensibly scouring the help wanted ads, though within a few minutes he was snoring.

I went back into the kitchen where my notebooks were spread out next to my Daily Racing Form. It was a Tuesday, a dark day at Aqueduct, but there was a carryover in the Pick 6 for Wednesday's card, meaning the pot was sweetened with forty-two thousand extra dollars. I had my work cut out for me.

I was completely stumped by the first leg of the six-race sequence, a full field of maiden statebred fillies going a mile. I considered giving up and simply planning a long series of trifecta and Pick 4 bets. But it seemed wasteful to neglect that little 42K pot of gold.

I dialed my friend Arthur's number.

I almost never actually call Arthur as we use text mes-

saging, his preferred method of communication. Even if
we're both at the track, sitting just a few feet away from
each other, he'll text message me. Usually asking my opinion of an over-bet favorite, but sometimes, particularly at
Saratoga, where the young girls are plentiful, what I think
his odds are of scoring with some twenty-year-old honey
in a strapless sundress.

"What?" Arthur answered.

"Arthur, it's Alice."

"Who?"

"Alice? Your friend?"

"Alice? Alice Hunter? You're calling me on the phone?"

"I know. It's a shock. I'm sorry. I need help."

"Tell me about it. The fourth at Aqueduct tomorrow,
right?"

"Oh. You too, huh?"

"Impossible pieces of shit."

"Right," I said.

I don't normally tolerate anyone calling horses pieces of
shit, nags, or pigs. But Arthur gets away with it because he's
even more derogatory when speaking of human beings.

"Don't be sensitive," said Arthur.

"Sensitive?"

"I could feel you recoiling over my slander of those
horses' good names."

"Don't get perceptive on me, Arthur, I rely on you for
complete cynicism and brutishness."

"That's cute," said Arthur, sounding slightly wounded.

I wondered if I had actually offended him. The tough guys
are the ones who melt when you least expect it.

"So you don't have any insights?" I asked Arthur.

"Maybe the three horse."

"A five-year-old making her second start? That's an un-
orthodox angle."

"If you're going to shoot down any ideas I have then
I'm hanging up."

"No, sorry, talk to me."

So he did. We went back and forth on a few less-than-stellar maidens. We decided to meet up at the Equestris Restaurant atop Aqueduct's clubhouse the next day at noon. To make things more interesting, we decided to pool our resources and play the Pick 6 together.

"Go do whatever it is you do with that flannelled bruiser of yours," said Arthur before hanging up.

"You talking to that Arthur idiot?" I spun around and found Clayton standing there, fully awake.

"Yes." I hated that Clayton hated Arthur.

"You gonna leave me for him?"

"For Arthur?" I asked, aghast.

"I'm sure women find him attractive."

"I'd probably break him," I said. Arthur is at least three inches shorter than I am and probably weighs less than I do. I don't like men who make me feel large. "Anyway, Arthur considers women over the age of twenty past their prime."

"So if he wasn't a short pedophile you'd fuck him?"

This was only the second time I'd heard Clayton say *fuck*.

"Don't joke about pedophilia. It's not funny. Arthur doesn't dip below legal."

Clayton grunted.

"Where's all this coming from?" I asked, moving to stand closer to him. I tried to be tender. I touched his face. Pushed a strand of hair off his wide forehead that shone greasy as an adolescent's.

We were gazing at each other and both jumped when someone knocked loudly on the door.

"Who the hell is that?" Clayton asked, as if I'd have any idea.

"Police," was the answer.

Clayton stared at me, like I'd called them.

"Shit," he said.

"Shhh," I cautioned since we were standing right near the door.

"Can I help you?" I asked, opening the door, acting slightly irritated but curious the way I imagined garden-variety law-abiding citizens might act.

"Clayton Marbler?" A plainclothes, mustachioed cop flashed his badge and looked past me toward Clayton. Behind him stood a tall brunette with a thin mouth.

"That's me," Clayton said.

I glanced over at his face. It was showing too much. He looked worried.

"What's this about?" I asked, playing the innocent girl-friend.

"Just a couple of questions. Could we come in?" asked the lanky brunette.

"Sure," I ushered them in.

The brunette sat at one end of the couch, the mustachioed partner at the other. Though the man was black and the woman white, there was a sameness about their small dark eyes and their tight, business-like mouths.

The male cop asked Clayton about Vito.

"Don't know him," Clayton shook his head.

"I do," I said, figuring they knew I knew him or, if they didn't, would soon find out. "He's an acquaintance from the racetrack."

"Right," said the brunette. "And Mr. Marbler, you've never met him?"

"You have met him, Clayton, remember? He came over to our table that day I brought you to the track?"

Clayton gave me the most wounded look I'd ever seen a human being give. But I was trying to save his ass. They knew I knew Vito. It would come out that Clayton had met him.

"Oh," Clayton said.

"The man is dead. You may have heard?" The male cop's eyes were tiny little slits now.

"No," Clayton said, a little too quickly.

"It was in the papers awhile back. Maybe you forgot?" The brunette this time.

"Oh. I don't read the paper," said Clayton.

This was true. But it seemed to make them even more suspicious. And their questions went on. And on. They never told us what led them to Clayton at this stage, weeks after the incident, just when he and I had started breathing easier.

"I'm going to call a lawyer," I told Clayton after the cops had left and we were sitting at the kitchen table, stunned and, for a time, speechless.

"How much does that cost?"

"Nothing yet. I have a friend who's a criminal defense lawyer."

"I'm not a criminal."

"You still need a criminal defense lawyer."

Clayton looked down toward his hands which were folded in his lap.

"What am I going to do?" he asked very quietly.

"It'll be all right," I lied. "I'll call Abe, my lawyer friend, then let's get out of the house. I'm almost done working for the day. Let's go to Central Park. Candy can run around, we can get some air. It's a pretty day," I said, like the beauty of any given day would matter to Clayton anytime in the immediate future.

"That's okay," he replied, barely a whisper. "You go on. I'll be here."

I tried to cajole him. It got me nowhere. He went to the couch and plopped down, face first.

I put in a call to Abe, told him the situation. Abe grunted.

"Doesn't look good after him not coming forward right away. Makes it look like it wasn't an accident. What, he thought he'd just get away with it?"

"It *was* an accident, Abe."

"Right. Well, if they pull him in for questioning, just tell him not to answer anything and call me."

"How much?"

"How much what?"

"What's it gonna cost?"

"It goes to trial, we're talking some bucks."

"Trial?" I nearly screamed. "They just asked him some questions."

"I'm giving you a worst-case scenario, Alice. You know me. Glass-half-empty kinda guy."

I thanked Abe and hung up. I wrote his name and number on a piece of paper then walked into the living room to give it to Clayton.

"This is the lawyer's name and number. If the cops try talking to you again, just call Abe."

Clayton barely lifted his head.

"I thought you were going to the park," he said.

"I am. What, are you trying to get rid of me?"

"I just don't want to bring you down," he said so quietly I could barely hear him.

"Don't be depressing, Clayton, you'll make it worse," I snapped, then felt bad and tried to think of something soothing to say. Nothing came to mind.

"Okay then," I said, "I'm going."

"Okay."

I took my red coat off the hook, put Candy's leash on, and went out the door. My neck was hurting and my shoulders were up to my ears.

Technically, dogs aren't allowed on the subway unless they're contained in a crate or bag. But I'd frequently taken Candy on, bagless and crateless, and no one had bothered me about it. She looks harmless enough, though if you're a squirrel, or another small, fast-moving thing, she's lethal.

Every imbecile in the city was in Central Park so I took Candy onto a wooded path then let her go even though off-leash hours weren't in effect yet. Another benefit of having a little dog, I'm less likely to get a ticket for letting her run loose.

We'd been walking for about twenty minutes, through wooded areas in the upper quadrant of the park, trying to pretend the place was ours alone, when I saw a guy down on all four with his head in some bushes. Next to him stood a thick brown dog. It was a strange sight. Man and dog on all fours. He was probably some insane person digging for treasure as his poor dog looked on.

Freak, I thought. As I walked past him, he craned his neck, saw me, and asked if I could help him. I imagined something sinister or disgusting and made a grunting sound, not wanting to just totally ignore the guy on the off chance he had a legitimate reason for being on all fours in the shrubbery, but not wanting to seem like some sunny-dispositioned bleeding heart who'd just humor whatever lunacy he had in mind.

"There's a dog here that needs help," the guy said.

That got my attention. I took a step closer and saw a black-and-white pit bull lying in the shrubbery with blood seeping out of his belly.

"Oh, shit," I said.

"Can you get a cop?" the guy asked.

"Yeah, I'll be right back."

I headed out to the roadway, frantically searching for a police officer.

"Have you seen any cops anywhere in the park?" I asked a woman who was jogging by slowly. She looked at me like I was an insect and kept moving. I asked a tourist, who cold-shouldered me too. Finally, I pulled my phone out and dialed 911. They told me to dial 311. 311 said they'd call Animal Control.

"No, no, don't do that, never mind," I told the 311 operator, imagining the dog being taken in by the kill shelter and immediately put to death.

I called information, got the number for the ASPCA,

and explained the situation. They said they'd send a humane officer.

"How soon?" I asked, anxious over the dog's fate. But the woman at the other end had already hung up.

Candy trotted at my side as I hurried back to the bleeding dog and the man.

"How is he?" I asked, leaning into the bushes.

"Not good. Look," he said, indicating a bloody footprint on the dog's white haunch, "he was kicked. And apparently dragged—his paw pads are bleeding."

The dog was staring ahead and looked resigned to death.

I thought I might vomit. I put my hand over my mouth.

"The ASPCA is coming," I said when I could speak again.

"The ASPCA? What about the cops?"

"Couldn't find one. Anyway, they'd just call Animal Control and the dog would be put to death since he's a pit bull and has clearly been abused."

I saw the guy glance over at his own dog and wince, probably imagining it being put to death. I looked down at Candy. She was uncharacteristically still.

The afternoon had suddenly turned much cooler and the park didn't seem lovely anymore. The dog's breathing was labored.

After what felt like hours, but was in fact only about twenty minutes, two humane law enforcement officers appeared. A man and a woman. The man looked sick to his stomach. The woman was matter of fact, poring over the dog's injuries before going back to the van to get some equipment. The guy and I stood back as they moved the dog and carried him over to their van. The animal just stared ahead, long past caring what any human did to him.

The female officer asked for my name and contact information then walked over to the guy to do the same.

"Thank you," she said to both of us.

"Yeah," I replied weakly.

The guy nodded at the officer then we both watched as the ASPCA van pulled away. We looked at each other. He shook his head. "That was awful," he said softly.

"Yes." There was an awkward moment. Like we were supposed to do something now, make some sort of pact for future dog rescues, at least introduce ourselves. But we didn't. He, I imagine, was sick to his stomach same as I was.

"Take care," he said. He was holding his dog's lead closely, as if afraid something awful might befall her too. He nodded then turned and walked away.

For a little while, Candy and I stayed rooted to our spot. It was nearly dusk now. The park was still infested with joggers and bike riders and a few straggling tourists. The sky was turning to ink.

A moment later, my phone rang in my pocket. I flipped it open without looking at the caller ID.

"You ready?" came a male voice.

"Ready?"

"For the Pick 6. It's me. Arthur. Hello?"

"Arthur. Hi. I just saw an abused dog."

"Oh." He knew something of my background, how my mother rescues dogs, how we're the sort of people with empathy for animals directly proportionate to our indifference to human beings. "Can you talk?" he added after an appropriate pause.

"I guess. I feel a little sick. But go ahead. Talk."

Arthur rattled off a series of theses about the horses running at Aqueduct the next day. He asked if I had come up with any insights.

"I did. But I'd have to look at my notes at home."

"All right. I can tell your heart isn't in it right now. Please sleep well and wake up clear headed."

I told Arthur I'd see him tomorrow, closed my phone,

then picked Candy up and squeezed her to my chest. She looked at me evenly, puzzled by the sudden hug, but not opposed to it.

I came home to an empty apartment. No sign of Clayton, no note. Maybe he'd gone out job hunting, though it was late in the day for that unless he was applying for some sort of graveyard shift. I pictured him working in a factory. Earning minimum wage. Coming home exhausted and defeated but still gentle and sweet because Clayton is always gentle and sweet, yet another thing that's made it difficult to truly get rid of him.

I took raw chicken necks out of the fridge, rinsed them, and fed them to Candy. In fact, raw chicken necks were the only things in the fridge. It was sad. It indicated that Clayton and I were living like dirty teenagers, incapable of taking care of ourselves, letting things slide.

I glanced at the answering machine and noticed the message light blinking.

Clayton was at the police station.

"I'm being held for questioning, Alice," the message said. His voice was small and scared. "Don't come. I've called the lawyer. I'll work it out."

"Oh no. " I said it aloud, but quietly, as if afraid the gods would hear and take the dread in my voice as affirmation of my paramour's guilt. Because some days I believe there are divinities everywhere. Religion upsets me, but a sense of awe at what is greater than me does not.

I called my lawyer friend Abe. He was on his way to the station.

"If there's bail I can get money," I told him.

"Un huh," he said. "They're just questioning him right now. But I'll let you know."

"They came here this afternoon to question him. And then returned a few hours later and took him away. What could they have learned?"

"Alice, I have no way of knowing that yet," Abe said patiently.

"Right. Should I come with you to the police station?"

"No," said Abe. "How much do you like this guy, Alice?"

"Why?"

"Well, he could be in big trouble. You got that, right?"

"He didn't do anything," I said. "I told you, it was an accident."

"He should have told the truth from day one. It looks bad now, Al. I'll call you when there's something to report."

I hung the phone up. I looked at Candy who was licking a trail of grease on the fridge door. I was a disgusting person with a trail of grease on her fridge.

I lumbered through my evening. I didn't know if Abe would spring Clayton. I kept toying with the idea of going to the station. Of being the supportive partner in spite of Clayton's wish that I not do this. I knew he didn't want me to see him like that. He hadn't had any shame about my seeing him living in a parking lot earlier in our dalliance, but the parking lot was his choice. The cops are not. His is a strange sense of pride, but it does exist.

I buried myself in work. I took out two years' worth of notebooks to find the speed figures I had made for some of the horses who hadn't been running at Aqueduct recently. I went online to watch race replays.

I passed the rest of the evening trying to lose myself in horses as represented by a series of numbers. I'd go for ten minute stretches of complete immersion, then my stomach would knot and I would think of the injured dog from the park or Clayton's face.

At some point, Abe called to tell me that Clayton was being arrested for manslaughter. There was evidence. A footprint.

My stomach knotted once more. "Shit," I said.

"Sorry, Alice. Bail will be set tomorrow. He'll spend the night in jail."

"Shit," I repeated.

"Alice?" Abe said.

"Yeah?"

"You know I'm not the advice type, but . . ."

"But?"

"Nah. None of my business. Good night. Try to get some sleep."

"Right," I said.

I popped a sleeping pill and drank some Scotch. Put a disc of Bach toccatas on the stereo. The music helped. I realized I'd listened to very little Bach since Clayton had moved in. He was not a Bach type of guy. He didn't complain, but I could sense that the music didn't compute for him and this upset me. So I hardly ever played it.

I managed some sleep around 1 a.m., Candy curled near my feet.

The sky over Aqueduct was the color of dead television. Or maybe it was me. I plodded up the escalator to the second, third, and then fourth floor. Entered the restaurant through the big glass doors. Offered Manny, the maître d', an anemic smile.

"What's wrong, Miss Hunter?"

"Bad week, Manny."

"Sorry to hear it. We've got a good omelet on the menu today."

"Thanks, Manny. I'm meeting Arthur."

"Right over there." He motioned to a table where I saw Arthur, hunched over his notebooks.

I slinked into a seat across from him.

"Hey, Alice," he said without looking up.

"Hi, Arthur."

He must have sensed something in my tone because he tore himself away from his notebook, glanced up at me, and did a double take.

"What's wrong with you?"

"Do I look wrong?"

"Alice, you look like shit."

"Dammit," I said, "I never hit the Pick 6 when I look like shit."

"What happened?" Arthur squinted at me. "What's the matter with you?" He gestured at me like I was covered in sores.

I told him that I was waiting for Clayton to be sprung from jail. That I had spent the morning getting the 50K in bail money after the judge had thankfully reduced the bail from the initial 100K. It was the money I'd squirreled away from my last Pick 6 hit, the money that was meant for a cabin in the woods where, from time to time, Candy and I could go hole up doing nothing, just taking in the air.

"Maybe we shouldn't be doing this," Arthur said, dead serious. "Your heart isn't in it."

"My heart is always in handicapping, Arthur. In fact, that's the only place it is. Besides, this kind of thing focuses me."

"Disaster and drama?"

"Exactly. The worse things are going for me in the outside world, the better I can concentrate on horse flesh."

Big Arthur didn't look convinced. Our wagering strategy was very serious business.

"Really," I said, "I'm fine."

"Yeah," he replied slowly, "okay. Let's do it."

My looking like shit didn't seem to be affecting me adversely. Arthur and I made it through the first four legs of the Pick 6 and were holding our breath during the eighth race, with the 2-1 favorite we hadn't used in the lead all the way around the track. With just an eighth of a mile to go, the horse we needed, a 6-1 dead closer, came flying up on the outside and got his nose on the wire first. Once the race was official, we sat looking at each other in complete silence. Arthur was pale. I'm sure I was pale. As we contemplated the finale, the ninth race, in which we had used just three horses, Arthur looked like he was going to vomit.

"Who the fuck is that?" he started screaming ninety seconds into the ninth race, with a horse we needed struggling on the lead as another horse came trundling up on his right.

"Shit," I said, until I saw the horse's number. It was a longshot I had insisted we use. He had the most awkward gallop I'd ever seen, like a washing machine on four legs, but he was doing it willingly, his ears forward as he passed the tiring leaders and won by half a length.

"Yes!" Arthur screamed when he finally realized that we had the horse on our ticket.

It wasn't a life-changing score, but it sure didn't suck, particularly on a day when I'd had to surrender fifty grand to spring my paramour from jail. Arthur and I would be splitting forty-two thousand and change. He wanted to celebrate.

"Let's get dinner. Champagne. Lap dances," he said.

"I'll have to take a rain check on that, Arthur."

"Aw, come on, Alice."

"Sorry."

"Well, give me a hug then."

I didn't move. Not that I was opposed to actually touching Arthur, just that his asking for a hug was so uncharacteristic, I thought he was joking.

"Don't look at me like that, I'm serious."

"Oh." I went over to Arthur's side of the table and we hugged awkwardly.

"Let's not do that again," he cracked after we'd let our arms fall to our sides.

I smiled. Then turned to head to the subway. It would have been glamorous to go pick up a big suitcase of cash but that's not how we do it. The money would be put in Arthur's New York Racing Association betting account and he'd give me a check for my share minus the substantial taxes. And it'd be just like a regular job. A lucrative week at a regular job, but still, just a job.

When I got home, Candy went crazy, dancing around in circles, letting out excited yelps and trying to jump up into my arms. I picked her up and let her lick my ear. As I held her, I walked over to the answering machine. Clayton had left a message. He was out on bail but he'd driven his van to the parking lot and was going to spend the night there, in his van. He sounded more depressed than I'd ever heard him.

Part of me wanted to go find him in his parking lot. Another part of me was relieved.

I didn't know what to do so I put Candy's leash on and took her out for a walk.

Night had fallen and the daytime bustle of trucks and commerce had died down. There was pink at the sky's edges, the rest was swallowed in ink.

I didn't feel like I'd just made twenty-one thousand dollars.

As Candy and I climbed back up the stairs to the apartment, I could hear the phone ringing. I jammed my key in the door, got it open, and raced to the phone.

"Yeah," I said, expecting Abe or Clayton.

"Miss Hunter?"

"Yeah?"

"This is Humane Officer Serling from the ASPCA."

"Oh, hi, yes, is the dog okay?"

"He's doing all right, yes. Not great. Had some internal injuries. But he made it through surgery and is recovering well. Thank you for your help. But that's not why I'm calling."

"Oh?"

"William Nichols asked me to give you his phone number."

"Who?"

"The man who was with you with the battered dog? He said he had something important to tell you. Asked for your number. I wasn't going to give out your number but said I'd pass his along to you."

"Oh," I said, not sure what to think, "okay." I wrote down the number. Humane Officer Serling and I spoke about the dog a little longer. He told me that, after fully recovering, the dog would be evaluated by the adoption experts and, providing he didn't have any insurmountable issues, be put into the adoption pool. And no. He would not be put to death.

I hung up and stared at the piece of paper where I'd written down the lunatic's phone number. What did he want?

I dialed.

"Yes?" He sounded terse.

"This is Alice Hunter. From Central Park. The dog."

"Thanks for calling."

"What's up?"

"I think we should get some coffee. We experienced a strange slice of life together. We should discuss."

"Oh?"

"Yes," he said.

I shrugged. Then realized he couldn't see me.

"Okay," I said. "When?"

"I have some free time tonight."

"Ah."

"Ah? Is that a *yes* or a *buzz off you jackass*?"

"A yes." I felt a curious tingling in my spine. I thought of Clayton in his parking lot.

William told me he had a car and could come over to Long Island City. I told him about the café around the corner and we agreed to meet there at 9:00.

I was surprised when I walked into the café and realized

William Nichols was attractive. He was long and lanky. His hair was brown going gray, eyes brown and a little slanted.

We shook hands. He had big, slightly beat-up hands.

I thought about Clayton's hands. They were a different kind of big.

"I felt like we should debrief," William said.

"The thought occurred to me when we were still in the park. Maybe we should make a pact for future rescue missions," I suggested.

"No. I don't want to see that kind of thing again."

"You're right. I don't either. Bad idea. Let's think of something else."

He laughed. His eyes lit up. He had a gap between his front teeth.

The waitress, a tiny Goth girl with pierced eyebrows, took our coffee orders.

"Did the humane officer tell you about the dog's surgery?" William asked.

"Yeah. Said there were internal injuries but the dog made it through okay."

"And will be evaluated and put into the adoption pool."

"Yes," I said.

"It's strange to consider the effort that's gone to taking care of this animal. I'm all for it and more, but a corresponding humane treatment of humans would be a nice thing."

"I'm all for the humane treatment of small humans or old humans, but I guess I don't have a lot of mercy for those in-between humans who are doing awful things. Like whoever beat that dog. He'll probably go and get another dog and start the cycle all over again. Or evolve up the food chain and start beating up women and kids."

William nodded. "True. I'm just wondering why it's generally easier to treat animals well than it is to treat humans well. I'd say that it's the fur, but I'm not inclined to be all that nice to really hairy people."

I laughed. And speculated about when I would announce that I have a live-in felon boyfriend.

"You have a spouse," he said then, apparently clairvoyant as well as attractive and ethically responsible.

"A spouse? Like a husband ? No."

"A paramour. A devotee."

"That's more like it. Yes."

"Live-in?"

"Yes."

"That doesn't make me happy."

"Me either."

He smiled, then frowned. "Then why do you have him?"

"It just happened."

"You don't strike me as a person who just lets things happen."

"You'd be surprised. I can be slothful about certain things. I hope that doesn't disappoint you."

He said nothing.

The Goth girl brought our coffee and we sipped in silence for a few minutes.

He asked what I do for a living. I shrugged and told him, expecting the traditional response, the one where people act as if I've just admitted to raging leprosy or an active heroin addiction. But not William. He was fascinated.

"And you?" I asked, after I'd gone into the particulars of my work.

"Architect. As you may have guessed by now."

"Guessed why?"

"My stern and organized personality."

"I just thought you were German."

He laughed. We sure were laughing a lot.

"Now what?" I asked after I'd had half my coffee.

"We've debriefed, I suppose."

"And that's it?"

"You're encumbered."

"Encumbered?"

"The paramour slash devotee."

"Right," I said.

William paid for our coffees then walked me home. We reached my stoop and stood staring at each other. My eyes drifted to his neck. The skin was very soft looking.

"Can I kiss your neck?"

He tilted his head. "I typically don't allow women who are otherwise encumbered to nuzzle on my person."

"Right," I said.

"But I might be persuaded to make an exception."

He leaned over and kissed me, softly. Then lingering. Then lips parting. The taste of his tongue. The smell of his skin. My knees literally weakened.

When we finally pulled apart, I weaved slightly, dazed.

"Okay," he said, "see ya."

"See ya." I turned and stuck my key in the door. I climbed up to my apartment. Candy danced. I patted her and scratched her neck. I sat down at the kitchen table, put my head in my hands, and moaned.

The phone rang.

"Yes," I said breathlessly, eagerly, hungrily.

"Hi, Alice," came Clayton's low and slow voice.

A deflated "Oh" escaped my lips.

"What's wrong?"

"Nothing. Are you all right?"

"Just wallowing in self-pity in the parking lot."

I smiled. Then realized he couldn't see me smiling.

"You don't have to do that," I said.

"Okay. Is it all right if I come over?"

"You do actually live here."

"I know, but I shouldn't. I forced myself on you. Repeatedly."

"That's not entirely true."
"But it's sort of true?"
"No, Clayton, no. Just come home already, will you?"
I hung up the phone.
I closed my eyes.

4. KIMBERLY

Carlos, the Chihuahua, was barking frenetically and Jimmy, the Newfoundland mix, was spinning around in circles in the living room of my Woodstock house. The misbehavior of the disparately sized dogs incited the fifteen other dogs to riot as my girlfriend, Betina, a German blonde, stood naked in the middle of the room. She was staring ahead and leaning as far to one side as a person can lean without falling over.

"Betina," I said, but I spoke too softly, she couldn't hear me over the din of the dogs.

For a moment, I blocked out the sound of the animals and just watched Betina. Her long limbs were bronzed even though they hadn't seen sun in months. Her belly had a tiny bit of pouching, as if she'd gorged on cookie dough while I was out earlier. She was lovely. And she was sick.

I imagined Joe, the composer living in the little wooden house next door, gazing into my window and getting quite a show.

"Betina," I said again, coming to stand right in front of her.

She looked past me. She was smiling slightly, maybe watching some inner film, something starring Klaus Kinski, with whom she'd had a childhood obsession.

"Bee." I reached out and gently touched her shoulder.

She jumped and her eyes focused on me.

"Kimberly," she said.

"What's wrong, darling? What did you take?"

"Take?" She tilted her head.

"Let's get you to bed," I said gently, fearing a bad reaction from her. Sometimes she goes ballistic at any suggestion, no matter how reasonable.

"Okay," she said in a soft voice.

As we slowly walked from the living room toward the stairs, I glanced out the window and, sure enough, saw my neighbor Joe gazing over at us. He quickly looked away.

After I'd settled Betina into a nest of blankets on our king-sized bed, she admitted to having popped four Vicodins. At least she hadn't taken too many psychiatric meds. Those scare me more than Vicodin.

"Where'd you get Vicodin, Bee?"

"It's a secret." She giggled, then let her head fall back. Her blond hair went spilling all over the pillow.

"Do you think you can sleep now?" I asked. "I need to get the dogs out to run."

"Mmm," she sighed. Her eyes had already closed.

For a few minutes, I stood watching her features melt. She was on more meds than I could possibly name. There was an eating disorder, depression, manic episodes. Various doctors and drugs had kept her propped up through a successful modeling career, but once she hit age twenty-seven and went from a size zero to a size two, she started unraveling. Which is just when I met her.

She was sound asleep now. I tiptoed from the room then went downstairs, dogs at my heels. All those brown eyes staring. The smell of dogness permeating everything. I meant to march to the kitchen and begin leashing dogs for the walk but I felt so heavy, so exhausted. I plunked down onto the couch and was immediately blanketed by dogs. Chico and Harvey, two unrelated but same-colored caramel pit bulls, wedged between the back of the couch and my side. Jimmy, the Newfoundland, tried to lick my face, and Ira, the three-legged hound mix, stood balefully to the side, shimmering with the need for attention but too polite to throw himself at me like the others.

"Come here, buddy," I said, looking at Ira and patting the couch.

He came over. More graceful and agile on three legs than some dogs are on four. He peered at me with undiluted love pouring from his enormous eyes. I petted his face and his long, silky, spotted ears. He was the most well-adjusted and well-behaved of the pack but no one was ever interested in taking him and I had long stopped talking him up to potential adopters. I rarely admitted it, but I didn't want to give him up.

While the four dogs around me were contented, the rest were dancing and fidgeting. I had to get up off the couch and take them out.

I'd just managed to stand up when the phone rang.

"Hi, Mom." It was my younger daughter, Eloise.

"Eloise. Hi."

"I'm on the bus. I'll be at your house in two hours. I was going to do an unscheduled drop-in to see how well you like it when the shoe is on the other foot, but I didn't want to find you doing anything nefarious, so I decided to warn you."

"There is nothing nefarious about me, Eloise, surely you know that by now. And I'm thrilled that you're coming up," I said, though this wasn't strictly true in light of Betina's meltdown. "I should warn you that my girlfriend is, um . . ."

"Off her meds?"

"No. On too many."

"Oh."

There was no love lost between Eloise and Betina. They'd met only twice and it hadn't gone well either time.

"I know you don't like her, Eloise, but please try to be nice."

"She's fine, Mom. She's just ditzy. But I'll be nice."

"Betina is a very intelligent woman," I said defensively. It was possible this was true, but Betina had never been emotionally well enough to demonstrate much depth of character. She was too full of need. And I'd fallen for that. "By the way, Eloise," I added, "why are you coming here? Are you all right? Are you still shaken about the trapeze instructor?"

"Do I need a reason?"

"Of course not. But I know you. Nothing short of disaster would motivate you to come see your poor old mother in the woods."

"I am still shaken about Indio. And I've had my heart broken by a new guy."

"Oh, Eloise, I'm so sorry."

"It's fine," my daughter said. "I'll see you in two hours, Mom. I'll take a cab from the bus stop."

"I could come get you."

"I know you could. But you have all those savage beasts to tend to. I'll take a cab."

After hanging up, I tiptoed back upstairs to make sure Betina was still sleeping. She was on her back, looking rubbery and very much asleep.

I put a few dogs on the back porch and some others in the guest room then leashed the rest and led them to the dog van, a big old purple Econoline from the 1980s. It isn't pretty and it smells terrible, but it's the only way I can shuttle half a dozen dogs at a time to the various trails and parks I take them.

Jimmy and Chico and Harvey and Arturo and Ira and Lucy and Carlos all arranged themselves in the back of the van, with Carlos waiting exactly three seconds before jumping into the front passenger seat then growling toothlessly at any other dog who dreamed of trying to join him there. Of course, the rest of the dogs knew that Carlos didn't have the firepower in his twelve-pound body to back up his threats, but they deferred to him for reasons I didn't entirely understand.

As I went to turn the key in the ignition, I worried

about leaving Betina alone in her condition. I pictured her wandering out of the house and down Byrdcliffe Road, half-naked and stoned. I got back out of the van and, as all the dogs gave me solemn, guilt-inducing looks, went next door to Joe's house.

Joe's is a brown wood-shingled house with purple trim. It looks like something out of a demented fairy tale, particularly when one gets close enough to hear the swells of piano music coming from its entrails.

Whatever Joe was playing sounded beautiful, and for a moment I stood on his front porch listening. I felt bad interrupting but he had, time and again, told me he welcomes interruptions. And this would be the first. I waited for a lull in his playing and pounded on the door. I heard him make some loud exclamation then come running.

He pulled the door open and blinked out at me. "What's wrong?"

"Oh, I didn't mean to scare you, sorry."

"I'm sorry I was looking at your naked girlfriend," Joe blurted out. He even blushed slightly, which was an odd thing to witness on a man in his fifties.

"I don't devote my time to spying on you two, but I just happened to glance out the window and there she was. It was difficult not to notice." He looked so sheepish; his rugged face, which always looks hangdog anyway, was really hanging now. His graying brown hair was falling into his eyes, his broad shoulders sagged.

"I know. I didn't come over to upbraid you. I'm worried about her and am wondering if you could check on her."

I explained what had happened and asked if he could look in on her in half an hour.

He solemnly told me he would keep an eye on her.

"Not too close an eye, she's all doped up. If she tries throwing herself at you, please don't succumb to her."

"I would most certainly not succumb to your girlfriend."

"Why? She's not cute enough for you?" I was suddenly incensed.

"Kim," he said, exasperated, "she's your girlfriend! I like you too much to mess around with your girlfriend. Anyway, you're more my type."

"Since when do you prefer short fifty-three-year-olds to lithe young blondes?"

"I mean emotionally. Betina is a bit . . . well, I don't know. I just paid you a compliment. Must you put me on the spot?"

"Sorry," I said. "And thank you."

I walked back to my van. The dogs all danced. With the exception of Carlos, who was trying to take up as much of the passenger seat as possible.

I drove down the hill, onto Glasco Turnpike, then took Route 212 to Rabbit Hole, a winding road flanked by state land on one side and a rushing creek on the other. Just three miles long, it ends at the trailhead of a massive nature preserve. It's my favorite spot to take the dogs as very few out-of-towners know of or use the trail and, most days, I have the whole gorgeous place to myself.

I let the beasts out of the van and they tumbled forth into the bright spring day. Most of them knew the way but I had to keep Arturo, the Italian greyhound, on a leash since I'd only had him a few days and had no idea if he'd come back if I let him loose in the woods.

We walked along for a half mile until we reached the creek. The only way across was to either wade through the icy, rushing, thigh-high water or hop from one rock to the next. Two of the dogs sloshed through, the others jumped rock to rock. I hopped, with Arturo clutched under one arm. I thought of the time I'd brought my daughters on this trail. Alice had turned up her nose at the idea of jumping across mossy rocks while Eloise gamely hopped in spite of the physical problems that have plagued her ever since she fell in a manhole. Alice eventually deigned to make the crossing and did it effortlessly as she does most things once she puts her mind to them.

The dogs were all bounding up the narrow, lush trail. To the left, the creek roared, savage after days of rain. To the right, mossy hills rose up and slender waterfalls spouted from their sides. The pack and I had been walking for at least an hour before I thought of Betina. I felt guilty realizing I hadn't worried about her all this time and decided to turn back. I picked up the pace and soon we had arrived back at the creek crossing. As I stood, trying to remember which rocks I'd hopped across the first time, I saw a tall woman purposefully striding along the trail on the other side of the creek. She was carrying something that looked like a dollhouse and, as I pondered what anyone would be doing carrying a dollhouse on a hiking trail several miles deep into the woods, she gracefully hopped from rock to rock, crossing the creek in three bounds.

"Hello!" she said brightly.

"Hi," I said back. She was very pretty. Tall with long blond hair. Dressed sensibly but not cheaply. There was something familiar about her.

"What beauties!" she said, bending down to pet Harvey. "Oh, and aren't you exquisite," she added, delicately patting the top of Arturo's head.

I worried that the nervous little dog would bite her out of fear, but he seemed in awe of this leggy woman who was, I realized, carrying a gingerbread house. This was really no better than a dollhouse on the scale of appropriate things to carry on a trail. And I kept waiting, as the woman and I chatted about the dogs, for her to explain why she was carrying such a thing. She did not volunteer this information.

"What are you doing with a gingerbread house?" I finally asked.

"Oh," she said, looking down at it and smiling, "I'm taking it to the lean-to up the trail."

"Ah," I said. Her explanation was even more bizarre than the act of carrying a gingerbread house, but now I was stunned by the realization that this leggy, gingerbread-house-carrying woman was in fact Ava Larkin, the movie star. I don't know why I hadn't put it together sooner. It was common knowledge that she owned a beautiful farmhouse on Rabbit Hole Road. I just hadn't expected to find a certified movie star striding down the trail. And she wasn't acting like a movie star. Not that I really knew what movie stars acted like. Alice briefly dated one. He had worn a baseball cap and sunglasses everywhere he went and that was about all I had determined about him before my daughter broke it off when he professed his love.

"I'm Ava," Ava Larkin said after we chatted for a few more minutes.

"Yes, I just realized who you are. I'm Kimberly Hunter."

"Nice name."

"You too."

Ava Larkin decided to abort her mission of transporting the gingerbread house to the lean-to and instead accompanied the dogs and me back toward the trailhead, gabbing away. Maybe she was starved for company. Maybe she had to stay locked up in her house on Rabbit Hole Road lest lunatics accost her. Whatever the case, she was easy to talk to. She loved dogs, animals of all kinds, she said. She was a Buddhist and had a regular yoga practice. She was, essentially, standard Woodstock fare. Except for the movie star part.

She was only in Woodstock a little while longer then had to fly to Canada to work on a film.

"Some asshole who wants to fuck me is directing," she said. Her pretty, pale face suddenly hardened, the blue eyes narrowed, and the astonishing cheekbones looked like they'd hurt you. It was odd to hear her suddenly using strong language; she'd seemed so gentle and mild-mannered.

"So tell me something, Kimberly," Ava said then, "do you need some work?"

"Work?"

"You mentioned working at a pet food store. That can't be very lucrative."

"It's not," I shrugged. "I was a social worker. For years. It tired me too much. I prefer living on very little and having a simple life."

"So you're not looking for a job?"

"Well, no, not really, but what job?"

"I need a local assistant. Everything from feeding my chickens for the long stretches of time when I'm not here, to dealing with whatever bills come, to running errands for me when I'm in town. Now and then I might need you to go down to the city."

I frowned. Not that the thought of this was unpleasant, more that it seemed astronomically unlikely that I would go hiking, encounter a glamorous movie star, and be offered a job by her.

"I haven't offended you, have I?" Ava asked. Now she was completely sweet and thoughtful again.

"Not at all. It's just somewhat surprising." I stared at the gingerbread house. What did her wanting to carry a gingerbread house to a lean-to portend about what it might be like to work for her, to be suddenly thrust into her life?

"I'll admit," I added, "I'd be nervous to give notice at the pet food store in the event it doesn't work out between us."

"Oh, you wouldn't have to. Not right now. Like I said, I'm going to Canada. You can make your own hours when I'm away and then we'll take it from there. And figure out salary and such. For now, would $400 a week be all right for tending to the chickens and keeping an eye on the house?"

"That's more than generous."

Ava Larkin beamed, and then looped her arm through

my elbow as if we were old pals. "Do you have time to stop in now?"

I almost said yes, and then remembered Betina.

"My girlfriend isn't feeling well," I said. I wondered if she would react adversely to my being gay. "But I could check on her and come back. I have more dogs to run anyway."

If my gayness bothered Ava Larkin in the slightest, she didn't show it. She walked me back to my van at the trail-head parking lot.

"That's my place," she said, pointing to the exquisite white farmhouse atop a hill down the road. "Just come by when you can."

"Would you like a ride back over there?" I asked, even though it was barely a quarter of a mile.

"Thank you, no. I need to walk." She said it like she meant it. Like she would very possibly unravel if she didn't walk.

We shook hands formally, and then I loaded the dogs back into the van and drove back to Byrdcliffe.

I came home to find Joe and Betina sitting in the living room having tea. Betina was fully clothed and looked completely normal. The Vicodin seemed to have worn off. I hadn't been gone *that* long. I didn't know how the storm had passed so quickly.

Betina, acting like an ordinary, balanced human being, offered to make me a cup of tea and trotted off to the kitchen.

I sat down on the couch, sticking my arms straight out in front of me, palms forward, to indicate that I did not want dogs jumping on me.

"I came to check on her and she was fine," Joe told me. "She was vacuuming the living room."

"What?"

"I was vacuuming," Betina said, coming back into the room. "I know. I never do anything to make your life easier. I'm sorry, Kim."

"Uh . . ." I stammered, embarrassed at her making this kind of statement in front of Joe. "Thanks, Betina." Wishing to steer the conversation away from the sensitive and personal, I announced that I'd had a strange encounter on the Rabbit Hole trail.

"Oh?" Joe said politely.

"I ran into Ava Larkin. She was carrying a gingerbread house. On the trail. Then she offered me a job."

"Come again?" said Joe.

I explained in more detail.

"Just further evidence that your life is enchanted," said Joe.

"Enchanted? Me?"

"Full of lovely surprises," Joe said.

I squinted at him.

"It's true," Betina volunteered. "Strange things always happen to you, Kim. Some people attract great luck, others attract misfortune. You attract strange things. And dogs."

"I suppose," I shrugged. "I told Ava Larkin I'd stop by her house in a bit. But I wanted to come home first to check on you, Betina."

"I'm fine," she drawled.

"So I see. Well, I'm taking the second round of dogs now."

Joe gave me a worried look, the same kind of look Ira, the three-legged hound, might give me if he was unsure about what I wanted from him.

"You'll stay awhile? We'll talk more when I get back?" I asked Joe.

"Sure," he said, looking relieved to know what I wanted from him, which, in this instance, was more babysitting of my girlfriend, whose apparently stable condition I didn't entirely trust.

As I got ready to go out again, I pictured Betina seducing Joe the minute I left the house. She'd never expressed interest in Joe but her sexual history is dotted with instances of her having sex with, and often getting involved with, people just because they are there. Somehow, all this time, I'd been able to persuade myself that I was an exception to this emotional sloth of hers. Now, I doubted it very much.

I drove back to Rabbit Hole Road, parked the van, and let the second batch of dogs loose on the trail. They galloped and bounded and looked for squirrels for an hour before we headed back to the van and then down the road to Ava's. A long dirt and gravel driveway led to the big white farmhouse. There were several barns and chicken coops and, near one of the barns, a large pond I'd never realized was there. I parked the van and walked up to a big solid oak door with an old cast-iron knocker. Before I reached for the door, Ava opened up. She had changed into loungy-type clothes: a white tank top that showed off her very firm and prominent breasts, and a pair of white silky pajama pants.

"You can bring the dogs in," she said.

"They'll create chaos."

"I'm a fan of chaos."

I went to get the dogs. They scrambled in, a soundtrack of toenails against wood floors. I cringed. Ava Larkin had to have all sorts of priceless baubles and antiques that these savage, orphaned beasts would destroy with their whip-tails and drooling mouths. But Ava had asked for it and just smiled her beautiful movie star smile as the animals wreaked havoc.

We went to sit in her well-appointed kitchen. A huge barn-wood table stood in the middle of the room. There was a Vulcan stove and an old porcelain sink. The fridge looked to be from the 1950s and was avocado green. There was ample counter space and handsome cabinets of bleached wood. Cast-iron pots of every description hung from overhead racks. Some of the dogs immediately settled down, but Skipper, a black Lab, and Rosemary, the shepherd, were off on some sort of exploratory mission. I expressed concern over their making a mess but Ava Larkin just waved her hand, "It's fine, stop worrying."

In some ways, she was even better looking in life than on screen. Now and then, as she explained some detail of the chicken feeding or the management of potential gas leaks, I would imagine that I'd stepped into one of the many films I'd seen her in—maybe that Sofia Coppola movie where she'd played the chanteuse/hit woman, or the Ridley Scott movie where she'd been a seventeenth-century courtesan, or even the Spike Jonze movie where she'd had hairy armpits and fifty pet rats.

After about an hour, when she'd shown me around the property and introduced me to the chickens, Ava Larkin gave me keys and the code to the alarm.

"Just in case. I mean, I'll still be here for at least another week and we'll spend more time going over things, but I'm sometimes suddenly called into the city and I want you to be fully armed for dealing with my life if I have to leave sooner than planned."

Armed for dealing with her life? I pictured myself riddled with bullet holes. I'd be tending her chickens and a psychotic stalker would mistake me for her and kill me. Of course, there was no physical resemblance. But still.

"Are you all right?" she asked.

"Oh, yes, I'm fine."

She scrutinized me. "Is something about this making you uncomfortable?"

"You don't have any stalkers, do you?"

She smiled. "Not recently, no. No one will be camped out up the hill with an AK-47 aimed at the house, if that's what you're afraid of."

"The thought crossed my mind."

"Strange world we live in, isn't it? Celebrity. It's an uncomfortable skin."

"I can't even imagine."

"No," Ava said, a little sadly, "you can't. But, of course,

I asked for it, tried for it, wanted it. It's a certain kind of freedom. It's a trade-off. One I'm willing to live with."

This struck me as a sensible outlook. I had always presumed stunningly gorgeous women to be incapable of sense. Maybe it was just the stunning women I attract, like Betina for example.

Ava accompanied me outside as I herded the dogs back to the van.

"I feel very good about this," she said as I climbed into my vehicle.

"That's surprising, if you think about it," I replied. "You just met me on a trail in the woods and have no idea who I am or what I'm capable of."

"You're trying to scare me?" She looked delighted.

"No," I smiled, "just marveling at your openness, I suppose."

"Thank you, Kimberly."

We shook hands. As I pulled out of her driveway, Ava Larkin stood smiling and waving, like a dignitary from the beautiful world.

I came home, unleashed the dogs, removed my hiking boots, and walked into the living room to find that Eloise had arrived and was installed on the couch with a pit bull in her lap. Betina was nowhere to be found but Joe was sitting opposite Eloise, in an armchair, with Carlos in his lap.

"You look beautiful," I told my daughter as I leaned over to kiss her cheek.

"I doubt that."

"Eloise, you have to learn to accept compliments."

"Why?"

"Oh, you're going to be a barrel of laughs to have around."

"Mom," she said, "don't talk to me like that in front of Joe. He barely knows me. What will he think?"

"What will you think, Joe?" I turned to look at my neighbor.

"I'm remaining neutral over here." He tapped the arms of his chair as if they were hunks of Switzerland.

"Smart man," Eloise said approvingly.

I studied my daughter, looking for traces of the heartbreak she'd alluded to over the phone. She is so small and delicate that she always looks at least slightly broken. I'm petite, but my olive complexion makes me look sturdier than my tiny, birdlike daughter with her nearly black hair and impossibly white skin. Eloise is drop-dead beautiful but doesn't seem to take her good looks very seriously, and I've seen her go out with men who would be considered hideous by most standards.

"Where did Betina go?" I asked, and as if on cue, I heard drawers opening and closing and a door slamming upstairs.

"She said she had to go to the bathroom. Twenty minutes ago," Eloise said.

I saw Joe and Eloise both giving cautious glances in my direction while refraining from commenting further.

"I should get back to work," Joe said after we heard another door slam upstairs.

"Sure," I said. "Thanks, Joe."

"Stop by later if you want," Joe offered.

"Okay, maybe I will," I said, realizing that I meant this and also realizing that, by having asked Joe to check on Betina earlier, I had opened up some sort of door with him. Some door to a friendship potentially deeper than that of mere neighbors.

"He's nice," Eloise commented after Joe had left and I was leashing up the last round of dogs.

"Yes, he's a good man."

"Aren't you going to see why Betina's slamming doors?" Eloise asked.

"She has days like this," I said with a shrug.

"Oh, Mom."

"Oh, Mom *what?*"

"Nothing." Eloise was looking at me from under her bangs. "Do you want help walking the infirm dogs?" she asked, motioning at Chariot, the husky with a weak hind end, Heather, the blind retriever, and Chicken, the ancient greyhound.

"You can just go work if you'd like," I told her, knowing that on the rare occasion when she does visit, Eloise likes to hole up in the guest room, obsessively working on her stuffed animals. "But thank you for the offer."

I got the aged and infirm dogs out, came back in, and fed all the animals, then, exhausted, climbed upstairs where I hoped to find my girlfriend in a slightly sane state.

Betina was sitting at the edge of the bed, naked. Next to her was the battered green suitcase she loved, half filled with clothes and toiletries. For a moment, I felt optimistic: Maybe she was moving out. The next moment, I felt guilty for this thought. And the moment after that, irrationally enough, I wanted to make love with her. I am usually not even vaguely attracted to her when she's in one of her fugues.

"Are you going somewhere?" I asked.

Her legs were dangling over the edge of the bed like those of a doll on a shelf.

"Yes, I think so."

"Where?" I didn't wait for her to answer, just reached down and pinched one of her tiny, pale pink nipples. She looked up at me, surprised but not, apparently repulsed. I couldn't remember the last time we'd had sex. I put my left palm under her chin, tilted her face up, then leaned down and kissed her deeply. She responded. I bit her bottom lip. I bit her neck. I sucked on her collarbone and pushed her back on the bed. I ran my hands up and down her stomach then put my right hand between her legs. She was wet. She wiggled. She moaned. She suddenly sat up, squashing my hand.

"No," she said, "I'm not even gay."

"What?"

"I'm not even gay. I don't know why I keep fucking you and living with you."

"Oh," I said, hurt and relieved at the same time.

"I thought I loved you."

"Yes. So did I."

"You mean you don't love me?" Now she looked wounded.

"Oh, I do, I suppose. I don't know. I really don't know anymore."

"This is so sad," she said.

It was the sanest thing she'd said in weeks.

She was sitting at the edge of the bed again, legs spread slightly.

"I'm going to live in the monastery."

"Excuse me?"

"With the Buddhists."

"But you're not a Buddhist. You hate meditation. And religion."

"It doesn't matter. I want to sleep on a narrow bed with scratchy sheets. I want silence."

"Ah," I said. "Which Buddhists, anyway?"

"The ones on top of Overlook Mountain."

"Oh." This meant she wasn't going far. Four miles away, to be exact. I figured the moment the reality of a Buddhist monastery sank in, she might decide she is gay after all and attempt returning to my home and hearth.

"When did you decide all this?"

"Right before taking the Vicodin. I thought I should knock myself out for a little while, enjoy a break from reality before setting off on my new life."

I stared at her, baffled.

"Is there something I should be saying now?" I asked. Once she walked out that door, I wasn't sure I'd ever want to see her again. I almost felt like my daughter Alice, who is so deeply definitive in the ending of affections, who goes from hot to frozen in a blink. Maybe this abrupt ending of love would bring me closer to my emotionally savage daughter. Maybe she would laud my ferocity.

"There is not much left that is to say," Betina answered.

In our first weeks together, I'd been charmed by her mentally translating from German to English before speaking and therefore structuring sentences in strange ways. Now, I just wanted to correct her.

"I do need a ride to the monastery," Betina added.

I had forced her to learn how to drive but she'd never really taken to it, what with the winding, shoulder-less roads of Ulster County. Her not driving had created yet another dependence, one I initially found endearing but eventually irritating.

"Of course," I said. "Is that all you're taking?" I motioned at the green suitcase.

"For now."

"This may sound harsh, Betina, but I'd prefer if you weren't coming back and forth all the time. If we're going to break up, I'd like to do it definitively." I was slightly incredulous to be speaking these awful things. They must have been welling up inside me for eons. I wish I'd known.

She gave me a hurt look.

"I'm not saying this to be cruel."

"You're not? I thought you loved me, Kimberly, how can you say these things?"

"You're the one who is quite suddenly moving out."

"And you do not seem sad by this."

"Saddened," I corrected.

She gave me another hurt look. And then, begrudgingly, started packing bags and boxes. We agreed that she could leave some things in the garage and, after calling me to arrange it, come pick the stuff up. We said these end-of-relationship things so calmly, as if we'd been rehearsing them for months. I started marveling at the finality of it all, at the wild sense of freedom that was beginning to expand inside me.

It was 8 p.m., and I wondered if they'd let her in the monastery at such an hour but wasn't about to ask her this. Now that it was happening, I wanted it over, wanted her out. If the monastery was closed, I knew I'd be half tempted to simply leave her there out front.

But they let her in. Maybe she was better prepared for all this than I'd thought, maybe she'd been planning it for weeks. As we came around the final hairpin turn and were confronted with the vast complex of buildings, some of them pretty, some of them uglier than a Motel 6 in North Dakota, I saw that they were waiting for her. A monk and two men in regular clothing helped unload her things from the hatch of my second car, my beloved and filthy Honda. There was an awkward moment with her new Buddhist friends standing expectantly, waiting to show her inside, and Betina and I staring at each other like dogs who felt animosity but were too tired to fight. In the end, she turned without a word and walked into the monastery, the monk on one side of her, the two civilians on the other.

As I drove down the mountain, taking care along the switchbacks and hairpin turns, I almost wanted to burst into song. But my singing voice is awful. I switched the radio on. A rabidly cheerful Beatles song came on.

I pulled into my driveway and saw lights on up in the guest room. Not that I expected Eloise to be asleep by 10 p.m., but if she had suddenly become an early-to-bed type, I wouldn't have been shocked. I wouldn't have been shocked if she'd converted to Orthodox Judaism, renounced sex, or declared herself a presidential candidate. I never knew what to expect of the young woman I had given birth to twenty-nine years earlier.

I went into the house wondering if I'd feel Betina's absence. But all I felt was dogs. Everywhere the eye rested, dogs, dogs, and more dogs. It shouldn't have come as a surprise, but sometimes it still does. I patted a few heads and rubbed one belly then went upstairs, followed by two pit bulls and a Chihuahua, to check on my daughter.

"Yes, Mom," Eloise answered when I knocked at the door.

I opened up and found her sprawled on top of the quilt, lying on her back, wearing nothing but a long T-shirt. There was a half-stitched stuffed animal on the nightstand, pieces of fabric on the floor. The dogs bounded onto the bed and started wagging their tails.

"What are you doing?"

"Working on that roach and not getting anywhere," she said, exasperatedly motioning at the headless animal on the nightstand. "What are *you* doing? What gives with your girlfriend?"

"She moved out."

"She what?"

I told my daughter. About Betina's sudden announcement, about my relief at hearing it.

"Shit, Mom. This all happened when I was vegetating in here?"

"Yes."

"And you're okay with all this? What, are you turning into Alice?"

"I felt I was turning into both you and Alice. You're a bit capricious too, you know."

"But I just had my heart broken. That has to count for something. Has to indicate that there is a capacity for love inside my tiny, shrewish heart."

"Maybe." I sat down at the edge of the bed and Eloise hugged me. Chico, one of the pit bulls, tried to get in there between us. I pushed the beast back and embraced my daughter.

"Tell me about him," I said.

"Billy Rotten."

"Well, with a name like that, what did you expect?"

"It's not his actual name. Just a moniker I gave him. He *is* called Billy. But not Rotten."

My daughter told me of her tumultuous and passionate one-night stand culminating in this Billy Rotten character kicking her out into the cold at the crack of dawn.

"But that's awful, Elo. How could that happen to you?"

"I was vulnerable, I guess. Because of Indio. It's awful to lose someone. Even when you've stopped loving him."

"You have had a terrible few weeks."

"I don't mean to sound like I'm kicking you out of my room or anything, but I'm exhausted, I need to sleep," Eloise said after a while.

"Sure." I got up.

"Don't be forlorn."

"Do I look forlorn?"

"Not really."

I smiled. "Good night, Elo."

"Night, Mom."

I started to usher the dogs out of the room but Eloise said she wanted them there. She'd been dogless for an entire week since Otis, the ridgeback I'd brought her, had been adopted by a family in Riverdale. Now, it seemed, my daughter needed some dog love.

I went downstairs where there was no shortage of dog love. They were all over me. Black fur and golden fur and spotted fur. Tongues and tails and licking and drooling. I felt like one of those people whose human relationships fail because all the available love inside them pours into animals.

It was a sobering thought.

I went into the downstairs bathroom and examined myself. My wild hair was hanging reasonably tamely around my shoulders. My aged neck didn't look too chickeny and the circles under my eyes were at a low ebb. I was presentable. I walked out the front door, across the low stone wall onto Joe's property, and knocked on his door. There was music pouring out of his house but it didn't sound like it was him playing. He was just listening, I supposed. For a moment I panicked, imagining that he was in there wooing some young woman and I would be the nutty middle-aged neighbor interloper.

"Hi," Joe said, pulling the door open.

"Hi back," I said. I looked him over.

"Will you stay awhile?" He asked, ushering me in.

"Maybe."

5. ELOISE

I was lying on the miserably hard bed in my mother's guest room with a one-eyed Chihuahua on my chest and two caramel-colored pit bulls snuggled next to me when I realized I simply didn't give a shit about Billy Rotten anymore. I wondered if I ever really had. If he hadn't just been some suitable vessel to pin my hopes on. I always have to have hope even if I don't know what I'm hoping for. Without this form of pathological optimism, the gun goes in my mouth just like my second boyfriend, Donny, who blew his head off with a hunting rifle at age nineteen.

The guest room mattress was too hard so I sat up and went to the closet to look for a quilt I might cover the mattress with. For a wacky, ex-hippie-drug-addict lesbian, my mother has stern ideas about sleeping and what is best for one's body. Her own mattress is like a bed of rock and the guest mattress isn't much gentler.

There weren't any extra quilts in the guest room so I went to look in the hall closet. My three dog guardians followed and a bunch of other dogs, hearing us stir, came bounding up the stairs. I was nearly knocked down by Timber, a big, shaggy Newfoundland mix who completely fails to understand his own strength.

The hall closet was taken up with dog crates and old clothes. I tiptoed toward my mother's room to see if she was still up. The bedroom was empty though. I wondered if she had raced back up to the monastery to retrieve her lunatic girlfriend.

"Mom?" I called out. Nothing.

I went down to the living room where I was immediately surrounded by dogs. It was late, the house was quiet; I'm sure the beasts had been sound asleep, but a human stirring was reason enough for most of them to get up and see if their services might be needed. Ira, Mom's favorite, came over to lick my hand. Lucy, the elegant Ibizan hound, leapt off the couch and raced ahead of me into the kitchen, hoping for an unscheduled feeding. As I opened up the fridge to stare in, about ten muzzles tried poking in there and Arturo, the Italian greyhound, tried to climb into the produce bin. I ushered all the dogs out of the kitchen and closed the door so I could study Mom's food in peace. My realization that I no longer cared about Billy had made me yearn for a celebratory meal, ideally a hunk of birthday cake with white icing. But there weren't any cakes in the fridge. In fact, there was nothing but sober, healthy food: rennet-free cheeses, organic eggs, veggies, and juices. I closed the fridge and started looking through cupboards. More organic stuff. Grains and dried goods and dozens of things I had no desire for.

The dogs suddenly started making a racket in the living room. There was barking, toenails scraping against the wood floor, and an apparent consensus to try knocking down the door to the kitchen. A moment later my mother came in, looking extremely disheveled. Her sweater was on backwards, her hair was a mess, and she had a crazy look in her eyes.

"Mom, where were you?"

"Nowhere," she said.

"That's impossible."

"Okay. Next door," she amended.

"Next door? At Joe's?"

"Yes."

"What were you guys doing? Heroin?"

"No."

"Mother, you're being monosyllabic and incommunicative."

"It's my right," she said, reaching behind her to open the door to the kitchen, at which the dog cavalry charged in.

"It is?"

"Of course," she replied, absentmindedly reaching down to pat several dogs' haunches and shoulders.

"Fine."

"What were you looking for?" she asked, squatting down to look into the eyes of Chicken, the aged brindled greyhound.

"A giant cake with white icing."

"Ah." Normally, she'd want to know why and would spend some time trying to solve the problem of there not being a giant cake with white icing on the premises. She might run to nearest store to buy one, or dig out a recipe book and begin baking one on the spot.

I started feeling a little peevish that my mother was not acting like my mother. She'd more than made up for her bad parenting in my early years once she started attending Narcotics Anonymous. She truly worked hard at repairing damages and building relationships with Alice and me and had become the mother everyone dreams of, one I can talk to, cry with, or be a child with. One I can expect to bake me a cake at 1 a.m. after I have shown up unannounced at her house on the very night her girlfriend has moved out. But she wasn't acting like the mother I had grown to trust. She was some crazy-haired harridan.

"Mom, what's with you?" I asked, studying her. I hadn't seen her look this wild since her druggie days when emotional torpor made bathing and grooming repellant to her.

"Don't pry, Eloise, it's unattractive. Maybe that's why that rotten guy dumped you."

I was stunned.

"Oh, Elo," she added, the moment she saw my expression. "I'm sorry, that was cruel. Please forgive me."

She reached across the kitchen table to try to take my hand. I didn't let her.

"Yes. That was cruel. But obviously it's something you feel. I'm sorry." I got up and started walking out of the kitchen.

"Eloise, please don't."

I kept walking. I heard my mother get up to follow me. Gone were all my luxurious, frivolous yearnings for cake and icing. I was hurt to the core. Maybe I *am* intrusive, I thought, maybe I demand too much too soon from people. Maybe I should be put to death. Maybe the hunting rifle to the temple would suit me after all.

"I made love with Joe," my mother said to my back, "that's why I'm on edge. But it's no reason for me to make cruel remarks that have no basis in truth. That was awful of me."

"You had sex with Joe?" I turned around, sufficiently stunned by this news to put aside the verbal blow my mother had just dealt me.

"Yes. I don't know why." She looked down at the floor.

"Well?"

"Well what?"

"Was it good?"

"Shockingly so."

"Really?" I pictured Joe. He was a handsome guy, I guess, I just had never thought of him in sexual terms. Not so much because he's old, more because I've known him a long time. He's like wallpaper to me and, I had always assumed, my mother as well.

"Really . . . Elo," she said, touching my face, "I'm so sorry. I was an evil bitch to say what I said. I was so preoccupied by what I'd just done with Joe that it made me irritable."

"Maybe I *am* too intrusive. Too needy. I demand everything from everyone."

"That's just not true, Eloise. The rotten guy was clearly a jackass."

"Yeah, probably. But I'm too tired to think about it now."

My mother studied me long and hard and, I suppose, satisfied that I had forgiven her lashing out, suggested we get some sleep.

As I settled back into the guest room, with not three but four dogs this time, I was too tired to dwell on what my mother had said or on her new adventures in heterosexuality. I was even too tired to mind the rock-hard bed and I fell into a deep sleep.

"You should come with me. It's a beautiful farm. You can see some chickens. Remember how you love chickens? Remember Bertha, your childhood chicken?"

"I have no memory of this alleged pet chicken," I told my mother. "I think it's another of your embellishments."

"Oh no," she shook her head, "no. You had a pet chicken when you were three. That is a fact of this family."

"If you say so," I replied, then scooped organic Cheerios-type cereal into my mouth.

"So you'll come with me to Ava Larkin's?"

"I guess so," I said reluctantly. I don't care for meeting famous people. One has to struggle to pretend it isn't surprising to be conversing with someone whose face is plastered across buses and buildings. I find it exhausting. But I didn't have anything better to do, so why not?

Twenty minutes later, as we pulled up in front of Ava Larkin's beautiful old farmhouse, I asked my mother if she had warned Ava that she was not only bringing an unruly pack of dogs with her, but a daughter as well.

"Oh, I'm sure it's fine," she said.

"Mom, that's no way to start a new tenure of employment, just showing up with your daughter in tow."

"You're not a toddler in swaddling clothes now, are you? She won't mind."

And, in fact, Ava Larkin did not seem to mind one bit.

"So nice to meet you," she said, flashing that million-dollar smile after she pulled open the big door to her farmhouse.

"You too," I flashed my own, considerably cheaper, smile.

Even though she was a certified movie star, Ava Larkin wasn't exactly traditional Hollywood fare. She was rangy with big breasts and her face was a little oddly shaped, like a strangely executed triangle. She was ridiculously beautiful though. And, I noticed, after she'd led us into the kitchen and offered us juice, she had a great ass. I envisioned telling my lesbian money manager Amy Ross about that. About how I had gay feelings for Ava Larkin's ass. I imagine most women must have gay feelings for Ava Larkin's ass though. I'm hardly being innovative in that.

I kept quiet as Ava and Mom gabbed about this and that and Ava presented Mom with a huge stack of bills that needed to be dealt with and then showed her to the office.

When Ava came back into the kitchen, I was still nursing my juice and marveling at the beauty of the kitchen where everything from the appliances to the taxicab-yellow walls was nicely done, but not overdone.

"So what do you do for a living?" Ava Larkin asked, sitting down across the table from me. "Or is that an obnoxious question?"

"No. It's not obnoxious. I make stuffed animals," I said with a shrug. I normally don't feel apologetic about my occupation but it would be hard to hold a candle to Ava Larkin's line of work.

"You do?" Ava's voice went into a higher register.

My making stuffed animals was apparently the most delightful thing she'd heard all week.

"Yeah, it's not profoundly lucrative or anything but it keeps me out of trouble."

Ava Larkin offered the million-dollar smile again. "I

have to show you something," she said, standing, "up-stairs."

I followed her up to the second floor. The ceilings were lower here and I probably wouldn't have noticed if Ava wasn't such a strapping lass. It's not like she was going to bang her head, but if she ever dated a basketball player, he'd have a problem. As I followed Ava down a long hall, I tried remembering who it was the media had linked her with most recently. There had been a husband for a while, Cooper Mavic, a movie star who also had a million-dollar smile, but that had ended badly—or so the tabloids said—when Cooper had an on-set affair with Angelina Jolie. He'd been followed by a Russian tennis star but, last I heard, that was off too.

"I don't show this to everyone," Ava Larkin said, opening the door to a small room and ushering me inside.

The room was packed with toys. There were shelves and tables. All covered in toys. Mostly high-end, hand-made stuffed animals, but some antique iron and wooden toys too. And there, in a place of honor on a middle shelf, was one of my animals—I called it the pit-mouse, a little gray mouse with the big powerful head of a pit bull terrier.

"I'm sure you think I'm insane now," Ava Larkin said. She looked really pleased at the prospect of my thinking her insane.

"Mildly, yes. People who collect things worry me some-times."

"I know. My father is one of them. I always vowed to never collect anything. There really isn't a bigger waste of time and energy. But suddenly, in my mid-twenties, after my first hit movie, I started buying toys. I can't really offer an explanation for it. I was not deprived of toys—or anything—as a child. I just like beautiful toys."

"I made that," I said, pointing to the pit-mouse.

"You did?" Ava nearly squealed as she picked up the

pit-mouse and gazed from it to me, as if looking for a re-semblance. "Eloise, this is beautiful work, really beautiful."

"Thanks." I felt myself blushing. I don't think I've blushed since the age of seven when the back of my dress got stuck in my tights and I walked around with my ass exposed until another kid pointed this out and laughed.

"You know," Ava said, "you can always come up here if you need a peaceful place to work. My house is your house. When I'm out of town or even when I'm here. There's plenty of room. I have four guest bedrooms. You could have a whole suite."

"That's very generous of you."

"Not entirely. I would harbor a slight hope of getting an animal out of it."

"Sure," I said, and I felt my mind instantly grappling with notions of a new and thoroughly unique animal for Ava Larkin.

"Girls?" I heard my mother calling from downstairs. "Anybody home?"

"We're upstairs, coming down," Ava called.

Several of the dogs started bounding up the stairs to look for us. Chico, the pit bull, found us first and immediately went to stand by Ava, pressing his body into her leg, asking her to pet him.

"I know I should take one of these dogs, it's just that my schedule and traveling wouldn't be fair to a companion animal. That's why I only have chickens."

"You could do like Oprah and have your own private jet so the dog could travel in the cabin with you."

"How rich do you think I am?" Ava asked, arching one of her delicate blond eyebrows. "Personal jets are still a ways off for me."

I liked how she said "a ways off," like she did plan to eventually rule the world, or at least be one of the rich and powerful people who can do things like buy airplanes. I'd only known her for about an hour but already had the sense that she'd do a far better job of being über-powerful than most über-powerful people.

"You have a talented daughter," Ava told my mother as we came back downstairs to convene in the kitchen.

"Yes," my mother agreed. "But did she tell you about the coma and the shattered pelvis?"

I thought about kicking my mother or punching her in the face. She was invariably embarrassing me in front of people by bringing up the manhole accident, like my nearly dying was the most interesting thing about me. Even though I do frequently trot this story out, I hate when my mother does it first. I know her bringing it up probably has something to do with what she went through—watching me for weeks struggling to stay alive. But still, it's embarrassing and I've asked her not to do it. I suppose she so wanted to impress her new boss the movie star that she couldn't control herself.

"Mom," I hissed at her.

"Coma?" Ava asked.

"I fell in a manhole. My pelvis was crushed and I was in a coma for weeks," I recited dutifully. "Then my ambulance-chaser lawyer sued the city and I got a million dollars. I still have a hitch in my step and some serious scarring."

"One point two million," my mother corrected.

"Wow," said Ava Larkin. "You're a girl of many gifts."

"Yeah, for tripping, falling, and getting hit in the head with foreign objects." I briefly mentioned the recent incident where a jug of maple syrup had landed on my head. Ava Larkin seemed impressed by this too. Her blue eyes were literally sparkling and there were two cherries of color on her cheeks. Why, I wondered, is this movie star apparently so enthralled by everything about me? Doesn't she ever leave the house?

Ava made us tea and gave us slices of the zucchini bread she had baked that morning. It tasted funny and this was a relief. If she'd been a good cook on top of everything else, I would have had to kill her on principle.

As Ava moved about in the kitchen, as she sat with us at the table, slouching a little, her large breasts prominent under a skimpy white tank top, I found I couldn't take my eyes off her. She was gorgeous but it was more than that. She was fascinating. Her face was expressive; showing joy one minute, worry the next. Her mouth always pouted slightly, and her pale hands moved around like nervous birds. She caught me looking at her several times and I turned away, embarrassed, even though she had to be used to being stared at.

My mother needed to get back home to tend to the rest of her dogs. As we headed to the door, Ava gave me a scrap of paper with all her phone numbers on it.

"Oh," I said, "thanks."

"Call me anytime."

"I will," I said, though this was a complete lie. I seldom call anyone and I certainly wasn't about to call Ava Larkin. What the hell would I say? She'd already heard my best stories.

My mother had gone ahead outside and was loading the dogs into the van when Ava asked if I would give her my phone number too.

"Oh," I said, taken aback, "sure."

She pulled her cell phone from a pocket in her cargo pants.

I recited my mobile and home numbers and watched as she entered them into her phone, squinting cutely as she did.

"Thanks," she said, then gave me a significant-seeming look.

I smiled. Felt myself blushing.

As I lay on the hard bed in Mom's guest room, Chico the pit bull on one side, Slim the whippet on the other, I realized that Ava was very possibly interested in me. And it seemed preposterous. I'm cute, even modestly successful, but I'm a girl and Ava Larkin, as far as I know, doesn't bat for the other team. Even if she does, it seems she'd want to hit up some fellow movie star, maybe some kittenish ingénue or a fellow lanky blonde with a ranch in Malibu. Power attracts power. And I don't have any.

Still, it was flattering. It's not every day a beautiful movie star hits on me.

I was about to get my phone out to call Amy Ross to tell her Ava Larkin had asked for my number when the phone rang. I looked at the caller ID. Alice.

"Hey," I said.

"You at Mom's?"

"Yeah."

"How is it?"

"Okay," I said. "She broke up with the German." I filled her in on Mom's emotional drama. "You know Ava Larkin?"

"Who?"

"The movie star? Ava Larkin?"

"Oh, right, yeah, what about her?"

"Mom's working for her."

"Come again?"

I told Alice the whole story, omitting the part about Ava Larkin asking for my phone number. My sister would have laughed at me, told me I was an idiot to think Ava was interested in me sexually. I *am* an idiot, but I'm not stupid.

"That sounds like Mom," Alice said when I'd finished with the story. "That kind of stuff always happens to her. She leads an enchanted life."

"Yeah," I said.

"And how is your rotten guy?" Alice asked dutifully.

"Still rotten. I mean, I guess he's still rotten. I don't know. I haven't talked to him, and as of last night, I'm over him."

"That's good to hear. Now it's my turn."

"Your turn what?"

"I met a guy."

"You mean other than your homicidal oaf?"

"Yeah." She told me about the guy. He sounded smart. She sounded smitten.

I had a pang of jealousy over it then remembered that Ava was possibly smitten with me and there was enough smitteness to go around.

"And what about Clayton's homicide rap?" I asked, feeling strange about uttering the phrase "homicide rap" like we were a family of felon-harborers and this sort of thing was commonplace.

"We're working to get it knocked down to manslaughter."

"But he's at your house? I mean, he's not in jail?"

"He's out on bail, yeah."

"So how are you seeing this other guy if Clayton's at your house?"

"Clayton and I broke up."

"And he still lives with you?"

"Where else is he going to go?"

"His own apartment maybe?"

"You know he doesn't have one."

"Make him get one."

"I can't make anyone do anything."

"Let's not get philosophical."

"What?" Alice snapped.

"I was trying to be funny."

"Oh."

"You don't sound so good, Alice."

"I'm struggling."

"You doing okay at the track?"

"It's been a bad week. But that's not the struggle."

"What's the struggle then?"

"I wish I knew. I'm fighting, but I don't know what I'm fighting."

"Oh." I made sympathetic noises and listened to my sister until she was done talking. I doubted I'd made her feel any better, but since I've dumped on her several thousand times, making her listen to a long litany of complaints when she really has better things to do, I tried to be helpful.

"Thank you, El," she said a few minutes later, "you're a good listener sometimes."

I felt slightly virtuous when we hung up.

The phone rang again. The incoming number was blocked but I instinctively knew it wasn't a telemarketer.

"Hello?"

"Eloise, hello, this is Ava."

"Hi, Ava," I said brightly, though what I felt was confused and stupid. And terribly flattered.

There was a tiny pause, a small intake of breath on Ava's part, then I could almost hear her deciding to plow ahead.

"What are you doing later?" she asked.

"Absolutely nothing."

"Will you be hungry?"

"Always," I said. My heart rate accelerated.

"Dinner?"

"Yes. Let's." I tried to sound calm.

"Do you have any preferences?"

Men, I thought.

"No. Me and Mom always eat at home so I don't know the local places."

"Maybe The Bear Café then," Ava said.

"Sounds ominous."

She laughed. "It's in Bearsville. A whole town of ominous. The food is good. Shall I pick you up? Maybe 7?"

"Sure, that'd be great." My stomach was knotted and I was surprised I could actually speak.

I explained how to find my mother's house and told Ava I was looking forward to seeing her later. I thought I might have even sounded coherent, collected.

I closed my phone and stared at it. I was amazed. Confused. Incredibly excited.

I got up from the hard bed and upended my backpack hoping that by some chance I'd brought decent clothes. I had not. I was used to wearing jeans and sweatshirts when visiting Woodstock. It's not exactly a formal place and it was unlikely my jeans would be snubbed at this ominous-sounding Bear Café, but still. I was having dinner with Ava Larkin. I didn't want to look like shit.

"Mom!" I raced out of the guest room.

"What?" she called up from somewhere downstairs.

"I need to go clothes shopping. Now."

I started down the stairs and saw my mother sitting in the middle of the living room floor, brushing Timber while half a dozen other dogs lay nearby, studying the grooming process.

My mother frowned at me and it was hard to tell if she was frowning at my disruption of a tender moment with the mutts or the notion that I suddenly required clothes shopping.

I was prepared to explain myself, to tell her that I was considering a lesbian liaison with her new employer, to get it all out in the open and wait for that knowing look that old lesbians give straight girls when they confess to finding another woman attractive. Except, of course, as of last night, my mother was no longer a card-carrying lesbian in the strict definition of things.

"You can take the Honda," my mother said, as if my sudden need to go shopping was completely normal.

"You mean drive?" I asked, aghast. I detest driving. I got a license a few years ago at Alice's urging after I'd had about my sixtieth bicycle accident riding my 1984 Peugeot ten-speed around Manhattan. I learned to drive and passed my test and have driven exactly twice since.

"Eloise, you are a licensed driver. You're almost thirty years old. Town is two miles away. You can do it."

"But Byrdcliffe Road is so twisty," I whined.

"You can walk. Or take my bike. Though please don't have an accident."

"Who are you and what have you done with my mother?" I asked, indignant.

She smiled. "I have things to do, Elo. Go on. Take the Honda. You'll be fine."

"Aren't you going to ask why I need to go shopping?"

"You're a beautiful young woman with a good career and more than a million dollars in the bank. As such, a sudden desire to go shopping is natural and probably even healthy. Buy me something."

I could see that my mother had no interest in extracting details from me, didn't, in fact, think there were any details, any secret Sapphic reasons for my shopping spree. I begrudgingly took the keys to the Honda from the wall hook near the kitchen door and, with much trepidation, got into the car.

I was pretty sure I was going to die or plow into one of the expensive houses dotting the sides of Upper Byrdcliffe Road and I did very nearly take out a rogue squirrel. I made it to town though, even found a parking spot that didn't require parallel parking.

Woodstock isn't exactly a hotbed of fashion but neither am I. I went into the lone decent clothing store, where a young girl with dyed black hair helped me find a slinky dark-red top and some form-fitting black jeans with skinny legs. I was in the dressing room, staring at myself and wondering if I was attractive enough, when it occurred to me to look at the price tags. The jeans were $220 and the top was nearly $300. Apparently, Ava Larkin isn't the only rich woman in Woodstock. I was about to take the clothes off and go look for a thrift store when I remembered that I am, by my standards at least, rich. Even though I love saying "I'm rich," I haven't had money long enough to not flinch at price tags.

"Where can I get shoes?" I asked the shopgirl as I handed her my credit card.

She made a sad face. "The city," she said. "But you can try the hippie shoe store across the street. They occasionally have something that isn't hideous. Or there's that sort of matronly women's clothing store down the block, they have decent shoes sometimes."

I did as the shopgirl suggested. The hippie shoe store was chock full of Birkenstocks, Keens, and other utilitarian and less-than-attractive footwear that was not suitable for a date with a movie star; and the salespeople were churlish. I had expected gregarious, eager hippies selling hippie shoes, but these people seemed to avidly hate customers and I was relieved I didn't have to validate their existence by buying ugly footwear from them.

The matronly women's clothing store had a few pair of vaguely sexy open-toed sandals, but it wasn't a warm day and the night would probably be downright cold. I decided my silver Camper sneakers would work fine, even give a nice tomboyish contrast to the sexy, femme outfit I was going to wear.

I got back in the car and found myself pulling down the sun visor to inspect myself, making sure my skin looked all right, that my hair didn't need trimming. After I'd flipped the sun visor back up, I realized I was going insane. Or at the very least, putting an awful lot of thought and worry into a date with a girl. It was weird. Disquieting. I half wanted to call Amy Ross to get girl-on-girl tips. I'd had little flings with girls, but those were in the distant past and had been fueled by booze. I wasn't sure I would know what to do. I wasn't sure I wanted to know what to do.

Fuck, I thought, what am I doing?

I drove back up to my mother's without taking out any trees, pedestrians, or small animals. I walked into the house just in time to say goodbye to my mother, who was heading out to a Narcotics Anonymous meeting. "I might not be here when you get back," I told her in a nearly threatening voice. I really wanted her to ask where I was going and with whom.

"Okay, you have fun," my mother said breezily, leaving me standing there with my shopping bags and only the dogs to tell my troubles to.

Harvey, the pit bull, blinked at me. The one-eyed Chihuahua, Carlos, wagged his stubby tail.

At precisely 7 p.m., a white Volvo 240 wagon pulled into the driveway. The fact that Ava Larkin was driving an old beat-up Volvo, when she could have driven any car she desired, made my chest constrict with fondness.

"Nice car," I said, coming out the door.

"Thanks," she beamed through the open driver's side window.

Her long blond hair was down and a little messed up from the wind. She was wearing a white sweater. I could feel its softness from five feet away.

"Get in," she said.

I did as I was told.

"Hi," she said as I slid into the passenger seat.

"Hi," I said, feeling like a thirteen-year-old girl.

We chatted throughout the short drive to the Bear Café. She wanted to know more about Mom's dogs. I told her how Mom periodically shows up on my doorstep, uninvited and unannounced, toting some mutt she needs me to give a foster home to.

"My mother is always sitting on top of mountains somewhere," Ava said a bit wistfully. "Her Buddhist stuff."

"My mom's girlfriend just left her for a monastery," I explained. "So my mom went and had sex with the next-door neighbor. A man." Seconds after the words left my mouth, I felt like an indiscreet dunderhead for spilling my mother's private life out to this woman who was, after all, her new employer.

But Ava didn't seem to give it much thought. She had pulled into the vast parking lot of the Bear Café, wedging the Volvo between a Land Rover and a BMW.

As we walked over to the restaurant, housed in a one-story wooden building perched over a creek, I wondered if people were going to recognize Ava, hound her for autographs, stare.

"Nice to see you, Ava," the hostess greeted her like any regular customer. Warm but not fawning.

We were shown to a table overlooking the creek. Ava moved gracefully, her long form flowing from standing to sitting. The creek roiled outside the window, pushing, forcing its way mightily along. My stomach was coiled and my palms were moist.

"I'm vegan most of the time," Ava announced after the waiter, a ridiculously beautiful young blond boy, brought us menus. "Once in a while I eat dairy."

I'd been vegetarian so long I never even thought about it anymore. Mom had been vegetarian since before I was born and even though she told me to go out and gorge on burgers if I so chose, I only did it once. It was gross. Neither my mother nor Alice nor I seem to require meat. Mom once theorized that the lack of meat in our childhood diet might be partially responsible for our rapaciousness where men are concerned. But I was feeling rapacious about Ava Larkin too. And she's no man.

"The stuffed animal business is frustrating," I said at one point, as we dug into our entrees, mine a pleasant risotto with yams, hers a seitan steak, "it's all up to the buyers, and toy store buyers are a fickle bunch. I've done well, but not as well as I should."

"You're doing perfectly," Ava said.

She was looking right into me, the blue eyes big and beautiful. I was beginning to simultaneously melt and tingle when she reached over and traced my cheek with her finger. I nearly passed out.

She didn't look the slightest bit abashed over the gesture, didn't seem the slightest bit abashed over our obviously being on a date in a small town where surely everyone in the place knew who she was. No. Ava Larkin wasn't an abashed type. I thought of her in the red catsuit she had worn in that Spike Jonze movie. I remembered that, at the time, I had thought Ava particularly stunning in her outrageous costume. I had admired her form and her ability as an actress even though I have always been a bit of a snob about actors, putting them into a pile with architects and lead singers in rock bands as pathological attention-getters. But she really wasn't the woman in the red catsuit now. She was just a girl I was on a date with.

We were sharing a crème brûlée when a lanky man with a shaved head skulked over to our table. I saw him coming before Ava did and, even though he was a nice-looking lanky man, I immediately assumed him to be some ne'er-do-well autograph seeker, some potential borderline stalker. I could feel myself frowning as he made eye contact with Ava. But she just beamed, jumped up, and threw her arms around him. "Josh," she said, "where the hell have you been?"

As the lanky Josh enfolded my date in his arms I felt a ridiculous and violent pang of jealousy.

"I've been here," Josh said, when the two finally drew apart. "Haven't heard from you though, Little Miss."

He calls her Little Miss? I thought, nearly enraged.

"Eloise, this is my friend Josh. Josh is an incredible guitar player."

Guitar player? I thought. *She's throwing me over for a guitar player?*

"Nice to meet you." I forced myself to smile at Josh.

Ava and Josh chatted for a good five minutes. They included me in their discussions of how late spring was and the new Nick Cave record and the first few months of the exhilarating new president's tenure. As the conversation progressed, Ava and I continued on with sharing the crème brûlée and, at one point, I saw Josh look from the dessert to Ava to me and I could see a bulb lighting in his mind. I wondered if he hoped for a threesome. I know I didn't.

Eventually, Josh ambled back to the table where he'd been sitting with a guy with a nose ring. Ava insisted on paying our check and we rose to leave. We walked out into the brisk, starless night. A small, furtive-looking man was on the front patio of the restaurant huffing a cigarette.

"Do you smoke?" Ava asked as we walked by the man.

"Sometimes," I said, "but not wholeheartedly. My sister does. Chimney."

"I smoke for little periods of time. Then my skin gets dry and old-looking and I quit and vow never to do it again."

As I considered the sheer impossibility of Ava Larkin's luminous, pale skin ever looking dry or old, even should she live to the age of 108, I also considered what her lips might taste like.

When we arrived at the car, Ava grabbed my arm. I wheeled around and practically lunged at her. Our mouths came together and our bodies touched. She tasted like crème brûlée. She put her hands on my ass. I put one on her hip and the other under her shirt, touching the tender skin of her stomach. She bit my lips lightly, then pulled back a little.

"Since neither one of us is a man, we can fuck on the first date, right?" she said.

I looked at her, tilting my head.

"We can, but what's our not being men have to do with it?" I asked, puzzled.

"Because men lose interest the moment they've conquered, whereas women's interest just increases after sex. It's a biological thing."

"Oh, whatever you say. I'd walk off the edge of the world with you right now."

"I wouldn't ask such things of you," she said softly.

I woke up to find a monster licking my face. Chico the pit bull. His massive pink tongue issuing forth from the massive pink mouth, an intimidating sight if I hadn't completely trusted the beast.

"Off me, animal," I gently pushed him away.

I was on the hard bed in Mom's guest room and had fallen asleep around noon shortly after coming back from Ava's. She and I hadn't done a lot of sleeping. There had been kissing and biting and coming, there had been the lovely sight of her blond hair mixing with my dark brown hair on the pillow when I woke up, and then a long peaceful half hour as I lay there watching her sleep, on her back, large breasts like melting butter. She had very little pubic hair, just a tiny landing strip even more rigorously tended than my own. She probably had a personal waxer come over and remove every hair from her body. I always do a home job, heating wax in a double boiler on my stove, dripping the yellow goo of it everywhere, and sometimes doing a downright rotten job, slathering it on unevenly with the result of a dent in the symmetry of my own landing strip.

Chico jumped off the bed and went to sniff through my backpack. I sat up and looked at my inner thighs where there were bruises. Ava's appetite, as voracious as mine, had caused her to nearly draw blood with her love bites. I stared at the bite-shaped bruises, purple, a little blue, actual tooth marks in one of them.

"Hellooooo," I heard Mom come in downstairs.

"I'm here, Mom," I called out. I got off the bed, pulled my jeans on, and went out into the hall, Chico dancing at my side, excited that I was finally up.

Chico bounded down the stairs ahead of me as the half dozen dogs who'd been out with my mother raced up to sniff and lick at me. Ira, the three-legged hound, jumped up on me, putting his one good leg on my stomach and looking up at me searchingly.

"And where, pray tell, did you spend the night?" my mother asked.

I had called her late at night, leaving a message that I'd be out and no to worry—but I hadn't mentioned that I was shacking up with Ava Larkin.

"At a friend's."

"The Irish guy?"

"No," I said. It was a reasonable assumption on her part since the Irish guy, Gerard, was the only person I knew living in the area and he was, according to my mother, a dead ringer for Viggo Mortensen, who my mother thought one of the sexiest men to ever live.

"Well, where were you, Elo?"

I finally had my mother's attention.

"Ava Larkin's."

"Ava's? Why?" My mother looked thoroughly confused.

"Just hanging out," I shrugged.

"Just hanging out all . . ." My mother stopped in midsentence when the lightbulb went off. "You mean you *had sex* with Ava Larkin?" She actually shrieked.

"Yeah," I shrugged again, like it was every day that I had sex with a female movie star.

"I'm not really sure what shocks me more here," Mom said, looking at me and blinking rapidly, "the gender of the person in question or how quickly you operate."

"I wasn't operating!" I protested. "She asked me out."

"Since when do you like girls?"

"I just like Ava. She's gorgeous. She's smart."

"She's filthy rich and she's my boss," Mom said. She had put her left fist on her hip. Her eyes were bright and her big curly hair had, I swear, gotten bigger and curlier. She was verging on looking like Malcolm Gladwell.

"I don't think this will compromise your work situation. Anyway, she goes to Canada soon."

"But what about when you break up with her? She'll fire me."

"Break up with her? It's not like we're an official item."

"Well, what are you?"

"I dunno," I shrugged yet again. I felt pretty shruggish.

"When will you find out?"

"You want me to have a monogamy talk with a girl?"

"Is that what you want?"

"I don't know, Mom, I just fucked her last night, I have to digest it."

She rolled her eyes. "Heathens. You and your sister. Savages. Devil-spawn."

"That's not polite, Mom. I feel very tenderly toward Ava."

"You're about as tender as a bag of rocks."

"Isn't the expression *stupid* as a bag of rocks?"

"I didn't know there was such an expression."

"Well, it's not nice for you to compare your youngest daughter to a bag of rocks, Mom, you're really getting mean in your dotage."

She laughed.

I laughed.

Chico let out a sharp, excited bark.

6. ALICE

"Look at this piece of shit!" Arthur jumped to his feet and waved his fist at the glass window overlooking the track. "Bum!" he screamed.

Arthur had gone against his own contrarian grain and bet the odds on the Todd Pletcher–trained favorite. It was backfiring. The horse, a splashy bay colt with a white blaze, had broken alertly out of the gate, gone to the lead, and stayed there for six furlongs, only to start running backwards in the last eighth of a mile and managing, in the end, to beat just one horse, a 70-1 longshot.

At the table next to ours sat three well-fed, wealthy-looking matrons in pantsuits. They were all staring at Arthur who was so inured to these sorts of shocked looks that he truly did not notice. I offered the matrons a smile of enormous wattage. They looked away.

Arthur stormed from our table, presumably to go huff cigarettes on the back terrace. I considered joining him but I had weaned myself down to three cigarettes a day now that I was doing some yoga and had even started going back to the gym for kickboxing class where Pedro, the kickboxing coach, had smelled cigarettes on me one day and commented, "Alice, you're a beautiful woman and you have some athletic potential, why you want to destroy yourself with cancer sticks is beyond me."

"I can't help myself, Pedro," I said, "it's the unbearable lightness of being. It really gets me down."

This was lost on Pedro, who frowned then turned his attentions to another student.

Arthur came back to the table. He was grimacing but

had gotten over the initial shock of the bum horse losing.

"Who do you think is gonna call you?" he asked irately, motioning at my phone which I'd been looking down at.

"A friend."

"I thought the homicidal oaf broke up with you."

This was true. Just a few days after I'd met and kissed William, the dog rescuer in Central Park, Clayton had come home, flopped onto the couch, and announced it wasn't working between us. I'd told him he could continue living with me. On the couch. And I'd tried not to think about the slight chest constriction I felt at that moment. It was probably just a heart arrhythmia.

"Clayton did break up with me," I confirmed for Arthur.

"But you have a new victim."

"Possibly."

"And you're waiting for him to call and fawn over you after you had your way with him all night long?"

"I haven't had my way with him."

"Ah. So you're still in the delusional state, suspending disbelief. Telling yourself this time it will be different."

"You're such a cheerful companion, Arthur."

"That's what you love about me." He glanced at the video monitor then started scribbling furiously in the margins of his Daily Racing Form. His big, tinted eyeglasses were sliding down to the edge of his nose and a vein on his forehead was throbbing like a gorged flower stem.

"Arthur," I said.

"What?" He didn't look up.

"I have to go."

"Go where?" He still didn't look up.

"Home."

"Why?"

Now I had his attention.

"I'm bored and cold."

"Thanks a lot."

"I don't mean by you. I just can't focus."

"You still coasting off that Pick 4 last week?"

I hadn't even told Arthur when I'd hit an insanely lu-crative Pick 4 a week earlier, on a day when he had been having particularly rotten luck.

"Yeah," I said tentatively.

He nodded.

"All right then. Off with you." He waved a hand at me. "I'll go find George to tell my troubles to."

George, Arthur's much-abused friend, is an antisocial antiques dealer slash gambler who Arthur has known for years. George is one of those hangdog types, perpetually prowling the track, preferring lurking to sitting down. When Arthur runs out of turf writers or trainer friends to talk to, he finds George and makes his shy, quiet friend sit at the table listening to his theories and tales of tough beats.

"See you, Arthur," I said, bending down to peck him on the cheek.

He grunted and waved his hand at me again, as if wav-ing off a gnat.

I went down the escalator, past the kiosk selling pro-grams, and outside, through the drizzle and onto the sub-way platform. The sky was low and threatening. A very fat man was sitting on one of the wooden benches, rocking back and forth. I pictured the late Vito on the platform. His protuberant belly, his quaking jowls. His big, messy body on the train tracks, blood and brain matter mixing with garbage and grease. I shivered. I flipped my phone open and dialed home, wondering if Clayton would answer. He did not.

The train car was sparsely populated, just three kids in huge sweatshirts, two old men, and one beautiful young African-looking woman the kids kept stealing glances at.

The fringes of Queens rolled by the train windows.

When I got home, Candy did a wild, jubilant dance

then launched herself into my arms. I cradled her and let her lick my nose.

"Clayton?" I called out. Nothing.

I put Candy down. She wiggled in place for several seconds, then ran to the door and eagerly looked from it to me and back. I got her leash off a hook and took her out to pee. We walked over to the river where I stared at the skyline blending into the slate-gray sky. Candy sniffed, dug a hole in a flowerbed belonging to a hideous condo high-rise, and barked at a Rottweiler and his human. The cold, which had gotten in my bones at Aqueduct, hadn't left. I started jogging, Candy trotted at my side, her curled white tail high in the air, chin up, obviously proud of her station in life.

I was still cold after jogging for a few a few blocks so I broke into a flat-out run. Candy skipped along next to me, excited by this sudden bout of activity, now and then jumping up to bite at her leash. It was still drizzling and my hair was getting wet and whipping across my face. The air smelled like rotten eggs. Candy had pinned her ears back like a racehorse. We must have looked a little mad. But there wasn't anyone to see us.

By the time I got back home, the dog and I were completely soaked. We took the stairs two at a time. I unlocked the door and called out to Clayton. Nothing.

I went into the bathroom and turned on the water in the tub.

"Sorry, but you're filthy," I told the dog. I deposited her in the tub. Her tail sagged and she pulled down the corners of her mouth as I used the shower sprayer to hose her down. She gave me an insulted and hurt look as I soaped her up with dog shampoo then hosed her again. When I'd rinsed all the brownish water off her, I let her jump out of the tub. She shook, spraying water all over everything. I engulfed her in a huge bath towel and dried her.

I turned the shower back on, stripped off my wet

clothes, and got in. I stood under the showerhead for a very long time.

I was still cold.

When my skin had turned red and my feet were pruned, I stepped out of the shower and wrapped myself in a towel. I had just started brushing my hair when I heard Candy let out an excited yelp and then heard the front door open.

"Clayton?" I called out.

"Hi, Alice." He sounded defeated.

I found him standing just inside the front door, shoulders sagging, hair falling in his face.

"Hi," he said lifelessly, "thought you were at the track."

"I left. It was cold and boring."

"Oh." He wasn't looking at me.

No one seemed to want to look at me today. Had I been struck hideous in my sleep? I self-consciously ran my fingers through my wet hair.

"What's wrong, Clayton?"

"I can't take being a burden to you anymore, Alice, it makes me feel like a creep. I have to sort myself out."

"Okay," I said slowly, not sure where he was headed with this particular line of thinking.

"I'm gonna put the van back in the parking lot and live there for a while."

"That's absurd, Clayton."

"You need your freedom."

"You can still be my roommate."

"I don't want to be your roommate."

I had spent most of our relationship trying to get rid of Clayton, and now, even though I was interested in someone else, I didn't want him to move out.

"I don't want you to go," I said, surprising myself.

"Why?"

"I like you."

"You got a funny way of showing it."

"I'm sorry. I don't do that well with interpersonal relationships."

"No kidding."

"But I don't want you to live in a parking lot."

"I did get some work," Clayton said. "A carpenter friend of mine needs some help. I'm going to go with him tonight to give an estimate on a job. Then I'll have at least a few days' work helping him."

"That's great," I said, trying to sound genuinely enthusiastic.

"I can give you some money for bills."

"You don't have to."

"I want to."

"Okay. So you'll stay?"

He finally looked me in the eyes. He was searching for something. I doubt he found it. But he agreed that he would stay on, sleeping on the couch. I felt inexplicable relief.

I went back into the bathroom to finish drying off. I slathered myself in body lotion, brushed my hair thoroughly, then put on the jeans and T-shirt I had hanging on a hook in the bathroom. They were relatively clean. Or, at least, I couldn't remember the last time I'd worn them.

"You want me to make some dinner?" Clayton asked when I came out.

"Dinner?" I said dumbly. For one thing, it was not yet 5 p.m., and for another, I had never seen Clayton cook anything.

"I'm trying to pull my weight here, Alice."

"That's okay. I'm not hungry yet. But thank you."

"I'd cook something later but I have to go out and do that job estimate in an hour."

"Don't worry about it." I felt uncomfortable with this new mutual solicitousness. Clayton had, I suppose, always been solicitous, but he'd never gone so far as to offer to cook. And I had never been at all solicitous. I tried that sort of thing on for size in a few past relationships and it had always backfired. Whenever I went out of my way for some guy, he took it as a sign to walk all over me. So I'd cut solicitousness from my repertoire several years earlier and never looked back.

"Well . . ." Clayton's arms were hanging loose at his sides and he was looking down at his feet. "I guess I'll take a shower."

"Okay," I said softly. I didn't know where I was getting this new inclination toward being empathetic to the big oaf. Maybe I was getting some sort of sickness, some disease of the brain, a particularly insidious tumor that would make itself known only by changing my behavior.

I went into the bedroom and sprawled face first on the bed. Candy was nesting on one of the pillows, licking herself. Her wet fur had left moisture all over the covers.

When I woke up it was nearly dark out and Clayton was gone. I got up and wandered room to room like a ghost. Normally, I'd be hard at work on the next day's races but I didn't think I could focus. Candy followed me as I wandered, wondering what the restlessness was about and if it could possibly lead to something good for her, like a walk or a meal of gooey meat.

I eventually settled in front of the computer and checked my e-mail. I'd sent William a note reiterating that I am single, since he'd seemed reluctant to believe it. Apparently, he was still reluctant.

He'd sent a return note stating that even if Clayton and I had downgraded to an "open" relationship, he didn't perceive me as unencumbered.

I wasn't sure where he'd gotten the idea that Clayton and I were having an open relationship. Even though monogamy is a tenuous proposition at best, I am a monogamist. I thought I had made that clear to William. I would not be seeking to swap spit with him if Clayton hadn't broken up with me.

I MapQuested the address on the signature line of William's e-mail. I knew he had both an office and an apartment in the same building. There was a reasonably good chance he'd be there.

I went into the bedroom, threw open my closet door, and stared savagely at my clothes. My eye rested on a fetching knee-length red dress. It was sexy but understated, if a red dress can ever be understated. I changed my underwear, putting on matching black bra and thong. I looked at myself in the closet mirror.

Cheap slut. Tramp. In my head I could hear my mother jokingly admonishing me.

My hair needed a trim but I didn't imagine William would be scrutinizing my split ends. That was the sort of thing I only had to worry about when having a dinner with one of my gay male friends. Gay men are relentless in their attention to the details of their female friends' appearances. Heterosexual males don't do much more than take in the tits, the ass, and the mouth.

My eyes weren't too puffy and my eyebrows, which had started getting thicker when I hit thirty-five, looked like they were having a tame evening. I had shaved my legs a day earlier, had a bikini wax last week. The yoga and kickboxing had made me a little less bony and more toned, or so I imagined. I felt about as comely as I ever feel. I pulled the dress over my head then put on my suede knee-high boots.

As I stood near the front door, hesitating, Candy looked up at me expectantly and wagged her tail.

I was a rapacious woman in a red dress, I might as well take my little dog too.

I put Candy's leash on and we walked to the subway. I picked her up and carried her under my arm like a football as I went through the turnstile. The man in the token booth either didn't notice or didn't care about my canine companion.

On the 7 train, an elderly woman complimented Candy's good looks.

"What a beautiful dog. Looks like an artic fox."

"Thank you," I said, even though I'm never sure how to respond to such things. It's not like I had anything to do with my little mutt's attractiveness.

At 42nd Street, I switched to the F train that brought us down to the Lower East Side. I walked up from the city's murky bowels and into a night that wasn't much brighter. I put Candy down. She sniffed at the pavement and seemed to make a face.

I remembered Ridge Street from long ago when, in my early teens, I'd had a junkie boyfriend whom I'd accompanied to score heroin. Puerto Rican and Dominican boys with firearms stood on corners watching for police cruisers and potential undercover cops while dozens of junkies, thin and smelling of death, lined up, waiting to buy little glassine baggies. Now, with shiny stores and eateries lining every block, it was hard to remember the area's past.

The building was a four-story brick, narrow but sturdy-looking. In the ground floor window stood a discreet placard reading, *Nichols Architecture*. There was a light on even though it was nearly 9 p.m.

I rang the buzzer. Nothing happened.

Candy looked from me to the door, wondering what was taking so long, eager to go in and explore this new place.

I felt like a jackass in a red dress. I considered what to do next. Maybe go to one of the few remaining bodegas and buy some cigarettes, then smoke, and walk my mutt down the once-scary streets, maybe even head up to 7th and B to see if, by some miracle, the horseshoe bar was still there.

Just as I was about to turn around and start walking uptown, there was a humming sound and I realized someone had answered the buzzer. I pushed the door open and walked into the hall, where I found William peering out from his office.

"Nice dress," he said, not showing the least surprise at my materializing there uninvited.

"Thanks."

"I was just firing off irate e-mails, come in while I finish up."

His big pit bull was standing at the door, wagging her tail. Candy approached warily and, when William's dog sniffed at her head, growled slightly. The big dog backed off.

"Sorry, Candy has that little-dog Napoleon-complex thing."

"Gumdrop doesn't care. She's the easiest-going dog I've ever known," William said. "Make yourself comfortable." He motioned at a low, modern gray couch that didn't look designed for comfort.

I sat down. Candy jumped into my lap; Gumdrop came and stood near us, wagging her tail.

William's office was clean and completely devoid of clutter. Sleek, modern wood shelves were lined with manuals and books. A slender, elegant desk held an enormous desktop Mac.

William had gone right back to what he was doing. I realized I'd expected that the mere sight of me would melt him. Not that I am known for making men melt on the spot, but once they're interested in me, it usually takes a bulldozer to drag them away.

I gave William thirty seconds more, then stood up.

"I'm not sure why I dropped in unannounced, you obviously have work to do," I said, walking toward the door.

He swiveled his chair around to face me. "What?" He looked at me like I was insane.

"We'll see each other some other time."

"Don't be ridiculous. I need ten seconds, then I'll give you my undivided attention."

He looked right into me as he said it. I sighed and sat back down. I stared at the bookshelves.

William finally got up from his hi-tech office chair and came to sit next to me on the couch. He touched my face.

"Hello, Alice."

"Hi, William."

He leaned closer and kissed me lightly.

I kissed him back, hard.

He put one hand on my chest and pushed me away.

"What's your status?" he asked.

"Status?"

"The live-in companion."

"He's still living in but he isn't a companion. At least not with any romantic implications. I thought I had made that clear."

"You did. But I still hesitate to put myself at your mercy."

"Mercy? There's no mercy involved."

"That's what I'm afraid of."

I laughed.

"Come," he said, getting to his feet and taking my hands in his.

We went up three flights to the top floor of the small building. William unlocked the door and opened up into a small but surgically tidy apartment furnished similarly to the office.

"Oh," I said, "it's nice."

"You say that as if you're surprised."

"I'm surprised at the tidiness."

"Why?"

"I don't know many tidy people." I shrugged and looked at him.

"Well, now you know one."

He seemed proud of this attribute. But it worried me slightly. The only extremely tidy men I knew were gay or weird.

But William didn't seem gay and, as far as I could tell,

was in possession of his faculties. And he really was easy
on the eyes. Those broad shoulders, that long neck. The
wide-set, light-brown eyes.

I came closer to him and kissed his neck. The skin was
so soft.

He looked at me, then, seeming to reach a decision,
put his hands on my hips and steered me toward the front
of the apartment where the bedroom was. He pushed me
down onto the bed, then lay next to me. For a few minutes
we stayed like that, looking at each other, wordless. Then
he pulled me on top of him. I lifted his sweater and buried
my face in his chest. It was hairless and soft without being
feminine.

He sat up halfway, pulled my dress over my head, and
examined me.

"You look like a wood nymph," he said as he ran his
hand from my stomach down to the tip of my left foot.

"A wood nymph?"

"A slightly otherworldly creature. Delicate but capable
of building a shack from sticks."

"Wood nymphs build shacks? Don't they just live in
trees or something?"

"I admit I'm not as well-versed as I should be in the
habits of nymphs. I imagine them as capable but lovely
creatures."

"Thank you, I think."

He bit my neck and put a hand inside my thong. I was
ridiculously wet. I fumbled with the buttons on his jeans,
letting out a sigh of relief when I'd gotten them undone and
reached my hand inside his boxers. His cock was thick. I
craved him.

He flipped me onto my stomach, ran his hands down
my back and ass and legs. I kept reaching out, trying to
grab hold of him, any part of him, but he batted my hands
away.

"Shhhh," he said, "let me explore."

He bit the backs of my thighs. He put a pillow under my hips, elevating my ass, and entered me from behind. Very slowly. Teasing. Torturing.

Every time I tried reaching back to touch some part of him, he'd slap my hands away; at one point, he pinned them under his own as he slid in and out of me.

Eventually, he relented. He flipped me over, then pulled me on top of him. He'd been tormenting me long enough that within a few moments of straddling him, I came.

I didn't look at him. That would have been too much, but as my body collapsed forward onto his, I buried my face in his neck.

He wasn't done with me. He let me lie on my side, recovering, as he slid in behind me. He fucked me like that for about ten minutes then, finally, let himself come.

He held me tightly.

I closed my eyes.

I woke up and squinted into the darkness of the room. Candy was curled up at the edge of the bed but William was nowhere to be found. And I couldn't see a clock anywhere.

I got up, turned on a very modern and beautiful bedside lamp, and started rooting around for my strewn panties and dress.

"Hey, what are you doing?" William appeared in the bedroom door.

He was completely naked. His body wasn't perfect, there was a hint of spare tire around his middle, but he was at ease with himself. I wanted him again.

"Why'd you put this back on?" he asked as he tackled me back to the bed and put his hand under the dress and inside my thong.

"It's illegal to walk the streets naked," I said before completely losing the power of speech as he put his mouth between my legs.

At some point, after sating each other again, after lying entwined and touching each other's faces, I asked what time he thought it was.

"Why? Where do you have to go?" He propped up on his elbow and stared at me almost menacingly.

"Home. To work. I was distracted thinking of you all afternoon and didn't do my work for tomorrow's races."

"Ah."

I wasn't sure he believed me.

"So." I said, "any idea what time it is?"

"About 11."

"Oh. My powers won't be at their peak."

"Your powers are most assuredly at their peak," he said, scooping his hand under the small of my back and squeezing me to him.

We stayed entwined for another half hour before I finally forced myself up and out of the bed. I had convinced myself that I had to get home to work. There was a carryover in the Pick 6. Arthur had text-messaged asking if I wanted to work on it with him. I didn't. But now I told myself I was going to. I told myself that Clayton had nothing to do with my needing to leave this man who turned me upside down.

"See you," I said as I stood near the door, Candy at my side.

William kissed me. He kissed my mouth, my forehead, my cheeks, my neck.

"Yes," he said, "you will see me."

I liked the verging-on-threatening tone.

I walked out onto Ridge Street. It was a dark but warm night. Not a person or cab in sight. Candy squatted in the street and peed, then sniffed at everything as we walked north up to Houston where I hailed a taxi. The driver, a cadaverously thin man whose skin was as gray as his hair, didn't fly into a rage when I told him I was going to Queens. In fact, he barely paused in the intense conversation he was having into the headset of his cell phone.

I wondered, as I often do, who cab drivers find to talk on the phone with them, seemingly endlessly, in the middle of the night.

The apartment was dark when I came in. I saw Clayton lying on the couch, on his side, his back to me. He was wearing his clothes and didn't have anything covering him.

I quietly went about my nighttime ablutions, washing my face and applying liberal doses of night cream. I inspected myself in the mirror and found my pasty skin was glowing a little. The circles under my eyes weren't visible. I looked happy.

That's ridiculous, Alice, I told myself.

I went into the bedroom and got in bed without even thinking about doing any work on tomorrow's races. I rested my head in a nest of soft pillows and fell right to sleep, Candy curled at my feet.

7. KIMBERLY

"Are you pregnant?" Joe asked.

"Hardly," I said, gazing up at him from my position on the bathroom floor where, after vomiting prodigiously, I had crumbled next to the toilet.

"It'd be cute if we had a kid," Joe said.

"Joe, you can't be serious."

"Why not?"

"I'm menopausal."

"I hear some women get pregnant even a year after their last period."

I stared up at him, dumbfounded.

"Joe," I said evenly, "my youngest daughter is nearly *thirty*. I'm not pregnant. It's just a flu."

"You sure?" Joe scrutinized me.

"Quite."

I thought of my daughter Alice's complaints about all men wanting to get her pregnant. I had always suspected she was exaggerating. The men who'd impregnated me had not intended to do so. But now, my fifty-six-year-old next-door neighbor Joe, with whom I'd been having a lovely fling for eight weeks, sincerely seemed to want me pregnant. I was sure it was a passing phase, a fleeting, whimsical wish, the kind one becomes prone to in advanced middle age.

As I thought all these things, Joe gazed down at me with what I strongly suspected was love. Love? It seemed so foreign after the Battle of Betina. And the Battle of Claire, Betina's predecessor, who had also been young and difficult. In retrospect, these relationships didn't really have as much to do with love as with conquering.

"Kim," Joe said, reaching for one of my hands and helping me to my feet, "I'm in love with you."

"Oh, Joe."

"*Oh, Joe?* What kind of response is that?"

"I'm fifty-three years old and I just vomited. I can't imagine anyone deciding to love me at this particular juncture."

"I didn't decide it. I just do."

"Oh, Joe." I reached up and touched his face.

"You keep saying that."

"I'm at a loss for words."

"Do you have any positive feelings for me?"

"Many. Yes. There is even a good chance I love you."

"A good chance?"

"Can I just brush my teeth and then we'll get out of the bathroom and discuss?"

"I suppose so." He gave me a wounded look then walked out of the bathroom, softly closing the door as he left.

I turned to the sink and took my toothbrush from the holder. Ours was the kind of relationship where I felt comfortable doing things like leaving a toothbrush. Not that I ever spend the night. When Joe and I want to sleep together all night, we do so next door, at my place, so as not to abandon the dogs. But leaving things at his place has made me feel girlish and I can't say that I've ever in my life felt girlish.

I scrubbed my teeth and ran a hand through my hair that had gotten lank over the last few months. I knew I looked awful so I didn't glance into the mirror.

"Okay," I said, coming out of the bathroom, "I'm all cleaned up."

Joe was sitting at the edge of the bed. He was wearing red boxer shorts. His graying brown hair was falling in his face. He looked sweet and sad.

"I don't mean to be cruel," I said, kneeling down in front of him and putting my hands on his knees.

"You're not cruel, Kim, I suppose you're just honest."

"I don't trust myself. I thought I loved Betina. And Claire before her. In retrospect, it was something else, a compulsion, but not love. So I'm hesitant."

Joe looked at me from under the fringe of his hair.

"Anyway, don't you think you're going to start longing for the young blondes you've favored the whole time I've known you?"

"How could you possibly be insecure?"

"That's not insecurity talking. I'm being pragmatic."

"No," Joe shook his head, "I like you better than them all."

"Oh, Joe."

"Let's take a vacation together."

"Vacation? I don't take vacations. I have seventeen dogs."

"Get your daughters to take care of them."

"Ha. Eloise has flitted off to Toronto to visit her movie star lesbian lover and there's no chance that Alice will do anything for anyone."

"How can you know that until you ask?"

"I know my daughters. I gave birth to them."

"Just ask. Ask Alice."

"Maybe," I said. I glanced at the clock on the bedside table and saw it was nearly 6 p.m. I had more dogs to exercise before nightfall.

"I know," Joe said, "you have to feed those beasts now. And I have work to do too. Can I come over later?"

I looked at him. At his sweet, handsome face. I couldn't believe I was here. Having a heterosexual relationship with an attractive, sane, solvent man who, by all indications, was taken with me.

"Sure," I said, "come over later."

I touched his face.

The dogs twirled and barked and jumped. Chico got down

on his back and exposed his belly, Carlos yapped, Ira stood off to the side looking at me with those huge, mournful brown eyes. I took a step toward Ira, but Jimmy, the nearly brainless Newfoundland, came crashing between us. Lucy growled at Jimmy, Chico jumped onto the couch, and all hell broke loose. I stood still and relaxed, took a deep breath, then let out a "Shhhh" and, to my amazement, the chaos stopped and all eyes turned to me.

If only my daughters had ever listened to me this way.

For the next two hours I fed and walked the dogs. When night fell, I turned on the backyard lights and took most of the animals out to play ball. I launched one ball after another till the huge yard was filled with flying dogs and tennis balls. At one point, I darted off to the edge of the yard to vomit. Then had to sit down on a rock for a minute until a spell of weakness passed. The dogs looked at me, some with concern, some with annoyance as my bout of unease had gotten in the way of ball-throwing.

At 8 p.m. the phone rang. A potential adopter for Lucy, the Ibizan hound who'd been abandoned at a veterinarian's office in Kingston.

"I love Ibizan hounds," the woman said.

"Do you have experience with the breed?"

"No, I just love them."

"They're high-energy dogs. They need to run, yet can't be let offleash in an unfenced area as they have a keen prey drive."

"Oh, that's okay," said the woman.

"Which part is okay?"

"All of it."

"Do you plan to spend two hours a day walking the dog?"

"Two hours?"

"Minimum. Almost all dogs need that much. With some, you can let them run offleash in the woods and they can burn off enough steam in an hour of running. With dogs like Lucy, you have to do a lot of walking. In addition to play time in a fenced yard, of course."

"Oh." The woman sounded deflated. They often do. They see pictures of these orphaned dogs on Petfinder, fall in love with a face without consideration for the needs that might accompany it.

"Why do you want to get a dog?" I asked.

"I grew up with dogs. I miss that dog energy."

"What kind did you grow up with?"

"Beagles."

"I have a beagle mix. Minnie. She will still need exercise but not as much as Lucy."

"I was hoping for something bigger. Could I at least meet Lucy?"

I agreed that she could come meet Lucy even though I had no intention of letting her have that particular dog. I would hope to match her up with one of the mellower beasts. Maybe Herman, a very shy sheepdog who just wanted to love somebody and detested excessive exercise. Or Simba, an aging black Lab who had lived his seven years with an elderly gentleman who thought that letting him out in the yard once a day was enough exercise. Simba had started enjoying our long daily walks but would never have rigorous exercise requirements like some of the others.

The woman, a bank teller named Sue who lived in nearby West Saugerties, was intent on coming by that evening. Since I'd already done my chores over at Ava's farm and taken care of most everything else I had on my plate for the day, I agreed.

When Joe came over two hours later, he found me on the couch, benevolently watching Sue, a thirtyish woman with frizzy red hair, as she sat on the floor, surrounded by dogs. I had given the woman my standard lecture on the true needs of dogs, that a dog, any dog, even a tiny lapdog, is an animal first and foremost and, as such, should not be left confined somewhere for hours at a time and then merely sent out to a small yard by way of exercise. Sue swore up and down that she knew a good dog walker who she'd hire to take the new pet out in the middle of the day and that she'd personally give it long walks both before and after work.

She seemed sincere enough and didn't balk when I told her I'd be checking up on the dog for the rest of its life. I had steered her toward Simba and Herman but it was Chico, the tan pit bull, who seemed to have stolen her heart. Chico had his big head in her lap and was looking up at her like she was a hunk of ham.

"Do you want me to come back later?" Joe had asked when I let him in.

"No, no, it's fine, you should see how this adoption process works."

"Why?"

"I don't know."

"Ah, okay then." He came in, shook Sue's hand, and sank into the couch. It was late now but Sue showed no sign of wanting to leave.

"Sue," I said gently, "I have to go to bed."

"Can I have Chico?"

"We can talk about it. You should go home and sleep on it. He's a wonderful dog but you will encounter pit bull prejudices, neighbors may make a fuss, home insurance will be hard to find."

"But he's a wonderful dog."

"Yes. But while it's perfectly legal for lunatics to purchase firearms, pit bulls have been banned in entire cities." I felt a rage coming on so I decided to nip it in the bud. I told Sue I'd call her in the morning. Chico and I walked her to the door. After I watched her get in her car and pull away, I turned to Joe.

"You know, I think we should take that vacation," I said.

Joe smiled.

* * *

The next morning, after Joe had left and I had vomited then gotten through the first round of dog chores, I obsessed over the idea of a vacation. I hadn't gone on one since 1989, when Anne, my second lesbian lover and first long-term girlfriend, inherited money from her grandmother and sprang for an extravagant trip to Nevis, a tiny lush Caribbean island where we plucked mangoes from trees and made love on the beach. As much as I had adored Anne, who had dumped me very suddenly after seven years, I wanted to take a vacation with Joe even more.

I was going into the city late that morning to drop off Arturo the Italian greyhound with a nice-sounding man who Eloise had approved as an adopter. The man owned a toy store where Arturo would spend his days at the man's side. I decided I would stop in on Alice and try to convince her to come care for the dogs so I could take this infamous vacation. It was important enough to warrant my calling her to make sure she'd be home.

"Hi, Mom," she said, sounding less than lively.

"What's wrong, Alice?"

"Clayton is going to prison. He pleaded guilty to involuntary manslaughter."

"Oh." I didn't know what to make of this. Alice hadn't seemed to think highly of her lover until he'd been arrested. I didn't like the idea of my daughter being so emotionally screwy that she only cared about someone who would soon be unavailable by reason of prison sentence. What's more, I'd heard from Eloise that Alice was seeing someone else.

"I'm sorry to hear that, Alice," I said, for lack of anything else to say.

"Yeah, thanks. What's up?"

"I was going to drop by and see you later."

"And you're calling first?"

"Yes. I'm turning over a new leaf. I also wanted to make sure you weren't going to be at the track."

"Mom, it's Tuesday."

"And?"

"Tuesday is a dark day."

"Right," I said, as if I had any idea what that meant. "So you'll be home?"

"What time?"

"Maybe 1 p.m. or so?"

"That's fine, Mom," she said in a defeated voice.

"Alice, are you all right?"

"No, Mom, I thought I made that clear. But I'll see you around 1."

I hung up and took a moment to torment myself over my poor parenting of Alice. I was so young when I had her. Seventeen. And her father, Sam, was just twenty. We moved in with his parents and tried to be a family, but Sam and I never really got along and the more he annoyed me and failed to understand me, the more I disliked him. We split up when Alice was four. Alice and I went to live with my folks for a while and then I left Alice there, with them, in what I thought would be a more stable environment, as I went off to San Francisco. I had told my parents I was going to nursing school but the truth was, I had met Jeff, Eloise's father, a guitar player in a psychedelic band. As Alice attended a rural elementary school in Pennsylvania, I gave birth to Eloise in Oakland, California. For a little while, Jeff and Eloise and I were a happy little family. But Jeff was a junkie and soon I became a junkie too. Eloise's formative years were spent watching her parents shoot up. Jeff died of an overdose when she was three.

I eventually pulled myself together. Eloise and I went back to Pennsylvania where we shared a room with Alice in my parents' house. But Alice was a stranger to us and she and I never developed the bond Eloise and I have. I eventually got clean in Narcotics Anonymous, became employable and trustworthy and even capable of parenting. But it was a little too late for Alice. Though she isn't an outright sociopath, I worry about her coldness and its counterpoint, the sudden flare-ups of emotion.

The dogs started milling around and barking and there was a knock at the door. I looked up at the kitchen clock and saw it was already 9 a.m. I opened the door for Gina, one of my pet supply store coworkers who was going to walk and tend to the dogs for me while I spent the day in the city.

"Gina, hi," I said, ushering my tiny friend into the kitchen. I am not a large woman, but Gina, who looks like a prepubescent Russian gymnast, makes me feel like a giantess.

"Hi, Kim." She barely moved her mouth when she spoke and her eyes were downcast.

"What's wrong?" I asked, immediately pouring her a cup of coffee. Gina fuels her tiny body with gallons of coffee each day. To better maintain her habit, she purchased an elaborate and exorbitant cappuccino machine for the pet store.

"Nothing." She sagged down onto one of the kitchen chairs and put her tiny hands around the coffee cup as if to heat them up, in spite of it being quite warm out. "I'm just low."

"Oh." I sat down opposite her. I was itching to get on the road, to drop Arturo off with his adopter and go see my errant daughter and then, very possibly, do something luxurious like get a pedicure from the cruel Korean women who have a shop near Alice's. But I could see that Gina needed me to extract information from her. Namely, what was making her low.

"Why are you low?" I pressed.

"I'm short," Gina said.

"What?"

"I'm short. I'll never get ahead in the world due to my diminutive size."

"Gina, that's ridiculous."

"No. It was cute when I was a teenager. Other kids called me Tiny Girl, like the Iggy Pop song "Tiny Girls," even though that song has little, if anything, to do with the actual size of the girls in question. As I got older, I started noticing that people would completely ignore me in social situations. Because they literally can't see me. I am so far below eye level."

"But you're very pretty. You're a head-turner. People notice you."

"Not unless they're short."

I really wasn't sure what to say. Gina is in fact extremely short. There's no denying it.

"What about jockeys?" I said, remembering what Alice had once told me about the athletic power of those small people.

"You're comparing me to a jockey?"

"No, Gina, I just mean that they are short yet very powerful."

"And unless they're on top of a horse, no one will even see them," Gina replied, disconsolate.

"What brought this on?" I asked, striving to sound patient and solicitous though I could feel the clock ticking and my pack of dogs eagerly waiting for something, anything, to happen.

"I'm interested in a tall guy."

"Well, I would hazard a guess he'll be interested in you too."

"No," she shook her head, "he doesn't even see me. I mean literally. I'm too short. He's too tall." She stared into space as she took several sips of her coffee. "Shit," she said then, "I'm sorry I'm so self-involved. How are you, Kim?" She looked at me then screwed up her forehead. "You don't look that good. Have you lost a lot of weight?"

"I've had some kind of flu but I'm fine."

"You still sleeping with a man?"

"Apparently, yes." I smiled.

"You don't seem to mind."

"No. You know, it's surprisingly nice. More than nice."

Gina smiled, showing her tiny, perfect teeth.

After giving her elaborate instructions on what to do with the dog pack in my absence, I put Arturo in the car and got on the road. I'd only gone one exit down the thruway when my cell phone rang. I wasn't going to answer it as I loathe people who talk on their phones while driving, but I glanced down and saw the incoming number. It was Sue, the accountant who was interested in Chico. I'd forgotten to call her.

There was a rest stop a few miles later and I pulled in, let Arturo out in case the excitement of the car ride had made him need to pee, and called Sue back. She said she had slept on it and called her mother and sister and ex-boyfriend and discussed it and, yes, she wanted the dog. I told her I'd send her the formal application that night. She sounded enthralled. I was glad for her. And for Chico.

The Toy Box was a small but lavish shop on Greenwich Avenue in the West Village. It was packed to the rafters with bright and beautiful toys, the sorts of things I would have liked to buy my girls when they were little but of course could not as I was destitute. I saw several of Eloise's animals prominently displayed and remembered that this was how Jerry, the toy store owner, had come to be interested in Arturo. He'd commented on so many of Elo's animals being dogs and they'd gotten to talking about my rescue work.

Jerry had a round but attractive face and bright blue eyes that smiled. When he saw Arturo, he looked as excited as Sue had sounded on the phone.

"Oh my god, he's even more magnificent in person. Or in dogdom," Jerry said, getting down on his haunches and putting his hand out, waiting for the delicate Italian greyhound to approach him.

Within seconds, Arturo was licking Jerry's hands and accepting the treats he had in his pockets.

"Oh, Kimberly," he said a few minutes later, as he sat behind the counter, Arturo perched in his lap, "you've made me a proud and happy man." He went on to extol Eloise's virtues. We exchanged some pleasantries and then, without turning back to look at Arturo, I left the toy store. I think people assume that animal rescuers become inured to feelings of loss after finding an animal a home, but it's a heartbreak each time, a small earthquake inside.

I had parked the Honda in an illegal spot on Christopher Street and was surprised to discover I had neither been towed nor ticketed. I got in and pointed the car east, toward Alice's in Queens.

There was traffic. Traffic heading east, traffic heading north, traffic getting onto the 59th Street Bridge. As I turned right off the bridge, into Long Island City, the mess thinned out. Now there were just occasional trucks, a few passenger cars, more sky. I found a parking spot across the street from Alice's, locked the Honda, and crossed over to the small, wood-sided house my first late husband left my daughter. I was glad for it. Glad that, after his many years of ne'er-do-wellism, Sam had at least managed to own a little property and see to it that his only daughter had a place to hang her hat and could even draw a steady income from the garden apartment rental. Though Alice never admits it, I suspect that the $1,400 a month the apartment brings in makes it possible for her to earn a living as a gambler, to endure long dry spells and still be able to pay her basic bills. But we never discuss this. Alice isn't a prideful sort of woman, at least not about most things, but she does feel superior to the vast majority of the population by virtue of being able to identify herself as a professional gambler on her tax returns. I suppose it is the quintessential act of getting over, and if she were an addict like me, it might be dangerous. But she's not. She's incredibly logical and levelheaded. Except where men are concerned.

I rang the bell and was buzzed in. As I climbed up the stairs, Alice's dog Candy came racing down the steps, wiggling and letting out excited barks. I scooped the small beast into my arms and let her lick my face, a thing I know Alice doesn't permit.

"You shouldn't encourage licking, Mom, most people don't care for that sort of thing."

She was standing at the top of the stairs, hands on her hips, looking down at me. She was wearing navy sweat pants that hung down so far over her narrow hips, I was surprised her pubic hair wasn't showing. Her long, skinny feet were bare and there was chipped red polish on her toes.

"Nice to see you too, darling," I said, reaching the top of the stairs. I deposited Candy on the floor, then kissed my daughter on each cheek.

"What possessed you to actually warn me you were coming?" Alice inquired as we went inside her apartment.

"I had to ask you something and wanted to make sure you'd be here."

"That sounds ominous."

"It isn't."

"So are you going to ask or just keep me in suspense?" Alice sat down on the couch and tucked her feet under her butt.

"I wonder if you'd come look after the dogs so I can take a vacation."

"Vacation?" Alice looked genuinely shocked.

"Yes. I need a vacation."

She considered this long and hard.

"Betina and I broke up," I said, warming myself up for telling her about Joe.

"I know. Eloise told me. And you're knocking boots with your neighbor Joe."

"Yes," I said, feeling mildly miffed that I wasn't getting

to tell her myself and that she seemed completely unfazed by my sleeping with a man.

"I can't keep track of you and Elo with all your gender switching. I may have curious taste in bed mates, but at least they're always the same gender."

"Don't feel superior about it. Maybe Eloise and I are just more open."

Alice rolled her eyes.

"Yes, Mom," she said then, "I'll watch your unruly hounds so you can go off and shag your neighbor on a beach somewhere."

"Don't make it sound so . . . so . . ."

"Debauched?"

"Exactly. I'm deeply fond of Joe."

"Mother, are you in love with a *man*?"

"You're being callous."

"I'm just asking a question. Tell me."

"I've come to realize I know nothing about love."

"You *love* him," Alice practically squealed.

Now it was my turn to roll my eyes.

"It's possible," I admitted.

Alice looked exceptionally pleased with this bit of information. I wasn't quite sure why.

"And what of *your* man?" I asked.

"William?"

"Who's William?"

"A guy I met."

"What about Clayton? This morning you were wistful and pining for Clayton."

"Clayton is in Rikers."

"So who is William?"

She told me. At length. More length than I suppose I really wanted or needed. Graphic details of their lovemaking, of his three cats and his pit bull and his small architectural firm.

"You're not listening to me, Mom," Alice said.

"Yes I am," I lied.

"Am I grossing you out?"

"Alice, I think it's nice that you sound genuinely moved by another human being. I admit that I don't trust it though. You have the most fickle heart of any individual I've ever known."

"I know," she said, surprising me with self-awareness. "William does something to me. Something I'm not sure I want done to me. But there's no question he does it."

"You barely know him."

"True," she shrugged. Then frowned. "What's wrong with you, Mom?"

"What do you mean?"

"You don't look that good."

"That's not nice."

"You look thin. A little sallow."

"I've had the flu."

"Oh?" She was really scrutinizing me.

"Nothing to worry about," I said, trying to look cheerful. "So," I added, changing the subject, "Arturo has a home and it looks like Chico does too, so it's only fifteen dogs."

"*Only* and *fifteen* do not normally go in the same sentence when talking about quantity of dogs, Mom. Anyway, I imagine you'll be going to the pound on your way out of town to pick up five three-legged pit bulls or something."

"No. I'm going to scale down a little."

"Really?" Alice looked incredulous.

I promised that she would only have to care for fifteen, maybe even fewer, depending on exactly when Joe and I ended up taking this vacation of ours. Not that Alice seemed to care. For once, she had made up her mind to help me and there didn't seem to be many conditions on her providing that help.

We talked about men, women, and dogs for another half hour and then I kissed my eldest goodbye and went back down to my car. I skipped the planned pedicure as

I wasn't feeling very well and wanted to get back on the thruway, back to Woodstock, back to the trees, the air, the dogs. And Joe.

Night had come, misty and cool, the many trees around my house rustling like clean sheets. Sue had dropped by, signed the adoption contract, and then whisked Chico off into the sunset. I'd watched the two drive away, pit bull and banker, in love. Eloise had called from Toronto to announce that she'd taken in a German shepherd she'd found in an alley behind the hotel where she was staying with Ava Larkin.

All was as it should be.

I settled the dogs in, then went over to Joe's.

I found him sitting at the piano. His button-down shirt was rumpled and his hair looked dirty. His glasses were perched crookedly on the tip of his nose.

"Hi," he looked up and offered a weak smile.

"Hi, yourself." I walked over and kissed him. His lips tasted like coffee.

He'd been working on a piano piece commissioned by a grande dame who'd been married to a minorly famous but now-dead composer. Lilian, the grande dame, missed having personalized compositions left on her pillow several times a month. Now, nearing the age of ninety, she went around plucking youngish composers from the New York scene, giving them small commissions to write her piano pieces that she then butchered in her overheated living room as her aged friends sat around sipping fruit-flavored liqueur. Joe was one of her favorites and she hired him at least three times a year but became more demanding each time, spending hours on the phone badly expressing what it was she wanted.

"You look exhausted," I said, sitting down next to him.

"I'm drained," he replied, petting my head.

In spite of not feeling well, I'd wanted him to ravage me. To put his hands all over my body. To prop me on top of him, to throw me face first on the bed. But that all evaporated now as I felt his exhaustion, and in place of the lust I'd been harboring a few minutes earlier, I felt a gentle tenderness, a desire to be kind to him for a very long time.

I kissed his neck and offered to make him some food as I was sure he hadn't eaten anything in hours.

"That's okay," he said softly, "just sit here with me, be with me, restore me."

We sat in silence for a few minutes. And then I felt awful. I had been keeping a secret from him. It wasn't fair.

"Joe," I said, looking over at his beautiful, tired face, "there's something I have to tell you."

He looked over at me with an almost hopeful expression, as if he expecting me to reveal some shocking but very good news.

I felt my heart breaking.

8. ALICE

I stumbled out of my mother's bed, tripped over Timber, the Newfoundland, and went sprawling onto the floor.

"What happened?" William asked in a groggy voice.

"I fell," I said, getting up and fumbling for the bedside lamp.

Timber was blinking up at me but seemed completely unharmed. My knee was throbbing and I'd probably have a bruise. It was the least of the indignities that had befallen me in the four days that I'd been dog sitting for my vacationing mother. Ira, her three-legged hound who was experiencing separation anxiety, had peed on me, the house's water heater had exploded, and Mom's ex-girlfriend had shown up in the yard, naked. But I'd dealt with these various horrors and, to soothe myself, invited William up. I hadn't seen much of him in the few weeks since we'd first slept together. In that time, I had been on a vicious losing streak at the track, Clayton had been in a fight at Rikers and lost half a finger, and Candy had contracted giardia, an intestinal ailment that gave her intense diarrhea. I'd actually been glad to escape to my mother's house atop a small mountain, gladder still when William had agreed to come up.

"Are you all right?" William asked.

"Fine. I'll probably have a bruise, but I'm fine."

"You look beautiful," he said, propping up on one elbow.

I squinted at him like he was a lunatic. Then I looked down at myself and realized I was wearing a slinky red nightgown. I'd found it hanging on a hook in the bathroom and had to assume it belonged to my mother. I'd never known her to own such a garment, but then again, I hadn't known her to sleep with men either.

"Thank you," I said, staring at William. He was naked, lolling there comfortably in spite of the slight wings of fat around his middle. I'm not a naked person. There's nothing wrong with my body. People seem to like it, and I don't particularly mind it, but I've always felt weird walking around with my ass hanging out. I wear nightgowns or pajamas to bed. I do enjoy skinny-dipping, but you won't find me at a nudist colony.

"Why don't you get back into bed?" William asked.

"I have to pee."

"Hurry," he said.

For what? I wondered. Though William was very pleasing in bed, he wasn't one of those prodigal lovers, like Clayton, for example, who, when things had been going reasonably well between us, wanted me in the morning, in the afternoon, outdoors, in my sleep, in the back of his van, etc.

I went into the hall and to the bathroom. I shut the door, turned on the light, and started running water in the sink. I didn't actually need to pee or wash my hands or face but I did need the white noise of running water to help me think. I was deeply confused. On one hand, I missed Clayton, but this missing seemed to have been engendered by his imprisonment, which might indicate that I am more emotionally ill than I ever suspected. On the other hand, there was William, reaching parts of me I didn't know existed. He disturbed and excited me on a molecular level. I liked his mind, I liked the intense and intimate sex, I even liked his dog, Gumdrop. I was in deep and I don't like to be in anything deep other than a Pick 6 carryover at Belmont Park.

I turned off the faucet and left the bathroom.

I tiptoed over Timber and climbed under the sheets. William had fallen back asleep. I lay on my side and stared at him. He didn't look idiotic in sleep. His wide, pale face was relaxed, his mouth was slack, but he wasn't drooling or doing anything disgusting, though I knew the disgusting was inevitable. Bathroom doors left open, stinky socks left strewn, drooling, belching, farting, general loss of inhibition. But I was actually contemplating the disgusting with William. William who I'd slept with just three times so far. William who I really didn't know or trust but possibly wanted to know and trust. It was too much to deal with. I closed my eyes and counted horses.

I opened one eye and peered at William. He was still sleeping. I touched his face. He stirred a little, let out a sigh. I started kissing his chest then biting his stomach. He came to life. Reached for my hips and hoisted me on top of him. I ground my body into his, then pushed forward, wanting to get closer and then closer still. I came like that, sprawled on top of him.

I started to wiggle off but he kept me there. He wasn't done with me.

I hoped he never would be.

Forty minutes later, William had gotten out of bed, showered, turned on his cell phone, cursed the lack of reception, and announced he had to go.

"Go?" I said. "What do you mean *go*? Go where?"

"I have to get back," he said, as if it were the most natural thing in the world. Even though it was Saturday and I couldn't imagine what might be so pressing for an architect on a Saturday.

"Oh?" I said, looking him over head to toe, trying to read his face, his body, his mind. *What the fuck?*

We hadn't talked about how long he'd stay, but I'd envisioned two nights. And now I was upset. At him for wanting to leave, and myself for not wanting him to.

I imagined my face was long, a little sullen looking, his cue to interject something like, *I wish I didn't have to go.*

He said nothing though, just put his toiletries kit into his overnight bag. The bag looked full, as if he'd planned to stay more than one night but had changed his mind.

"Walk me to my car?"

"Sure," I shrugged. I felt all my hopes shrivel up and trot off to a corner to die. I watched William as he put his bag into the backseat of his ancient Saab.

"Okay, bye," I said, giving him a hard look.

He put one hand under my chin and tilted it up. With the other hand, he brushed a strand of hair out of my eyes.

He kissed me very softly. I was stiff at first, then melted into the kiss. Just as I was about to suggest we return to bed, he pulled back.

"See you soon," he said. He got into his car, put it into reverse, and backed out of the driveway.

I stared after him, expecting him to turn around and come back.

He did not.

I went into the house and wandered from room to room, dogs following me as I went. I was restless. Surprised. Angry. I wanted to smash something. But I couldn't smash my mother's things.

For the first time, I really noticed my mother's deranged color scheme, the walls painted orange in one room, lime-green in the next, but all of it somehow actually working. It was a lovely house, I realized, one filled with my mother's relentless spirit.

I wandered back into the bedroom where the bed was still rumpled. Ira, the three-legged hound, jumped onto the bed and looked at me with huge brown eyes. He was soon joined by Harvey. They were willing me to pull myself together and take them out. But I felt lifeless and broken.

I shuffled into the bathroom and glanced at myself in

the mirror. I'd expected worse. My hair wasn't plastered to my head with grease and, for once, my face was free of blemishes.

I idly opened the medicine cabinet because medicine cabinets are always an interesting glimpse into the physical secrets of a house's inhabitants. Do they have headaches? Diarrhea? Itching? Something more ominous like a psychiatric disorder? I didn't know these sorts of details about my mother.

I'm not sure what I expected, but it wasn't what I found. The cabinet was chock full of prescription drugs. I didn't know what half of them were, but the other half were painkillers. Were they Betina's or was my mother working some local quack for opiate prescriptions? I examined a bottle of Oxycontin; Mom's name was on it. The prescription date was recent. *Take 1-2 every six hours for pain as needed.*

This explained my mother's looking thin and drawn.

I slammed the medicine cabinet door shut. I felt my stomach knotting up. I had met some of Mom's Narcotics Anonymous friends but it's not like I had their phone numbers to call and ask if she was on a relapse. Eloise probably didn't know any more than me and was still away somewhere with her movie star lover. My stomach knotted tighter. The dogs were swarming around me now, some whining softly, some just staring at me. Harvey grabbed the corner of a towel, pulled it off the towel rack, and engaged Lucy, the Ibizan hound, in a game of tug.

I sat down on the closed lid of the toilet and put my face in my hands. I probably should have cried but tears wouldn't come.

Harvey licked my bare foot. Candy put her front paws on my knee, and when I looked up from under my veil of hair, I saw that she was staring at me imploringly.

"All right," I said, slowly getting to my feet, "all right."

I stuffed my pockets with dog treats and shuffled into the kitchen. I put half the animals out on the sun porch where there were many beds and bowls of water and nothing to destroy. I shooed the other half outside and into my mother's van, where Candy reluctantly shared the front passenger seat with Carlos, the toothless Chihuahua.

I headed down Byrdcliffe Road toward Bearsville and Rabbit Hole Road. I know my mother takes the dogs there as a special treat and I remembered the time she had forced Eloise and me to go there for a mildly arduous hike involving several crossings of a raging creek.

It was a winding road with a swollen rushing creek on one side, pretty farmhouses on the other. I pulled into the dirt parking lot near the trailhead and unloaded the animals. I unleashed the dogs who would come back when called, and proceeded onto the trail, my arm nearly pulled from its socket by Rosemary, a German shepherd who wished dismemberment upon all squirrels.

We reached the first creek crossing, and while the water wasn't as high as I remembered, hopping from rock to rock still looked like a precarious operation. I had put on a pair of Mom's hideous Teva sandals, the kind of sensible footwear designed for this sort of thing, but the rocks in the creek were mossy and looked slippery. I pictured sliding into the water, losing control of Rosemary, and possibly cracking my skull open.

As I stood studying the rushing creek and breathing in the clean, sweet air, I suddenly choked up and tears came. I felt weak and squatted down on my haunches. Rosemary, sensing something, had grown perfectly still, as had the other two leashed dogs. Even some of the loose ones had hopped back across the creek and come to stand near me. The pack seemed to realize that the human was having a meltdown. This somehow made it worse. I wept.

I was lost inside myself when Rosemary pivoted her head and let out several sharp barks. I turned around and there, amazingly, was my sister, Eloise. She looked more beautiful than I'd ever seen her. She was wearing loose-fitting gray pants and a flowing white blouse. She was barefoot. She still had the hitch in her step but now it just seemed to add to the regalness of her bearing.

"Eloise?" I said, standing up.

Some of the loose dogs ran up to Eloise and surrounded her.

"Alice," she said, seeming unsurprised to find me on this remote trail, surrounded by dogs, with tears staining my cheeks.

"What are you doing here?" I asked as she came closer.

"Walking," she said dreamily. "Ava and I just got back. She's unpacking. I decided to stretch my legs."

I had forgotten that Ava Larkin's house sits near the mouth of the Rabbit Hole trail and that it was here that Mom met Ava in the first place.

"You're going to get foot diseases," I said, motioning at her bare feet.

She smiled a strange smile that seemed to say that kind of thing was beneath her. Her eyes were far away and sparkly at first, then she seemed to really see me for the first time and her face changed.

"Alice, you're *crying*?"

"I'm sad." I shrugged.

"What's the matter?"

"Let's walk, and I'll tell you," I said since the dogs were getting impatient.

I got Eloise to take two of them across the creek while I handled Rosemary. I remembered Elo struggling to cross the creek the time we'd come here with Mom, but that was pre-movie star lesbian lover Elo; this new Elo crossed barefoot with a dog in each hand and didn't miss a beat.

On the other side, we took up the narrow, slightly muddy path leading deep into the woods. The creek was at our left, a lush hill to our right, little waterfalls bursting from it every few steps.

"So?" said Eloise after we'd walked in silence for a few minutes.

"I think Mom's getting high again."

"No way."

"I think so." I told her about the pills.

"Maybe she's really in pain."

"We're all really in pain. But pain-meds pain? No. She'd have told us."

Eloise agreed that it was a worry. That, between taking up with a man, taking a vacation, and apparently taking pain meds, something had to be wrong with our mother.

"You think the relapse made her heterosexual?" my sister asked.

"What, because she'd have to be stoned to have sex with a man? Are you an expert on lesbianism now?"

"I'm not an expert on anything, Alice, that's your department," my sister said sadly. "I wasn't implying that it would take a drug relapse to make someone switch back to men. I just mean she's not in her right mind and she ended a long-term relationship, and, seemingly out of the blue, took up with someone of a different gender."

I said nothing.

"So you were crying over our mother?" Eloise asked after a couple more minutes of strolling in silence.

"Is it my crying you're skeptical about or my crying over our mother?"

"Well," Eloise said carefully, "a bit of both."

"Yes. I am crying over our mother. And there's the problem of that man," I added.

"Clayton?"

"Well, him, but William too. You know. The architect with the brown pit bull."

Suddenly, my sister's head pivoted on its neck so fast I thought it might twist off.

"Brown pit bull?" she practically hissed.

"Yes. Gumdrop," I said, frowning at Elo's reaction.

"Gumdrop?" She looked like she was going to pass out.

"What?" I asked. "What's wrong?"

"His name is William? As in Billy?"

"Not Billy. Just William."

"Sometimes he calls himself Billy. Must just depend which sister he's fucking."

"What?"

"Billy Rotten is an architect. I gave him Turbo, the brown pit bull. He called me not long ago, after not making contact for weeks, to tell me how well the dog was doing. He had changed her name to Gumdrop."

We had both stopped walking.

I felt the blood draining from my extremities. Eloise was no longer that peaceful-seeming being of a few minutes ago. Her face was twisted up and her eyes looked black.

"William is Billy Rotten?" I said dumbly.

"Evidently." Eloise looked furious.

"You know that I had no idea, right? He was just some guy I met in the park."

"He was just some guy I met in the park too. I guess that's his M.O.," Eloise said bitterly.

"But, Elo, you're with Ava now, do you really care?"

"Of course I care. He broke my heart and fucked my sister."

"I don't think he knows I'm your sister." I said it soothingly even though I was beginning to get angry with her. After all, I was the one actively sleeping with the guy. I was the one who had to put everything about William into a new context, a context that included his being intimate with my baby sister. I felt betrayed. By William but, somehow, by Eloise too. I knew this wasn't logical and was probably also exactly what she was feeling. But there it was.

We had started moving again though it wasn't the companionable walk we'd embarked on a few minutes earlier. The woods seemed darker, the dogs did not look quite as carefree, and Eloise wasn't walking as lightly on her bare feet. Her limp was pronounced now.

She cursed when she stepped on something sharp, then, just as we came to the second creek crossing, announced she was turning back.

"You're not actually angry with me, Eloise, are you?" She was. But by asking, I thought maybe I could point to the ridiculousness of such a stance.

She didn't even dignify me with an answer. She shrugged and started walking the other way.

"Elo, come on, what about Mom? We have to talk," I called after her.

She turned back around. "Talk to someone else, I'm sick of your shit."

I stood there, stunned under a canopy of beautiful trees.

I'd walked all the dogs and given medicine to the ones that needed it. I had tried calling Eloise's cell phone but it went straight to voicemail. I considered calling William but didn't even know where to begin. What would I ask? Why did you leave? Why did you fuck my sister and leave her too?

I toyed with the idea of taking some of Mom's pills. Knocking myself out for a day or two until I could forget that this day had ever happened. But there were the dogs to deal with. And I don't like losing time the way drug addicts do. I don't mind a buzz sometimes, but total annihilation? I never really did understand that.

I was at a loss. I skulked into the living room, turned on the TV and found TVG, the racing channel, among the hundreds of channels Mom gets through her satellite dish. I hadn't even planned on wagering, had expected to spend the day with William, but with the afternoon's jaws yawning wide, the only sensible thing to was throw myself head-first into horses. I put my laptop on the coffee table and pulled up one of my online wagering accounts; in a matter of moments, I was getting lost in the numbers. There was horseflesh on the TV, live odds and past performances from the Daily Racing Form on my computer screen. I was at peace. Or, at least, I was doing what usually puts me at peace. After hitting two lucrative trifectas, I signed onto my Gmail account. Nothing good. Nothing from William. Nothing from Eloisc, and, of course, nothing from Clayton. I didn't know what the Rikers Island e-mail policy might be but Clayton had never been interested in computers, e-mail, or any form of non-tactile communication anyway.

I went back to wagering, managing to hit the $1,265 late Pick 4 at Belmont. I hadn't really done my homework so it was mostly dumb luck. I hate dumb luck. It never makes me feel better.

I walked the dogs again. Four at a time, in shifts, along Upper Byrdcliffe Road and part of the way up the Mt. Guardian trail. By the time I'd walked and fed all fifteen dogs, it was dark out and I felt somberness creeping up on me. They say old people and crazy people get disjointed when darkness falls. I am probably both at this point.

I wanted to call someone, but who? Arthur was one of the few people I knew who was both in the country and speaking to me. But I didn't feel like talking about Todd Pletcher–trained horses or teenage girls. So I didn't call him.

I pictured my mother. Tried to put myself inside her head, to figure out what exactly she was up to with the pills, the man, the vacation. I remembered Eloise and I meeting her outside a church down on Route 212 where she attended Narcotics Anonymous. I glanced up at the clock on the wall. It was close to 8 p.m. I could go loiter outside the church where I might recognize some of Mom's NA friends as they drifted out of the meeting. I could accost one of them, see if they knew what my mother was up to. It was probably some sort of infraction of their traditions to tell an outsider what was going on with one of their members, but it's not like I was a law enforcement officer. I had a right to know.

I arranged Mom's dogs in various rooms throughout the house then leashed Candy and put her in the backseat of my mother's Honda. My little mutt sat down and regally lifted her muzzle in the air.

As I pulled into the church parking lot, people were emerging. Most of the men had strange facial hair and the women looked like biker chicks. They were congregating in little groups, some smoking, some standing near motorcycles. They looked like a bunch of thugs. Mom always says the people in AA are more upstanding but proportionally duller. So she goes to NA.

I noticed a familiar-looking girl who was wearing sunglasses even though the sun was almost gone. I remembered Mom talking to her though her name wasn't coming to me. As I got out of the car, telling Candy to stay put, the tall, willowy girl detached herself from the people she'd been chatting with and started heading toward a gold-colored Subaru.

"Hey," I said, feeling like some sort of weirdo.

The girl frowned and stopped in her tracks.

"I'm Kim Hunter's daughter. Alice. I think I met you once."

"Oh," the girl said. "Right." She was very pretty with sharp cheekbones and fawn-colored hair. She was wearing a printed dress and ballet slippers.

"Could I talk to you for a second? I just want to ask you something about my mother."

The girl removed her sunglasses and leveled her gaze at me. Her eyes were a piercing blue.

"What's up?" she asked.

"I found pills in my mom's medicine chest." I decided it was probably best to get straight to the point.

"Oh?" she said cautiously.

"Painkillers. A lot of them."

"And?"

"And I'm wondering if my mom is on a relapse. She's been behaving erratically. My sister and I are worried."

Bringing Eloise into it seemed to legitimize the whole thing somehow.

"What are you doing right now?" the tall girl asked.

"Doing?"

"I mean, do you want to go to town and grab a coffee? We can talk."

My heart sank since surely her wanting to talk to me over coffee signaled something significant to talk *about*.

"Sure, okay."

"I'm Ida," she said, extending a hand to shake.

Ida? I thought. I would have imagined her to be an Isabelle or at the very least a Julia, but never an Ida.

We agreed to meet at Joshua's, a café in town, and I got back into the Honda where Candy greeted me as if I'd been gone for weeks. I returned the effusive greetings then put the car in drive.

Town was packed even though it was a weekday. It was June now and all the city people had opened up their summer houses and were swelling the tiny local economy with their needs for lawn-care products, organic foods, and ice cream. The municipal parking lot was full but I crammed the Honda into a dubious spot near a fire lane. I found some dog treats in my pocket, cracked the windows, and told Candy I'd be back soon.

Ida was already there in the café, standing at the counter ordering a coffee. I ordered one too and we made our way to a table.

"I'm up here watching my mom's dogs while she's on vacation," I explained.

"I know, it's a small town."

"Oh," I said, wondering what else she knew.

"Yes, I know about your sister and Ava Larkin too."

"You do?" I felt myself screwing my face up and immediately tried to stop. Ida had an unlined, untroubled face, the kind that made someone like me self-conscious.

"Yes. Well, for one, your mom and I are friends. But I'd probably know anyway. Not that many of the locals ever actually see Ava Larkin, but her landscaper apparently saw her making out with Eloise, who he'd met once through your mom. As a result, the entire town knows." Ida smiled a little wistfully. "I never thought I'd like this kind of thing, this small-town thing. But I do. I love it."

"You came from the city?"

She nodded and took a huge, unladylike gulp of her coffee. There's nothing more wonderful than an elegant woman slugging a beverage back like a redneck.

"I'm from the South but I started modeling when I was fifteen so I moved to Manhattan. I had a good run and a severe heroin problem . . . I know. Heroin-addict model. Boring."

I laughed.

"I lost most of my teeth by age twenty-eight and by thirty I was living on people's couches with all my possessions in a black garbage bag. But I still wore cute little Prada dresses. Well, *one* cute little Prada dress. It probably didn't smell very good."

She flashed a smile. She had plenty of teeth.

"Fake," she said, flicking a fingernail against a front tooth. "Somewhere in there I managed to fall in love. In spite of the drugs and the insanity. I married my husband five years ago and went into NA. We bought a house up here and never looked back. Now I'm forty and I garden and work at the Historical Society and fuck my husband and like it." She grinned.

She started asking me about myself. I wanted to know about my mother but didn't want to be rude, and anyway, it seemed like Ida was warming herself up for it, evaluating me, deciding whether or not she could trust me. I told her about my life. She cocked an eyebrow at my occupation as most people in twelve-step programs do. I told her about Clayton and even about William and the fact that he'd slept with both Eloise and me.

"Shit," Ida whistled through her teeth. "That's messy."

"Yeah," I shrugged, "it is."

"But you want to know what's up with your mom."

"Yes. It really freaked me out finding all those pain pills."

"The only reason I'm going to tell you this is that I've actually seriously considered tracking down your number and calling you to tell you," Ida said.

I braced myself for the details. How Mom had been popping pills for the last three years but none of us had noticed.

"When you showed up outside the meeting, it seemed like a sign I should tell you. Even though I don't believe in signs."

I nodded, waiting for her to get on with it.

"Your mom has cancer."

9. ELOISE

I was sitting on a tree stump, guzzling Pepsi from a plastic quart bottle as I watched Ava wielding a chainsaw. She was wearing cut-offs, a white tank top, work gloves, and protective goggles. It was possibly the sexiest sight I'd ever seen in my life. Sexy enough to momentarily take my mind off my wretched sister Alice who I'd been mentally cursing for thirty-six straight hours since running into her on the trail and finding out that she was sleeping with Billy Rotten. I wasn't sure who I felt more vehemently toward, Billy or my sister, who'd had the audacity to leave me seven phone messages since, all of which I'd deleted immediately.

"What are you looking at?" Ava had stopped chainsawing and noticed that I was staring at her.

"You," I said. "Want some?" I proffered the Pepsi.

"Get that vile swill away from me. Why are you putting that stuff in your beautiful body?"

"I turn to it when life throws me a curve ball."

"What curve ball?" She'd pulled the goggles up onto her forehead and was squinting at me. Her long skinny arms were shiny with sweat, strands of blond hair were glued to her cheeks.

"My sister," I said. I had mentioned running into and arguing with Alice but I hadn't told Ava what we'd had words about.

"What did your sister do?"

"She's seeing that guy I was with right before I met you."

"The late trapeze instructor?"

"No, Billy Rotten."

166 Maggie Estep

"Who is Billy Rotten?"

"I had a one-night stand with him. But a significant one-night stand."

Ava cocked an eyebrow.

"I really liked him but I couldn't bring myself to follow through with him. It was too soon after Indio's death. Or something. Yet Billy haunted me. Until I met you and forgot all about him. Still, it's not like I welcome the news of my sister sleeping with him."

"You introduced them to each other? And then Alice stole him?"

"No." I shook my head and explained the situation. How it was entirely possible that Billy didn't even know Alice was my sister and that it was extremely unlikely Alice realized that her William was my Billy.

"So why are you mad at her?" Ava frowned.

"I'm not sure," I admitted. "I don't even know why I got so bent out of shape about Billy in the first place."

"Are you in love with him?" Ava put a hand on her hip. She didn't have much in the way of hips, had the classic fashion-model figure of a twelve-year-old boy, but even so, she looked stern with that hand on that hip.

"Of course not."

"So why exactly are you mad at your sister?"

"She's always doing the same things I do, only better. Plus, Mom asked her to dog sit, not me. Alice is just better at everything."

Ava had both hands on her hips now and was frowning.

"Eloise," she said, "your mother couldn't ask you to dog sit because you were in Canada with me. Also, I don't really understand the nature of big sister/little sister competitiveness since I only have a little brother, but from what you've told me in the past, your sister loves you. Maybe it's best to remember that."

I looked at my girlfriend, at her lovely, smooth, earnest face. I felt like a jackass.

"Would you stop being so magnanimous? Stop giving me hope for the human race."

Ava laughed then pulled her goggles back over her eyes and picked up the chainsaw.

"And my mom," I added, before she turned the machine back on, "Alice thinks she's fallen off the wagon. Alice found pills."

Ava put the chainsaw down and pulled the goggles back up.

"When were you going to tell me this?"

"I had to mull it over awhile first."

Ava sighed, took off her work gloves, came over, and put an arm around me.

"Darling, you have to learn to tell me everything or I will fear for the longevity of our love."

"Okay," I nodded dumbly.

I told her about the pills and some of the details of mom's druggie past. Details I had glossed over in light of the fact that my mother is now Ava's employee.

After I'd gone on for several minutes, Ava cut in: "Your mom is innocent until proven guilty of all this. What's more, she may have a legitimate need for the pain pills. I would suggest talking it over with her and not jumping to horrific conclusions."

"Stop being so clear-headed," I said.

"Go call your sister and make nice and let me get this wood cut." She pulled the goggles down once more.

I kissed her before she picked the chainsaw back up. Her goggles bumped my forehead.

"Go on," she said, reaching around to pat me on the ass, "I've got to get this done."

I started to walk away then paused, looking back at her. She'd turned the chainsaw on and was grimacing as she attacked an oversized log. She had, she'd told me, learned to use a chainsaw for some movie she'd been in ten years earlier. It was amazing to me that actors learned useful life skills for the sake of make-believe.

I headed into the house where I was effusively greeted by Ron, the shepherd mix Ava and I had adopted in Toronto.

"Shhhh," I said, turning my back to him so he couldn't jump on me. He was an intelligent and willing dog but he hadn't mastered house manners just yet. Ava and I had found him in a parking lot behind the fancy hotel where we'd been staying during her shoot. Without too much coaxing, he followed us back inside the hotel and the elevator operator said not one word as we ascended to the penthouse.

Later on, after getting a production assistant to go out and find a leash and collar for the dog, who Ava promptly named Ron after a screenwriter friend of hers, Ava agreed to let me call up various local shelters and rescue organizations to alert them about the found blond shepherd mix. Since Ron was vastly underweight and hadn't had a nail trim or a brushing in many months, it seemed unlikely he was someone's beloved lost pet. Twenty-four hours later, when no one came looking for him, Ava declared that we would take him home to Woodstock where he would become our dog.

Ron was still trying to jump up on me.

"Shhhh," I said again, standing with my arms loose at my sides, not looking him in the eyes.

He circled me a few times and then, since that wasn't yielding any results, sat and looked at me expectantly.

"Good boy." I patted the top of his silky head. The dog had been starved and abandoned but he wasn't stupid.

Ron followed as I went into the kitchen where I'd left my cell phone. I opened it up and saw that Alice had called twice more. I dialed Mom's number. The machine came on telling me my mother was away for another five days.

"Alice," I spoke into the machine, "this is Eloise."

"Finally," she said, picking up.

I toyed with the idea of hanging up. What kind of greeting was that? Why was she always so abrupt?

"Why are you always so abrupt?" I asked.

"Mom has cancer."

"That's not funny, Alice, don't joke about things like that."

"I'm not. I talked to one of Mom's NA friends. Ida, the friend, told me. She didn't think it was right that Mom wasn't telling anyone."

"You're not serious."

"Eloise, I may be fucked up but I'm not *that* fucked up. Our mother has cancer of the esophagus. Late-stage cancer. She's going to die. Soon."

"No," I said.

"Yes."

"No," I said again.

"Yes, Eloise, yes."

I tried to absorb the information. My head was spinning and I felt nauseous. I found myself digging my hand into the fur on Ron's back. "We have to call her," I said.

"No. Ida made me promise not to talk to her about this until she'd come back from the vacation."

"That's ridiculous. Why?"

"It's probably the last vacation she'll take. She doesn't need her daughters calling her in hysterics."

"Alice, she failed to tell us she's dying, surely that merits a phone call."

"No, Eloise. It's fucked up that she didn't tell us, but it's even more fucked up that she's dying. I can't even imagine what she's gone through so I definitely cannot imagine how she'd have reached a decision not to tell us. But we're not calling her. Let her be."

I said nothing. I smoothed Ron's fur. Still holding the phone, I got down off the couch where I'd been sitting and moved closer to Ron, who was on the floor. He licked my nose.

"Are you there, Elo?"

"I am."

"Why don't I come by?"

"Come by?"

"Come by and see you. Or you come here. We're sisters. We should be together. I wouldn't have told you this over the phone if I thought you'd agree to see me without hearing it first."

"I'm sorry I've been an ass," I said. "Yes, come by. Or do you want me to come there?"

"I have to get some dogs out anyway. I'll take them down the trail by Ava's then stop by."

"I can walk with you, if you don't mind."

"That would be nice," said Alice. "I'll come pick you up? Twenty minutes?"

"Yes." I hung the phone up gingerly, as if putting it down with any force might drive nails into my mother's coffin.

I have known since I first started knowing things that there was a good chance I would one day see my mother die, but considering that she's only twenty-four years my senior, I didn't think it would happen until I was verging on old myself.

I wanted to get up off the floor but I couldn't. Ron sat at my side, still, contented. I don't know if he sensed my heartbreak the way certain service dogs sense an oncoming epileptic fit. Maybe he did. Whatever the case, having his fur-covered body next to me was soothing.

I'm not sure how long I was there, on the floor, next to the dog, lost in terrible thoughts, but I was snapped out of when Ron started barking and ran to the door.

Alice had arrived. She looked thin and had enormous dark circles under her eyes.

"Hi," she said. For a moment she stood there, almost appearing to weave in the doorway, then took a step closer and threw her arms around me.

For once, I didn't stiffen. We're not a family of huggers. Well, Mom has always been a hugger, became even more of one once she went into Narcotics Anonymous, but Alice and I have always been awkward about physical displays of affection—with each other and most everyone else except people we're sleeping with. Mom has never understood it. Not only did she provide the world with two *black-hearted harlots*, as she calls us, but physically undemonstrative ones at that.

Alice and I were still hugging when Ava came striding toward the house. I pulled back from my sister's embrace.

Ava still had the goggles on top of her head and the work gloves on.

"This is my sister Alice," I said, looking at my girlfriend over Alice's shoulder.

Alice turned around. "Hello," she said, automatically extending her hand.

"So nice to finally meet you." Ava threw her arms around her.

Ava is very much a hugger.

I could feel my sister's stiffness from where I was standing.

"Alice is here because our mother is sick," I said robotically while Ava was still hugging my sister.

"Sick? What's wrong?" Ava finally let my sister go and frowned, looking from me to Alice.

"Cancer," Alice said. "She's dying."

"What?" Ava's face fell.

Alice told her. I heard the facts rattled off like a series of small blows. I sat down on the nearest chair. Put my head in my hands.

"Oh my god, baby," I heard Ava say, and then she was kneeling down in front of me, putting her hands on my shoulders. She pulled me up off the chair and into an embrace. I let myself melt into her arms. I felt safer there. Momentarily forgot my sister. Then remembered, pulled back.

I told Ava that Alice and I were going for a walk down the trail. I saw questions forming in my girlfriend's mind but she thought better of asking them right then.

"Yes," she nodded, "do."

I brought Ron along. In spite of having only known the dog for two weeks, I already depended on his dogness. His solidness. I needed him.

Alice got Mom's dogs out of the van. Ron stood stoically letting the pit bull, the Lab mix, the Newfoundland, and the Ibizan hound sniff him, then he sniffed each of them in return.

As the dogs went through these formalities, Alice and I just stood there, mute and wounded.

We walked. Down Ava's long, snaking driveway, down the lovely magical Rabbit Hole trail. Neither of us said much. We were, for the first time in a long while, having a companionable, sisterly silence.

"Oh, Eloise." Ava was cradling my face in her hands, looking at me with so much tenderness I thought I might fall over.

By the time Alice and I had come back from our walk, Ava had made sandwiches, but neither Alice nor I could eat. We sat, all three around the kitchen table, Alice and I watching Ava eat. Eventually, Alice had gone back to Mom's house, back to the dogs. The dogs. Alice and I hadn't even talked about what would happen to them.

"The dogs," I heard myself murmuring, as Ava continued looking at me.

"The dogs?"

"I don't know what we'll do about them. If Mom only has months or maybe even weeks to live. Neither Alice nor I can accommodate so many dogs."

"I'll take them in here."

"What do you mean?"

"We'll take care of them. You and I."

"But Ava," I said, "you have another movie in three weeks."

"I'll cancel it."

"That's not necessary," I said, though I was moved. "Let's talk about something else." I pulled back and Ava's hands dropped away from my face.

"What?" Ava knitted her pretty eyebrows. "What do you mean?"

"My mother is dying. We've spent the afternoon talking about it. Let's not talk about it anymore. I can't."

"Oh."

"I don't want to dwell. It won't help. She's not dead yet anyway."

Ava's pretty mouth was forming an "o" of surprise.

"Don't look at me like that. Please."

She said nothing. But she kept looking.

"I want to go to the movies," I said. I did. I desperately wanted to go to the movies. I wanted to be lost.

"Okay," she replied carefully, "we can do that."

She started speaking to me very softly after that. As we went onto her computer to look up what was playing. As we sent Ron outside to pee. As Ava searched for her eyeglasses.

I didn't know if I could take Ava's level of empathy much longer. I started feeling claustrophobic. We were almost ready to go, Ava was just stuffing her wallet into her tote bag, when I felt my mouth opening and unpleasant words coming out.

"I need to go back to the city. I need to be alone."

"What?" Ava looked like I'd slapped her.

I *felt* like I'd slapped her. I didn't know where it was coming from. I needed to hurt her. And to get away from her.

Ava sank onto the living room couch. She was very pale.

"I didn't say I don't love you . . . And don't look at me like that."

I saw her wince. I wanted to go home. Back to my hole.

"But what about Ron?" Ava was saying.

I had packed up two bags. I had looked up the bus schedule online and gotten Ava to agree to drive me to Kingston to catch a late bus into Port Authority. She had stopped talking at a certain point. Had, in fact, disappeared to some other part of the house. But now, as I stood near the door, wondering if I had everything, Ava was playing the Ron card, as if he were our child, as if we'd had a long marriage and I was uprooting myself from a family. It was ridiculous and tragic.

"He likes you better anyway," I shrugged. "And I didn't say I'm not coming back." I was being cold. Cruel even.

Ava stood gazing down toward the floor. I didn't even look at Ron as I walked out the door.

I had been holed up for three days, alternately working on a new batch of stuffed animals and laying sprawled on the floor, listening to Lyle Lovett, crying over Indio, and vomiting. I had known for a while that I was pregnant. And, just as my mother had failed to tell people she was dying, so had I failed to tell anyone I'd been knocked up by Billy Rotten. The whole time I'd been with Ava, I'd been pregnant. She had once commented on how full my breasts were looking. I had just shrugged. I kept thinking I'd know what to do but that hadn't happened yet. I'd had an abortion when I was nineteen. The father was a creep, I was broke, I hadn't dwelled on it too long. Now, ten years later, I wasn't broke. The father was still a creep but so it goes. I'd figured I'd wake up one morning feeling ready to embrace motherhood. That hadn't happened either.

Ava hadn't called and I hadn't called her. It seemed like she'd been a dream, an invention, not a flesh-and-blood woman I had shared everything with for eight and a half weeks. A few times a day, I'd pick up my phone and start dialing her number. Then I'd slam it down. Every time it rang, I wondered if it would be her. Invariably, though, it was just Alice.

I had just brushed my teeth after vomiting when the phone rang.

"Are you coming or what? Mom will be back in four hours," Alice said into my ear.

"Yes," I heard myself answering, "I'm coming."

"There's a 2:30 bus that gets in at 5. I can pick you up and have you at the house when Mom walks in. I don't want to do this alone, Eloise."

"Two-thirty? What time is it now?"

"One forty-five. Hurry." She hung up in my ear.

I did as I was told.

I threw some things into an overnight bag then brought Hammie, my cat, downstairs to my neighbor Jeff who'd looked after her so much these last weeks; I was pretty sure Hammie actually preferred him to me. The cat didn't even give me a second glance, just rubbed against Jeff's calves and gazed up at him like he was a can of tuna.

I caught a cab and the young Puerto Rican driver was thrilled that I was in a hurry. He drove like a stock car driver all the way down. I gave him a huge tip and rushed into the station where I found an incredibly long line snaking up to the bus I needed.

I found a spot in the rear, with the smell of toilet seeping out from the little bathroom cubicle. I put on my iPod and took out a new pit-mouse I was working on. I saw the boisterous student-type girl sitting next to me stare at what I was doing. I reflected on the time, shortly after the settlement, when I was newly rich and had hired a limo to take me up to Mom's. It hadn't cost that much in the grand scheme of things, but I'd felt that if I kept spending that way, the money gods would be angry and some child would choke on one of my stuffed animals, the parents would sue me, and all my manhole money would be gone. So I've taken the bus ever since.

I had Prokofiev violin sonatas playing on my iPod, not the quietest music in the world, but it wasn't doing much to drown out the student next to me who was talking loudly to another girl sitting across the aisle.

I wanted to stab the girl for ruining my Prokofiev. Instead, I thought of Ava. I tried to picture what she'd do in this situation, how she might manage it with equanimity. Then I realized Ava wouldn't be on a packed bus, as her presence on Pine Hill Trailways would create hysteria once someone recognized her. I mused over the particulars of Ava's movie star life and wondered if she would be as easy-going and kind as she is if she did things like take crowded busses.

As the vehicle emerged from the Lincoln Tunnel and out into the grim, stumpy wilds of New Jersey, it occurred to me that Ava was infecting almost all my thoughts. Even in the days I'd been holed up in my apartment, deliberately not thinking of her, I had still carried her with me, was still strongly affected by her. I wondered if this is why I had left unceremoniously. Since love, to me, is parasitic and horrifying.

As the students kept on braying, I put the pit-mouse away and drifted off, coming to moments before the bus pulled into Woodstock. I rubbed my eyes, pulled my bags down from the overhead baggage holder, and stumbled down the narrow aisle and out of the bus. I saw Alice sitting at the far end of a bench, on the little triangle known as the green. The other end of the bench was occupied by a baby-faced skateboarder who was talking to two other baby-faced skateboarders in ill-fitting pants. Alice's little white spotted dog was at her feet and Alice was hunched, with her hair in her face. She didn't look up until I was standing right in front of her and Candy started making a fuss, pulling on the end of her leash in order to put her front paws on my legs and scratch at my jeans.

"Hi, Elo," Alice said lifelessly. "Mom just called. Fifteen minutes ago. She's extending her trip by three days."

My first instinct was to be angry with Alice for dragging me up there. Fortunately, I bit my tongue since, obviously, it wasn't Alice's fault, and a dying mother extending what was probably her last vacation was not someone I could be angry with either.

"I'm pregnant," I announced.

One of the skateboard kids looked over at me, grinned, made a thumbs-up, and said, "Right on, man."

Alice stared up at me without blinking.

"By a woman?" she asked, deadpan.

"By that fucking asshole."

"You mean William?"

"Yeah. Him."

The skateboard kids were now all listening in, so Alice got up.

"I parked behind Haust," she said, motioning at the hardware store.

We walked across the street, avoiding colliding with a homeless-looking woman in a giant winter parka who was standing in the middle of the road, directing traffic.

"You're gonna have the kid?" Alice asked after putting Candy in the backseat of Mom's Honda.

"I don't know. Should I?"

"Don't ask me, Eloise. I'm not a kid person, but obviously someone has to have them."

"Where's the asshole anyway? Have you talked to him?" I asked.

"Not a word. Two e-mails and one phone call unanswered."

"This may sound uncharitable but I admit I'm glad."

"Yes. That not only sounds uncharitable but it actually is uncharitable. Though I guess since the guy impregnated

178 ⚘ Maggie Estep

you, there are extenuating circumstances. But does this mean he doesn't know he knocked you up?"

"It does. Yes."

"Shit," said Alice as she pulled out of the parking lot and waited for the seemingly endless flow of cars on Tinker Street to let her turn. "That's a pretty valid excuse for a meltdown. I'm sorry, Elo. You know I had no idea that William was your Billy and of course I had no idea you were pregnant by him."

"I know," I sighed, "I know."

We fell silent for a bit, ignoring the five-hundred-pound gorilla of our dying mother as we drove up Rock City Road, left at Glasco Turnpike, and onto Upper Byrdcliffe Road, with its peaceful overhang of branches and dappled sunlight.

The dogs all went bonkers as we entered the house and Alice, doing an impressive imitation of Mom, went about quieting them down.

"I'm going to put my stuff upstairs," I told her, "I might as well stay until Mom gets back."

"Good," Alice nodded.

I trudged up to the guest room where I put my overnight bag on the unpleasantly hard bed then sat down and stared out the window at the massive evergreen that stood guard in front of the house. After a few moments, Alice appeared in the doorway.

"You should call that asshole, I think. Don't you?"

"Yeah?"

"Probably, yes."

"Won't he think I'm trying to get something from him?"

"I have no idea what he'll think, but I suppose, as awful as he is, he has a right to know." Alice shrugged.

"But know *what*? I don't even know if I'm going to have the kid."

"I think you are."

"I am?"

"I think so."

"Oh," I said, glad that my sister knew what I was doing. While her knowing what I'm going to do before I know is one of the things that gets me angry at her, it can also useful. "Then I suppose he should be told."

"What about your girlfriend?"

"I don't know what I'm doing about her either."

"Eloise, you're in love with the girl. Call her. Better yet, go see her."

Alice had never counseled me quite this extensively. We'd had a lifetime of gruffness between us. Love, yes, occasional snippets of something that could be construed as advice, but heartfelt counseling? No.

"What should I do first? Call the asshole or see if Ava still wants me?"

"Call the asshole. Go use the phone in Mom's room for privacy."

"Okay," I said, shrugging. I went into Mom's room and closed the door. Timber was asleep on the bed and Carlos, the one-eyed Chihuahua, was lying on a pile of laundry on the floor. Even though Alice's stuff was strewn around the room, it still felt like Mom. I lay face first on the bed and started weeping.

I was still crying when I sat up and pulled my cell phone from my jeans pocket to look up Billy's number.

I dialed and it went straight to voicemail.

"Hi, Billy," I said, hoping I didn't actually sound like I was weeping. "This is Eloise, could you call me please? It's important. I'm at my mother's house for a few days."

I left the number. Hung the phone up. Lay back down.

Timber licked my tears.

Alice eventually came in and found me like that, on the bed, puffy-eyed, with the black dog snuggled up next to me.

"You all right?" She came to sit at the edge of the bed.

"No."

"Mom, Billy, or Ava?"

"All of the above."

"Did you talk to Billy?"

"Left a message."

Alice sighed. "I'm going to play the late Pick 4 at Santa Anita," she said, "meaning I'll be absorbed for a couple of hours with the TV blaring, etc., so I wanted to see if you needed anything before I zone out."

"I'm going to go to Ava's."

"Good. She's there?"

"I don't even know. I'm just going to go over there." I said it a little defensively, daring Alice to tell me I should do otherwise.

She did not. She just nodded then went downstairs to gamble.

I washed my face, brushed my hair, then changed my underwear and T-shirt. It occurred to me I had no way to get to Ava's unless I braved it and drove Mom's Honda. The idea of driving all the way to Ava's, which had to be at least six miles of winding roads away, was a bit terrifying. But then again, so was the idea of not seeing Ava.

"Can I take Mom's Honda?" I asked Alice as I came down the stairs, half a dozen dogs on my heels.

She was slumped in front of her laptop. The TV was going and she was staring at the horses on the screen. She did not seem to hear me. I tried to see what was happening on the TV. I waited for the horses to cross the finish line, at which point my sister cursed volubly.

I cleared my throat. Alice, at last, noticed me.

"Mom's car? Mind if I take it?"

"Oh," Alice said, "of course not, go ahead."

I told her I wasn't sure when I'd be back. I don't think she heard me.

I took the keys from the little hook in the kitchen and, after shuffling dogs away from the door, walked to the car thinking about Alice's strange behavior. The main reason Mom and I had never worried too much about her gambling was that she never seemed strung out on it. We'd known her to have bad days, bad weeks, even bad months, but she never seemed to sink into a pit of depression about it. She just studied that much harder, took a deep breath, dove back in, and usually came out ahead sooner or later. She frowned on things like slot machines or any game that was purely chance. She never seemed to lose herself in gambling. Until now. She was gone, inside some other world, a world where, I'd guess, her paramour wasn't in jail, Mom wasn't dying, and she and I had not slept with the same man.

I got in the car and cautiously drove along Upper Byrdcliffe Road.

Pulling into Ava's driveway, I saw an unfamiliar Jeep parked at a haphazard angle in front of the house. It looked like whoever had driven the thing had been in a big hurry.

I hesitated at the front door. Part of me wanted to just barge on in and see what Ava was up to in there with this Jeep person. Though I didn't truly think she was up to anything with any person.

I was wrong.

After knocking several times, I finally heard Ava's voice call out, "Who?"

"It's Eloise," I said, not knowing what else to say.

I heard nothing else for what felt like many minutes. I was slightly sick to my stomach as I stared forlornly from the door to Mom's Honda wondering if I should hightail it back to Mom's, wondering if I hadn't made some terrible error in judgment, if, in fact, Ava had never loved me and was now shacked up with someone she did actually love.

Ava eventually opened the door. Her hair was all over the place and she was wearing only a long T-shirt. She looked at me and said nothing. Didn't invite me in, didn't greet me, just looked.

"Hi. I'm sorry," I said, "I had a meltdown." I opened my hands in an apologetic gesture.

"I have a friend over."

"I should have called, but I didn't want to have an awkward phone conversation."

I saw a battle in her eyes. I heard someone moving in the room behind her.

"Anyone I know?" I motioned with my chin at the insides of her house.

"Mark."

"Oh." I had no idea who Mark was but she said his name so unequivocally, he had to be meaningful.

"Can I come in?" I asked. I didn't *want* to come in, didn't want to see this Mark. I didn't want to see the end of Ava and me.

"Eloise," she said softly, looking up at me, "what are you doing?"

"I want to see you. I want to be with you. I didn't expect you to take up with some guy five minutes after I'd left. You should have known I'd come back."

"How should I have known that?"

"You just should have."

"That's asking a lot. You hurt me badly."

"I'm sorry. I'm a jerk."

"You think this sudden bout of humility will fix it?"

"I'm hoping."

"Come in, I guess," she shrugged and stepped back from the doorway.

The guy was standing in the middle of the living room. He was wearing khaki shorts, no shirt. He had dark wavy hair and was about Ava's height. He had a beautiful, lean upper body. He was handsome. I hated him.

"Mark," Ava said, "this is Eloise, my girlfriend."

Girlfriend? I thought ecstatically. *Really? Still?*

"Hello," said Mark, looking a little confused.

"I met Mark on the trail," Ava explained, waving her hand toward the outside.

"You meet a lot of people on that trail," I said, slitting my eyes at her.

"Yes," Ava replied solemnly, "that's true."

"She met my mother on that trail," I informed the illustrious half-naked Mark, "that's how Ava and I ended up meeting."

"Oh?" He was trying to be polite but seemed to be realizing he had fallen over his head into some pool of lesbian psychodrama.

"Mark's a composer," Ava said.

She had lit a cigarette. I didn't see where she'd gotten it. Maybe Mark the half-naked composer. Those types always smoke.

"That's nice," I said. I stared at the man, willing him to put his shirt on and leave.

He smiled at me, and, when I failed to smile back, looked away.

"Excuse me," he said, "I have to find my shirt."

Ava and I watched him walk up the stairs toward the bedroom.

"He's cute," I said resentfully.

"Has a girlfriend," Ava shrugged.

I felt relief.

"And you're not planning to have him fall in love with you and leave his girlfriend?"

"I hadn't gotten that far in my planning," Ava said.

Her eyes were sparkling now. She was enjoying herself. Then, suddenly, her eyes went dark.

"You're not here because of your mother . . . because your mother . . ."

"Died? No. Not yet. I'm here to see you."

The sparkle came back to her eyes and she took a step closer. I wanted to reach under her long T-shirt, cup my hands over her small but nicely shaped ass.

"I'm pregnant," I announced. "By that stupid guy. The one I had sex with once."

"What?"

"I'm pregnant."

"I heard that part. I just can't believe it. You had unprotected sex with a one-night stand?"

"Apparently."

"You're a whore."

"Not really."

"You're going to have a baby?"

"I guess."

"You're not saying it with much conviction."

"There are a few variables."

"Such as?"

"Such as what you would think about such a course of action."

"You'll have to be more specific."

"Okay. Can you and I be together if I have a kid?"

Ava looked at me through her long, light-brown eyelashes.

"Are you asking me to be the father of your baby?"

"Something like that."

"Wow. We're really lesbians now," she grinned.

"Do you like that idea?"

"Of being breeding lesbians? Sort of, yes." She had finally stubbed out the cigarette.

"Can we kiss and make up?"

"It's not going to be as easy as that, Elo. I'm damn glad to see you here, flattered that you're making these sorts of grand proposals, but you fucked me a few days ago."

"I'm sorry."

Ava was sitting on the couch now and I went to kneel in front of her. I put my hands on her bare knees and peered up into her vivid blue eyes. I slowly moved my hands up her thighs and a few inches under the T-shirt. She touched my face. I got up off my knees, straddled her, and kissed her.

Which is when the composer saw fit to come back down the stairs.

"Um, sorry . . . I . . . uh . . ."

He was standing at the foot of the stairs, turning from Ava and me to the door, as if afraid we'd attack him like wild dogs.

Ron, who must have been sleeping in another room somewhere, materialized at that moment, rushed over to greet me, then stood slowly wagging his tail, looking from me to the composer to Ava, registering his confusion by tilting his head.

Ava pushed me off her lap and stood up. The back of her T-shirt got stuck in her panties and her ass was hanging out as she walked over to Mark, put her hands on his shoulders, and said, "I'll talk to you soon?"

"Sure, yes," he answered, lightly pecking Ava on the cheek. "Nice to . . . uh . . . meet you," he added, smiling at me tentatively.

"Yes," I said, "a pleasure." I gave him a genuine smile this time.

As Ava saw the composer to the door, I called Ron over and hugged the furry blond beast. He licked my hands and forearms.

"I didn't actually have sex with him," Ava said after Mark closed the door.

"No? Why not?"

"Well," Ava shrugged, "we just hadn't gotten there yet when you knocked."

"Slut."

"He was a great kisser," Ava shrugged.

"No more kissing boys, okay?"

"Providing you don't pull any more stunts."

"Agreed."

She folded me into her arms.

10. KIMBERLY

Joe and I were lying on the beach outside Ginney's Motel on the tiny island of Nevis. The sun was setting, the ocean was calm, and I was losing strength by the minute.

I was resting my head on Joe's chest as he smoothed what was left of my hair that, between the humidity and the salt water, had to feel like a Brillo pad.

"I know you love me. You don't have to prove it by touching my hair."

"Shut up," he said, kissing my head.

His tenderness was heartbreaking.

When I'd finally told him about the cancer, he'd been furious. There were a few dark days when he wouldn't speak to me. I could see him, if I looked out my picture window, but he wouldn't look back across at me or answer the door. After three days, he walked into my kitchen one morning, stood with his head bowed to his chest, and started weeping.

I held him. We got through it, as much as two people can get through one of them dying.

Now Joe was watching me wind down. On the beach of a tiny, sweet Caribbean island where goats wandered and little Paso Fino horses plucked mangoes from trees.

This was our last night on the island after already extending our trip by three days. I had to go home and face all the people I hadn't told I was dying. I would have preferred driving shards of glass under my fingernails.

"What are you thinking about?" Joe said softly in my ear.

It was the kind of question teenage sweethearts asked

each other, not half-dead people in their fifties. It made me smile.

"I was thinking of driving shards of glass under my fingernails."

Joe's head swiveled. "What?"

"I'm dreading facing my daughters. And my NA friends. Everyone."

"Just tell them. Tell them you were convinced that keeping the cancer to yourself would make it go away."

"But it sounds so ridiculous now."

"It's the truth. It's what you thought."

I shrugged, then ran my palm down Joe's chest, feeling the hollowness of his belly, letting my hand travel inside his bathing suit.

"Kim, the goats will see us."

I put my face inches from his and looked inside him, trying to read what was there, wondering if it wasn't sick-making for him to be molested by a cancerous old woman. Death's approach has made me sexually rapacious. As if making love to Joe can stall the inevitable, the big black rabbit hole I am hurtling toward. Even though I spend most of the day feeling too sick to even move, I still want to ravage Joe. One always hears about great loves that come late in life. This one is almost too late. But it is here. I love Joe.

"Is my rapaciousness grossing you out, Joe?" I asked even though I didn't want to.

He sat bolt upright, displacing me from his chest.

"How can you ask such ridiculous questions? More to the point, how could you think something like that? You're the woman I love. You're dying. Touch me."

That shut me up for a while.

"Do I have to do this?" I asked Joe as he pulled into my driveway.

We'd been traveling all day, making our way back from

Nevis to JFK Airport, where Joe had left his car in long-term parking. We'd hit snarls of traffic and I wasn't feeling well, physical illness compounded by emotional unease as we got closer to Ulster County and the moment drew near for me to walk into my house and tell my daughter Alice that I was going to die.

"I don't think you'll feel good about yourself if you just up and die without warning your daughters."

"But I won't feel anything about myself. I'll be dead."

"There's no telling what goes on in the world of the dead. Feelings are certainly a possibility. Unlikely, I admit, but not entirely out of the question. Tell your daughter."

"And you'll come over in an hour to rescue me from Alice?"

"You make it sound like she's going to beat you up."

"She's not the most sensitive of creatures. Her anger will override whatever else she might feel."

"She's going to feel devastated and you're going to apologize for not telling her sooner. Then you're going to call Eloise and tell her too."

I felt sicker than I'd felt all day.

Joe kissed me lightly then shooed me out of the car.

When I pushed open the front door, there was an eerie lack of barking and only one dog, Ira, my faithful three-legged hound, greeted me. I had a paranoid moment and imagined that Alice, lost in a world of gambling and anger, had let all the dogs but Ira run away. Then I walked into the house and more dogs began appearing. Strolling lazily into the kitchen. Greeting me warmly, but not with the sort of over-the-top lunacy I'd expected.

I found Alice sprawled on the living room couch. There were dogs nestled next to her, dogs at her feet, dogs on the rug in front of the TV. A few got up to greet me, but the ones nearest Alice didn't budge other than to give a few half-hearted tail thumps, having apparently sworn allegiance to my daughter in my absence.

I patted some of the animals as I looked over at my sleeping daughter. The TV was on, tuned to the horse racing channel. There were horses pulling buggies. Trotters, I think. Or maybe pacers. I never can get the difference straight.

Alice being asleep seemed like a sign that I should simply go up to my bedroom to unpack and take some Vicodin. But my suitcase was suddenly too heavy. Even my smaller bag felt like it would pull my arm out of its socket. I was weak and exhausted.

I walked over to the stairs and slowly, very slowly, climbed up, leaving my bags behind. I tried to take my mind off the discomfort of the task by admiring the staircase. It was simple but beautiful, recently rebuilt by a woodworker friend who had hand-carved the banister. It had a life all its own. And it would outlive me by decades, if not centuries.

I finally reached the top of the stairs. My bedroom door was closed. I opened it, expecting to find dogs inside since I'd told Alice to rotate them from one room to the other several times a day to keep the pack dynamics in check. There were in fact five dogs but also my daughter Eloise, propped up in bed, reading one of her beloved Andrew Vachss novels.

"Mom," she said, as if she'd seen a ghost.

"Eloise, what are you doing here?" This I was not ready for. One daughter I could maybe handle. But two?

"Where's Alice?" Eloise asked rather than answering my question.

"Asleep on the couch."

"Let's wake her up," she said, jumping up from of the bed as if it were on fire.

I didn't know what to think or do, so as Eloise bolted from the room, I sat down on the bed and began petting the dogs, losing myself for a moment in their dogness. Timber and Lucy and Carlos and Harvey and Simba.

I was sitting in the middle of the bed, surrounded by dogs, when Eloise reappeared, Alice in tow. I toyed with the idea of putting it off, but then, before I could stop myself, I was blurting it out. The cancer. The metastasis. The brief round of chemo.

I would have kept going but Alice cut in: "We know, Mom."

"You what?"

"We know you're sick."

"You . . . oh?" They both nodded and looked down at their feet.

"And you're not furious with me?" I looked from Alice to Eloise and back.

Neither daughter said anything, then Alice shrugged. "Mom, I can't even begin to imagine what you went through or what led you to not telling us immediately."

Alice's apparent acceptance was so uncharacteristic it silenced me. The tenderness, the genuine love in this, pried me open and I started weeping. Which in turn engendered another thoroughly uncharacteristic move from my eldest, who sat down on the bed and hugged me. Eloise got in on it too and we became a snarled threesome of tears and the kind of grief I knew existed but didn't want to actually feel.

I held my daughters, feeling their limbs, their heartbeats, their tears. I couldn't remember the last time we had been like this.

I didn't want to let go.

By the time Joe came to check on us, we had stopped crying. We were all three in the kitchen and Alice was trying to make milkshakes. The dogs, every last one of them, had joined us and there really wasn't an ounce of space. Joe had to tiptoe over tails and haunches and muzzles resting on paws.

"What's going on in here?" he asked cheerfully, as if

this were any other night and my difficult daughters just happened to have both come to see me at the same time and we all three just happened to have had a fit of weeping, traces of which were still evident on our swollen, reddened faces.

"Alice is cooking," I said with a little smile as Joe came to stand at the back of my chair, resting his hands on top of my head.

"Hardly," Alice corrected. "I'm making milkshakes but even someone with my limited culinary skills does not call milkshake-making cooking."

Joe laughed. I laughed. Eloise laughed.

Since both the beds in my house were spoken for and the dogs would be looked after, I decided to sleep over at Joe's. Alice and Eloise said they'd tend to all the morning dog chores, leaving me to sleep in and relax. I thanked my girls, not telling them that I'm often afraid to sleep these days since every time I do, I wonder if I'll wake up.

All that night, Joe held me as fiercely as he could without choking me. We couldn't seem to get physically close enough to each other. I felt like he was trying to tie me to him, to keep me alive.

When morning came, I ignored it as long as I could and lay next to him, watching his fitful sleep, his eyelids fluttering, small, wounded sounds escaping his lips.

I slowly crept from the bed. I was in pain and needed to take something. I had Percocet in my bag. I got two out then padded into the kitchen to get a glass of water. I was nauseous and didn't know if I'd be able to swallow. I took one small sip of water. It stayed down. I was about to brave one of the pills when Joe came into the room.

"You okay?" He put his hand on the back of my neck and rubbed gently.

"Fine," I lied.

"Pain?" he asked, not believing my lie.

"Yes," I admitted, "but I'll be all right."

I swallowed one of the pills. Felt it traveling down my throat. Willed it to go all the way down and stay there. All the while, Joe was studying me, tilting his head just like the dogs do. I took the second pill and sat down at Joe's cheerful 1950s Formica table. My head felt heavy, so I rested it on the table, my forehead taking in the coolness of the Formica.

"I'm not dying. I mean, not right this minute," I said, speaking into the table, "my head just got heavy. I'm resting."

"What would make you happy today, Kim?" Joe asked softly.

"I can think of a lot of things," I said, briefly lifting my head to look at him. "I suppose I would like to spend time with my daughters. And my dogs. And later with you."

"But what about *you*?" I added. "Don't you have an awful lot of work to catch up on?"

Joe shrugged. I knew he did have work. A ton of it. I also knew he had no plans to tend to much of it while I was still alive.

"I want to do what you want to do," he said.

It was all so sad. I just wanted to shut it off. The fountain of fucking sadness.

I took a shower, put my dirty clothes back on, avoided looking in the mirror, then went into Joe's living room where I found him sitting at his piano, staring at the keys as if they were strangers.

"I'll spend a few hours with my girls," I told him. "Please play. Please?"

He nodded. I leaned over to kiss him.

He smelled so good it hurt.

I walked over to my house, stepping past the low stone wall separating my property from Joe's, slightly buzzed since the pills had hit me by now and I was actually enjoying them. It wouldn't last. Soon, the nausea would outweigh the pleasant oblivion. All the same, I was a recovering addict getting a free ride. It had taken a terminal illness to get that free ride, but some part of me, some still-sick part, didn't mind all that much.

I found both my daughters and nearly all the dogs gathered in the kitchen where Eloise was making eggs.

When I walked in, everyone seemed to freeze, as if afraid breathing might knock me over and kill me.

"Hi," I greeted brightly.

"Morning, Mom," Eloise said.

"Hi," Alice said.

Ira had run over when I walked in and I stood scratching his head. Timber deigned to get up and poke his muzzle into my thigh.

"Who's up for the Rabbit Hole trail?"

Both daughters looked at me like I was insane.

"What?" Eloise said.

"Mom, are you stoned?" Alice asked.

"I took two Percocet. I'm allowed. I have cancer."

"I wasn't questioning your taking medication, more like if you're really up for a trail."

"I'll be fine," I said defensively, even though I doubted I would be, "I want to walk. With the dogs. With both of you."

Eloise looked up from under her bangs and smiled sweetly.

Alice scowled then agreed that yes, we could all go to the trail.

The effort of pretending to feel well had drained me already and I went into the bathroom, I opened the medicine cabinet, and took another pain pill. I had built up a tolerance over the last few months. It wouldn't knock me out. But it was a balancing act, taking enough to dull the pain but not so much that I couldn't function. I hoped for the best.

When I came out of the bathroom, I found Eloise standing just outside the door. She rushed past me, barely making it to the toilet in time to vomit.

"Oh no, Elo, are you sick?" I had a sudden vision of my daughter being stricken with cancer as well.

Just as I was about to get furious with the gods, my daughter wiped her mouth, looked at me, and announced that she was pregnant.

She said it quietly and firmly the way she might have announced, when she was a teenager, that she was staying out late.

"Are you sure?" I inexplicably asked.

"Yes, Mom." She gave me a dirty look.

"Um, but haven't you been with a . . . uh . . . woman?"

"Yes. But before Ava I was with Billy Rotten. Well, for exactly one night."

"You got pregnant from a one-night stand?" I asked, aghast. "You made love with a stranger without a condom?"

"Mom."

"I'm sorry, Elo, I'm just . . . well, I'm happy. Of course. Um . . . You are . . . you are going to keep the baby?"

"Yes, Mom. With Ava."

"You're going to be lesbian parents? Jesus." I closed the toilet seat and sat down on the lid.

"Mom, are you okay?"

"Well," I said carefully, "I've taken three pain pills so my head is swimming. My previously heterosexual daughter is suddenly a lesbian but having a baby by a one-night stand. And I'm going to be a grandmother. Except I'll be dead by the time the baby is born, so technically I will not have been a grandmother to anything more than a fetus."

"Mom, please don't say that."

Eloise knelt before me and made the kinds of cooing sounds I hadn't heard from her since she was a baby.

"But Eloise, I told you. I have maybe a month left. Any day now I won't be able to get out of bed. I'm not going to see my grandchild. But the notion that you are having a baby is a very beautiful one."

I cupped my daughter's face in my hands. She was crying. I didn't want to start. It would make my face hurt and would tire me even more.

"Come on," I said, standing up, "let's try to walk some dogs."

I draped my arm around Eloise's shoulders. She went into the guest room to find her sneakers and I headed into the bedroom to put on baggy shorts.

I let Alice drive the van. I sat in the passenger seat and Eloise was in the back, tending to the dogs. We had brought all but the infirm ones for a total of eleven. They were a little boisterous.

I had asked Eloise if she wanted to stop by her girlfriend's on the way, see if Ava wanted to join us.

"No, Mom, you're not turning this into a social occasion, this is a family walk and though I hope Ava is becoming family, she isn't yet. So thank you, but no."

I was pleased. I wanted my girls and my dogs to myself but hadn't wanted Eloise to think I was shutting Ava out, particularly when we were passing right by her house.

As Alice piloted the van into the dirt lot at the Rabbit Hole trailhead, I felt a wave of nausea. I tried to will it away but I must have looked awful.

"Mom, what's wrong?" Alice asked.

"Just a little nauseous, it'll pass," I said.

Alice looked at me levelly for a moment. "Between you and Eloise, we need a vomitorium."

It made me laugh and gave me energy. I got out of the van. I wobbled a little, then took the leashes off Ira, Harvey, and Carlos, as my daughters wrangled the rest of the pack and we walked onto the rocky trail.

There had been rain the night before and the dense foliage and tall trees were bursting green. The stones of the rocky path were still wet and, between their slickness and the fuzziness from the pain pills, I had to think about where I put my feet.

We were silent until we reached the first creek crossing. There, we liberated all the dogs except Rosemary and Lucy, the Ibizan hound.

As I picked my way from rock to rock through the creek, the dogs ran and splashed and Harvey, in his exuberance, knocked Carlos into the water. The Chihuahua scrabbled then clung to a rock until Alice reached down and scooped him out, depositing him on the other side of the creek. Harvey, who seemed to actually realize what he'd done, stood by looking concerned, then licked the beleaguered Carlos once he was back on terra firma.

"So," I asked, as we walked up a slight incline, the dogs bounding and foraging for frogs and chipmunks, "what about these dogs?"

"What?" said Alice.

"They won't all have homes before I'm dead."

"Oh, Mom, please stop talking like that," Alice said.

"No, Al," Eloise came to my defense, "she's right. Denial is not helpful. Mom is going to die. These dogs need a caretaker. Ava and I can take three or four, but not all."

"You can?" I asked Eloise.

"Yes. Ava and I talked about it. The dog we rescued, Ron, is lonely. I'll be hanging around the house being pregnant and making stuffed animals. I may as well try to find homes for some of the dogs."

"So that's it?" You and Ava are just going to shack up and be domestic and have babies?" Alice said.

"One baby," Eloise replied. "Just one. No one has knocked Ava up yet. But yes. We're going to shack up and be domestic, Alice."

Alice actually stopped walking and stared at her sister. I could see how incomprehensible this was to my untamable eldest.

"Wow," said Alice.

It was possible there was a hint of envy in her voice. But it was likely just wishful thinking on my part. I didn't want my daughter to end up alone against her wishes. She liked being alone now, while she was still vibrant and could pick and choose bed mates as the urge struck her, but I wasn't sure how she'd feel twenty years down the line when her habitual solitude might become crippling and hard to shake.

"I want to help with the dogs too," Alice said after she'd paused long enough to process the concept of her little sister settling down.

"Thank you, Alice," I said, "maybe you could take Timber and Lucy—or whoever you think you might be able to find a home for."

"Whoever Eloise doesn't take."

"It'll be quite a crowd in your apartment," I said.

"I was hoping to stay at your place until all the dogs are sorted out."

"You? In the country for what could be months?"

"Is that really so shocking?"

"Yes," I said.

Eloise echoed the sentiment.

Alice shrugged. "I like it up here."

"But what about the track?"

"I can get by with computer and TV for a while. Plenty of handicappers never even go to the track."

"Well," I said slowly, "you girls are getting the house anyway, it would make me happy if one of you lived in it, at least for a little while. I've loved that house."

Both my daughters nodded but neither one said anything. As if by silent agreement, we all three seemed to focus entirely on the dogs, on their grace and energy, on Harvey's caramel coat gleaming under the bits of sun that reached through the trees, on Lucy's beautiful, loping gait, on their willingness to be happy and uncomplicated.

We reached the place where the trail narrows and dips

down into a little ravine choked with tree roots. Just as I put my right foot down to purchase, Harvey knocked into me and I tripped and went down into the ravine.

Everything turned black.

11. ALICE

My mother had fallen into the ravine and was lying on her side, unconscious. I felt my mouth hanging open but the rest of me was frozen.

I finally registered that my sister was screaming at me.

My eyes came into focus and I saw that Eloise was squatting down by our mother, whose face was turned toward the dirt. There was a gash on Mom's temple where she must have hit a rock as she fell.

"Is she . . . is she . . . ?"

"No, she's not dead," my sister said impatiently, "but she's unconscious. I don't know what to do."

Eloise looked up at me with huge, scared eyes. I was the big sister. I was supposed to be capable. But I was frozen.

The dogs were milling around and several had come over to sniff at our felled mother, forcing Eloise to shoo them away.

"Alice, help me." There were tears in her eyes.

I reached for the phone in the pocket of my pants.

"You won't get a signal here," Eloise said impatiently.

"So what do we do?"

"I think we should carry her back to the van and then take her to Ava's."

"Carry her? But you're not supposed to move someone who has fallen."

"She hasn't broken her neck, Alice."

"Do we know that for a fact? When jockeys fall on the track, they put them on a stretcher just in case."

"Can you refrain from comparing everything to horse racing? Our mother is dying."

"Okay, we'll carry her."

Our mother, who'd never weighed more than 110 pounds, weighed even less now. I lifted her upper body, cradling her head in the crook of my elbow, while my diminutive sister carried her inert legs. The dogs were confused and concerned; Harvey licked Mom's face, upsetting Eloise.

"No, Harvey, no!" she said.

The caramel-colored dog looked sheepish and put his head down.

We made very slow progress like that, hauling our mother along the narrow, rocky trail while trying to wrangle the dogs, all of whom we'd had to unleash. I kept imagining Rosemary taking off into the woods and Mom coming back to consciousness to find we'd lost her. But the dogs, their supremely honed instinct alerting them that all was not well with the humans, stayed close.

Eloise and I had to stop four times to rearrange Mom's weight. Around us, the woods seemed to have grown darker, the beautiful trail now ominous, as if harboring dangerous forest beasts who could smell our mother's weakness.

We had a particularly perilous creek crossing where I was sure we were going to drop our dying, unconscious mother into the rushing water. I almost told Elo about this nearly comical image I kept having, but she would not have gotten it, has never understood my macabre sense of humor and how holding onto a mental image of dropping my dying mother into a creek was somehow making it all slightly bearable.

We finally reached the trailhead parking lot and had to put Mom down on the ground while opening up the back of the van. Again, the dogs swarmed and busied themselves, trying to figure out how they could help with this unusual and worrisome procedure.

When we reached Ava's driveway, Eloise hopped out and unlatched the gate. Mom had told me that before installing the gate, Ava had all sorts of unwelcome drop-bys from the many locals who knew she lived there.

Eloise got back in and we drove up, got Mom out, and carried her to the front door where Ava, who must have heard us pull up, came out of the house.

"What happened?" was all she could manage as she froze there in the doorway.

Eloise and I carried our mother in, and just as we were lowering her onto the living room rug, she made a startled sound and her eyes focused on me.

"Oh?" she said.

"Are you okay, Mom?" I asked.

She suddenly sat bolt upright and I saw Eloise wince.

"Mom, careful, you fell on the trail, you hit your head," Eloise said. "Ava, call an ambulance."

"No!" our mother actually screamed. "Please, no. I'm fine."

My sister and I stared at her. There was blood crusted on the side of her face and she looked tinier than ever.

"Mom, please." Eloise was squatting down at her side. "You were unconscious, that means concussion, you need to be seen by someone."

"Eloise, I'm dying," Mom sounded exasperated, "what does a knock on the head matter?"

"I have a friend," Ava inserted, "Paul, he's a physician, lives nearby. I'm sure he'd come."

I looked over at the tall, pretty woman. I imagined she was the type who could get any man to go anywhere anytime. It wasn't till about age thirty that I discovered I could too, that this magical power isn't the exclusive domain of the achingly beautiful.

"How about that, Mom?" I said. "Can you at least let Ava's doctor friend look at you?"

She rolled her eyes, then gave a little shrug. "Okay."

Ava picked up a cordless phone off an end table and dialed from memory. There was a brief conversation and, after hanging up, Ava told us her friend would be over soon.

"He lives in Hurley," she said apologetically, "it's going to take him a few minutes to get here."

"Thank you, Ava," Mom said.

Eloise was still squatting by Mom's side. The dogs were milling all around and, I was sure, were about to break all sorts of valuable baubles, though to her credit, Ava didn't seem to have any ostentatious displays of wealth and fame lying around.

A few minutes passed with Mom growing increasingly coherent. Eloise had called Joe and he was on his way.

"By the way," Ava said, looking over at me from where she'd perched on the arm of a beautiful, deep-red couch, "it's nice to see you again, Alice."

"Likewise," I smiled at her. She really seemed all right. Like someone I could approve of for my baby sister. Though I was still thoroughly flabbergasted by Eloise suddenly turning gay and having a baby, I suppose I was glad she was doing these things with a ravishing movie star.

Eloise looked from me to Ava and glowered, like we were having social hour while Mom was sitting on a rug bleeding and, ultimately, dying.

At the risk of invoking Eloise's wrath, I suggested making tea and Ava and I went into her lovely kitchen to put the kettle on. I didn't know what to say to her and she seemed stumped about making conversation with me too.

"So," I finally said, "how did you and Eloise meet?" I knew the answer but didn't know how else to make small talk with the woman since I didn't feel like discussing my mother bleeding on her rug in the other room.

Ava told me, in lavish prose, about meeting my mother on the Rabbit Hole trail and then meeting Eloise shortly thereafter and how my sister took her breath away.

"I'm not fond of clichés but it truly was love at first sight," said the movie star.

"Yeah," I shrugged, "I've had that. I mean, maybe not love, but an instant and deep attraction."

"With your jailbird lover?" Ava said with a sly smile.

"Oh, you know about that, huh?"

"Yeah. I hope that's okay." She suddenly looked worried.

"It's fine. I'm not guarded about my personal life. But Eloise might make me sound like more of a harlot than I am."

Ava laughed, showing a row of beautiful, pearly teeth.

"But yes. I did have an instant attraction with my jailbird. I thought it would evaporate approximately thirty minutes after it first manifested, but there's something about him that gets to me."

"Oh?" Ava said, looking genuinely interested.

"It's disarming when people are simple. And I don't mean dumb. But he's a simple man with simple desires."

"I've had some of those."

For a minute, I glimpsed the true heartbreaking she-beast Ava must be, the beast that was in abeyance now that she was in love with my sister.

"What about the asshole?" Ava asked then.

"The asshole? You mean Billy Rotten, the baby father?"

Ava nodded.

"What about him?" I knew that Eloise had decided to give up trying to contact the jerk. Eloise hadn't asked me if I'd heard from him but I suppose her girlfriend wanted to know.

"What's your status with him?" she asked.

"There isn't any status. I haven't heard from him and I certainly don't intend to sleep with the guy who knocked up my sister, if that's what you're asking."

"It was."

I liked her forthrightness. She was, in the parlance of some of my racetrack acquaintances, a brassy broad.

The tea water was boiling and Ava had gotten four cups out.

"Should your mother drink tea?"

The question made me think of my mother in the dotage she would never have, as an octogenarian Eloise and I would have had to make basic decisions for, such as whether or not she should drink tea, when she should be bathed, what specialists she should see. I had never really thought about these things, particularly in light of the fact that Mom and I are so close in age. But for the first time, I realized that it would never come to that. My mother would not need her diaper changed, would not need me to oversee a retinue of doctors or consider nursing homes.

Having no idea if tea was recommended under the circumstances, I shrugged at Ava, who took it upon herself to brew a cup for Mom.

We'd all, including Mom, who had progressed to sitting on the couch now, started sipping our tea when Paul, the doctor, arrived.

He was of medium height and medium build, balding but pleasant looking with little round glasses and an old-fashioned doctor's bag. Ava engulfed him in a hug and we all thanked him for coming. Mom, who stared at him menacingly for a few seconds, warmed to him quickly. He took her into the guest room to examine her. Eloise and Ava and I tried to make small talk; I asked them about Ron, their recently adopted dog. Ava got Ron to come over and demonstrate his new trick of rolling over on his back and exposing himself. It made me think of all the times I had questioned the canine species' eagerness to do even the most absurd things we humans dreamt up to ask of them. I would have made a terrible dog.

Most of Mom's dogs had finished their explorations of Ava's house and had come back to the living room and we were all waiting there, quiet and vaguely desperate, when Mom and Paul emerged from the guest room.

"She'll be all right," Paul announced. "Under normal circumstances I'd want her admitted into the hospital. But

I understand her reticence. Just please call me if anything strange happens over the next twelve hours."

"Strange?" said my mother. "Strange things always happen to me. In fact, I can promise you something strange will happen to me in the next twelve hours," she added with pride.

Paul smiled and Eloise looked aghast once more. My poor sister, who has never been as emotionally shut down as me, was having a very hard time with everything and obviously thought we were all being way too lighthearted.

Ava accompanied Paul to the door, looping her arm through his and speaking to him softly. I saw Eloise shoot her a look. I entertained the idea of having a talk with my sister, of explaining to her that this would all be easier if she weren't so emotionally visceral about everything. But I realized Eloise would just accuse me of being a Neanderthal.

Mom's paramour pulled up just as Paul was getting into his car. I saw Ava introduce the two men, saw them speaking there under the glorious huge willow tree in front of Ava's house.

After Paul had gotten into his car and driven away, Joe came inside. He looked hollow and sad and I felt for him. He seemed to want and need to hover over Mom, so I told him he ought to take her home to his place and I would wrangle all the dogs back to Mom's. Both Joe and Mom looked at me gratefully and I felt strange in my unaccustomed role as dutiful, helpful daughter.

Ava and Eloise helped me usher all the animals back into the van.

"I'll be back at Mom's in a half hour or so," Eloise told me. I hadn't wanted to ask. Had wanted to leave her the option of staying behind with her girlfriend, but I was glad she was coming back to Mom's. I realized, for one of the first times in my life, that I didn't want to be alone.

As I got into the van and started the engine, I looked out at my little sister standing next to her ravishing girl-friend and felt a pang of envy. Eloise, in surrendering to loving Ava, was experiencing something foreign to me.

I pointed the van toward the road.

I needed to get groceries so I drove through town rather than taking the shorter way back to Mom's.

Town was packed, car traffic crawling along and the peculiar breed of dowdy white tourists that Woodstock attracts overflowing from the narrow sidewalks as they ambled past candle shops and dusty hippie stores whose survival is a mystery. Just past the village green, traffic was at a standstill as dozens of pedestrians slowly crossed the street. I looked around, trying to fathom what these people were doing here, and was startled by a familiar male figure. At first, it didn't quite register. The guy was holding hands with a woman in a green sundress who in turn was holding the hand of a little boy.

"Fuck," I said aloud when it sank in that it was William. Billy Rotten.

My first instinct was to jump out of the van, run up to him, and punch him in the mouth. A horn honked behind me and I drove forward, pulling off Tinker Street into the parking lot behind the hardware store. I shoved the van into a narrow space and got out of the vehicle as the dogs looked on expectantly.

"Stay," I said, "all of you stay."

I strode onto Tinker Street and literally came face to face with Billy and his wife and child.

His jaw went slack and his body stiffened visibly.

"Alice, hi."

"Hello," I snarled. I looked meaningfully at the woman at his side, then at the child. I didn't want to scar the child for life so I wasn't going to get too carried away. At least, I hoped I wasn't.

"This is my sister, Tess," Billy said then.

Shit, I thought.

"And my nephew Trevor," Billy indicated the child. "I wanted to show them Woodstock."

"Right," I said. I had no idea how to proceed.

"Is everything okay?" Billy asked as the sister smiled pleasantly and the child looked all around.

"Not really."

This wasn't the answer he was hoping for. He looked uncomfortable.

"My mother is dying of cancer and you screwed my baby sister."

"Uh . . ." Billy looked nervously at his own sister. Then at the kid. "What?"

"Eloise. My sister. Cute tiny girl with dark-brown hair? You met her in Central Park?"

"Uh . . . what?" Billy Rotten squinted.

"You don't remember?" I was just about screaming. Billy's sister had hustled her child a few feet away to look into a shop window.

"I . . . I'm confused," said Billy, glancing to see where his sister had gone, or maybe to take in the fact that the tension in our bodies was inciting passersby to stare.

"You had a one-night stand with Eloise, my little sister. Before having several-nights stands with me." With every fiber of my being, I was resisting telling him Eloise was pregnant. She had decided the guy was too much of a lout to be told and I didn't want to give him the opportunity to prove her wrong. I loathed him for making me feel things I was unaccustomed to feeling and then leaving me high and dry.

"Eloise is your sister?"

"Yes."

"What are the odds of that?"

"It's not funny, Billy, William, whoever the fuck you are."

"But it *is* strange."

"You're a flaming asshole."

"I've been told that."

I wanted to bash his skull in with a lead pipe.

"Alice," he said in an oily voice, "I'm sorry."

"For what?"

"All of it," he said, making a big helpless gesture. "You and me. Your sister. I didn't mean any harm."

"Oh, please."

"You scared me. I ran. Same, ironically, with your sister."

"That's ironic all right."

"What do you want me to say here?"

"I don't want you to say anything. I just thought you should know. You fucked me and you fucked my sister and we were both fucked up by it. Have a nice day." I turned and walked toward the van.

"Alice!" he called. Some tiny, idiotic part of me felt hopeful. Like he would come running to explain some unruly set of emotional problems that had led to his not calling me. I had, I realized, been hoping he was married, that this explained his disappearance. It was too harrowing to consider that after all my years of carefully selecting men who couldn't possibly hurt me, I had been duped, had fallen for someone who sat by laughing as I tumbled into the void.

"What?" I turned back for a second.

"I'm sorry."

"Big deal," I said, and then kept walking.

I sat clutching the steering wheel, choking the thing. Ira had jumped into the front passenger seat with Candy and Carlos. He licked me and, in his enthusiasm, bumped me hard in the chin.

"Away, beast."

"Where were you?" Eloise demanded when the dogs and I tumbled in through Mom's kitchen door. "I was worried."

"Went to the store."

I deposited the grocery bags on the kitchen table. After sitting in the van trying to breathe for close to forty-five minutes, I had finally snapped out of my stupor and driven to the grocery store.

"What's the matter with you? You look ashen," my sister said.

"I'm upset about Mom."

"It's about time."

"What's with you, Eloise?"

"What do you mean?"

"Why so snarky and vindictive?"

"Vindictive? Me?"

"Never mind." I didn't want a fight.

"Don't *never mind* the situation. What are you saying?"

"It's just . . ." I sighed.

"It's just what, Alice?"

"It's just that everyone experiences pain differently. Reacts to it differently. I realize you don't believe I actually have feelings and the concordant pain, but I do, Eloise. I don't appreciate your being judgmental about how I'm dealing with my grief."

I didn't look at her. Had taken a seat at the cheerful kitchen table and was gazing down at my hands that suddenly fascinated me.

"I'm sorry," I heard my sister say in a small voice.

I glanced up and saw how sheepish she was looking, how tiny and wounded, like a stabbed dove.

"It's okay," I said, reaching over and patting her hand.

We fell silent then. Awkward, embarrassed by having such a direct conversation.

"The dogs," I said, standing up, "I have to get the gimpy ones out."

"Oh, I did that already," Eloise shrugged.

I stopped in mid-stride. Unsure what to do now.

"Mom's at Joe's?" I asked, just for something to say.

"Yeah."

"When are you going back to Ava's?"

"I dunno. I thought I'd spend the night here. Be close to Mom in case anything comes up."

"Oh."

"Alice?" Eloise said then, which was weird, her using my name like that, making sure I paid close attention even though, obviously, I had to since I was standing right there.

"Yeah?" I was nervous, wondering if she somehow knew I had seen Billy.

"When are you going to see Clayton?" my sister asked.

"Clayton?" I was confused. "I don't know, why?"

"I think you should go see Clayton."

I tilted my head. "Why?"

"You just should." She didn't seem to want to elaborate.

I frowned at her for a few seconds, then started unpacking the groceries.

I showed the guard my driver's license and expected some sort of grief or request for more identification. I'd come armed with four pieces of ID, and had stripped my person of all metal objects, including my watch and any change in my pockets, doing whatever I could think to not set off any alarms or be forbidden from seeing Clayton after schlepping on the Rikers bus and waiting in a cold, fluorescent-lit room packed with broken, desperate people. My license was evidently enough and I was permitted to remove my shoes and go through the metal detector. I didn't set it off but was patted down anyway. Then sent to another room to wait. This second room was a bit smaller and brighter but not exactly cheerful. People, mostly black and Latina women with children, sat in molded plastic chairs, some striking up conversations with each other, some keeping to themselves. There was one other white person in the waiting room, a thin old man with a scar on his face who looked like he'd done time. A lot of time.

I'd wanted to come see Clayton without any fanfare, to just drop by unannounced, but discovered that not only did he have to put my name on a list of visitors he'd accept, but I had to figure out the visiting schedule that went according to the first letter of the inmate's last name. The M day was Thursday, so here I was. In a molded plastic chair. Feeling incredibly conspicuous with my straw-colored hair and the elegant blue pantsuit I'd donned for the occasion. Other women were looking at me resentfully, like I was some sort of slumming princess, which admittedly was how I felt even though it was probably the first time in my life I'd felt like anything resembling a princess.

My ass was beginning to throb from the chair's hardness when Clayton's name was finally called and I was permitted to walk through yet another door and into a big, cavernous room filled with little tables with more molded plastic chairs. It wasn't hard to pick Clayton out, between the bright orange jumpsuit and his whiteness. There was only one other white guy and he was short and squat with no hair.

My stomach churned when I first laid eyes on my big, jumpsuited oaf. Not in apprehension or revulsion. I was excited, almost exhilarated to see him. He looked beautiful to me and this was so startling that I stopped short before reaching the table he was sitting in front of.

He was looking up at me with no expression at all. He'd cut his hair into a crew cut about an inch long. It suited his big features. His dark eyes, which were so good at looking hurt, were immense and, in that moment, incredibly inviting. Except he wasn't looking at me invitingly. He was just staring, barely seeming to register that I was there.

I felt like I was walking in slow motion, every step taking several minutes. My chest constricted. The poor bastard, I thought. He's in prison. It hadn't really registered till this moment, just as Mom's rapidly approaching death hadn't fully registered until I realized I'd never watch her get old.

"Hi," I said, taking the chair opposite his at the table.

"Hi, Alice," he responded in that low, sad voice of his.

"You okay?" I asked, peering at him as if I'd never studied his face before, which, in fact, I probably hadn't. He'd always been a vague impression, an indistinct blur of man.

"I'm in prison, Alice," he said softly.

He looked at me for a second then looked back down at the table.

"I'm sorry about all this, Clayton."

"I got off pretty easy in the grand scheme of things."

"What's it like?" I asked, motioning around me.

"It's prison, Alice, what do you think it's like?"

"Oh," I said, sheepish. "What can I do?"

"What do you mean, what can you do?"

"To make the next ten months a bit more bearable."

"Nothing," he said with a shrug.

"Are you pissed at me, Clayton?"

"No." He still wouldn't look at me.

"You're not really talking to me."

"What do you want to talk about, Alice?" Now he *was* looking at me. "You've jerked my chain for months and I wouldn't be in prison if it weren't for you. I don't want to talk. In fact, I almost didn't put your name on the visitor's list."

I stared at him. "I'm sorry, Clayton, I'm fucked up. But I'm trying not to be."

"That's supposed to make it okay? You're sorry? I'm in prison and you're sorry?"

I said nothing and looked down at my lap. At the cool cotton of my dark-blue suit pants. I thought of the nice cream lace panties I was wearing. Not that I'd thought there'd be a chance to show them to Clayton, just that

I wanted to feel like a woman wearing nice underwear. From the looks of it, Clayton had no interest in ever seeing my underwear again. As I realized this, I felt my stomach knot up. *I love this guy*, I thought. And there wasn't a second thought, a second voice inside me kicking in to volubly ridicule this notion.

I sat absorbing the shock of it. Then I looked up at Clayton with his head hanging down toward his chest, his stubble of brown hair, his big shoulders hunched in the prison-issue orange jumpsuit.

"I love you, Clayton," I said.

His head snapped up and he narrowed his eyes. He didn't say anything for a few seconds. Then: "What was it you said when I told you I loved you? Something like *Shut up* or *What the fuck are you saying?*"

"I was wrong. I was reacting to you as if you were all the ones who came before you," I said quietly.

At the table next to us, a woman was reaching across to touch her orange-jumpsuited man. She started putting her fingers in his mouth. A guard came over. "No touching," he said. The woman sat back a few inches.

"I don't know why you're saying these things now, Alice, but it's no use. You killed whatever was there. Killed it dead." He shrugged again, then looked back down at his hands. "Anyway," he added, "I'm getting back with Becky. She's been coming to see me."

"Who?"

"My ex-wife. Becky. When I get out of here I'm moving in with her."

"The one who ran off with a plumber?"

"Yeah," Clayton lifted his chin a little, "I made her do it."

"You made your ex-wife run off with a plumber?"

"I kept going camping."

"Come again?"

"I kept going camping. Every weekend I'd go camping. Becky hated camping."

"Ah," I said. I'd never known camping to be a relation-ship crime.

"Now she says she doesn't mind. Whatever I need to do to keep my head on straight. She doesn't mind."

"Well, that's big of her."

"Don't be a fucking smart-ass."

"What do you want me to be?"

"Nothing."

"I guess that says it all." I went to push my molded plastic chair back. Then realized it was bolted to the floor. I stood up. I waited for Clayton to protest.

"Alice," he said in a quiet but firm voice. "Sit down."

I sat.

"Don't walk out of here hating me. I don't need that. I don't deserve it. I tried with you."

I looked at him. Waited for more. But that was it.

He was so handsome.

I stood up again. I walked away without turning back.

"What, you wanted to wait around for the inevitable bit-terness and disappointment to set in? I expect better of you." Arthur hadn't deigned to look up from his notes when I'd told him that I'd seen, and been blown off by, my jailbird paramour the day before.

We were at Belmont, in box seats Arthur had inherited for the afternoon. I'd called him up the day before, after getting off the Rikers bus. I'd planned to spend one night at home in Queens then head back up to Woodstock the next morning. But the whole Clayton episode had flattened me so much that I had to do something to feel like myself again—as opposed to some trampled, dejected *thing*. On the phone, Arthur hadn't asked how I was or what I was doing, had just told me what box he'd be in at Belmont the next day and that he expected to see me there around noon.

"I'm not myself, Arthur," I said now.

"You don't want me to actually believe you cared about this lumberjack, do you?"

"I liked him, Arthur."

"Oh, come on." Arthur rolled his eyes. "You couldn't have cared less until he got tired of being abused and took the unprecedented step of dumping you before you dumped him."

"That's actually not true," I said in a small, tired voice that didn't sound like me.

"Al, are you serious? Were you in love with this guy?" Arthur, for the first time in the long and brutal history of our friendship, was being sincere.

"I guess I was. Or something like that."

"Exactly," Arthur said victoriously, *"something like that.* You'll be fine in fifteen minutes. I'm proud of you for trying to show genuine feeling. It's kind of sexy. But you can stop now."

I smiled. But it wasn't fine. I had felt for Clayton. And for that awful William too. Maybe I was becoming one of those women I have long despised who goes through whorls of emotion each time she so much as kisses a guy. Maybe I was getting old and sensitive.

I shook the thought off and took out the red felt marker given me a few years earlier by the racing writer Steven Crist, whose box I'd once sat in at Saratoga. I'm not particularly superstitious, but it can't hurt to handicap with a pen given me by a man known as King of the Pick 6. I reviewed the bets I'd mapped out for the coming races and, for a little while, felt better.

But the racing gods weren't having it. I was off my game. I was emotional, and even though I'd never in my life let feelings leak into my handicapping, today I was doing exactly that.

I tried to pull myself together by taking a stroll out to the paddock. It was a beautiful, warm day, the sky an explosive blue. Even the grooms and assistant trainers leading the horses to the saddling stalls looked relaxed, nearly glad to be alive. I leaned over the railing at the front of the viewing area and stared ahead.

"What is wrong with you, Alice Hunter?" It was just after the fifth race. Arthur had gotten through the first two legs of the Pick 6 with a 12-1 shot followed by a 5-1. He was feeling magnanimous, deigning to notice my unfit condition and the fact that I had not cashed a single ticket.

"I told you, Arthur," I made a hopeless shrugging gesture, "I'm a mess."

Arthur actually looked at me, right at me.

"Don't for a minute try to convince yourself that it's the lumberjack you're upset about. Your mother is dying."

"Like I needed you to remind me."

"It's just helpful to face facts sometimes."

"Since when do *you* ever face a fact?"

To my surprise, Arthur's face clouded over and he looked away and, I could have sworn, his eyes were bright and wet.

"My father's very sick, Alice."

That silenced me. I felt like a heel. Arthur had mentioned his father's illness months earlier. He'd mentioned it in passing, just letting the announcement dangle there between bits of verbal race analysis, and I'd never pressed him for details. Even when I'd told him about Mom, he hadn't brought it up and, I had to admit, I'd forgotten.

"What's the situation?" I asked in a hushed voice.

"Hanging on by a thread. A month or two."

"Oh," I said, barely more than a whisper.

"So we're in the same boat."

"Yeah."

"And you do realize it's your mother you're upset about, right? Please tell me you do."

"Yeah," I acknowledged.

"Okay. Now do some fucking sensible wagering, would you?"

I smiled.

But I didn't have it in me.

I cashed a little exacta on the sixth race and called it a day.

"When will I see you again?" Arthur asked as I stood up to go.

"I don't know. Soon."

"Okay," he shrugged. "Take care of yourself, Alice."

It sounded strange to me. Like he never planned to see me again. Like we'd taken our relationship a little further than ever before by briefly alluding to our dying parents and now had to go our separate ways. We had sullied what had been a perfectly functional superficial liaison. I hesitated, looking down at Arthur, who was busy with his notebook.

"What?" He looked up.

"Nothing."

"I know. I love you too. Now beat it, punk."

It was dark by the time I pulled Mom's tired Honda into her driveway. I was exhausted, my back was stiff, and I desperately needed a cigarette.

I extracted myself from the car, slowly, like an ancient, crippled person, fished my cigarettes out of my bag, and fired one up. I hadn't wanted to stink up Mom's car and now the reward came in the form of long-craved nicotine. I leaned back against the vehicle and closed my eyes for all of two seconds before Eloise opened Mom's front door and Candy came racing out to greet me. She was squeaking and leaping into the air. I scooped her into my arms and let her lick my ears and chin. She nearly choked she was so excited.

"Hi, Elo," I said to my sister, who was leaning in the doorway, preventing the other dogs from bounding out.

"Hey," she replied. "How was Clayton?"

"Wants nothing to do with me."

"What?" Eloise tilted her head. At that moment, a dog I'd never seen before stuck his head between her knees and gazed out at me. He was white with a tan spot over his left eye. His enormous ears stood straight up like a rabbit's.

"Clayton gave me my walking papers," I said with ambivalence. I didn't want to go through the whole thing right this minute. "What's that?" I asked, indicating the big white dog head.

"Mickey. He was about to be put to sleep. Some friend of Mom's was frantically on the horn to all the crazy dog people in the state and Mom agreed to take him even though she can barely speak. I suppose this means, by extension, that you've agreed to take him. Ava and I have already picked out the ones we're taking."

"Oh." I stubbed out my cigarette, put Candy down, and walked up to the door. Eloise moved aside to let me in but Mickey just stood there, slowly wagging his very long tail.

"Hey, buddy," I said, squatting down next to the beast.

The skinny spotted pit bull didn't look me in the eyes, didn't even sniff me. Just stood there wagging and looking slightly past me, as I petted his broad but fleshless shoulders. His spine and ribs were sticking out and there were yellow stains all over his mostly white coat. After I'd been petting him for several minutes, he carefully reached his muzzle toward my face and licked my ear.

All the while, both Candy and Eloise were staring at me.

"What's his story?" I asked my sister. "Where'd he come from?"

"A cop found him in the Bronx. Brought him to the pound. He was in there two weeks and had one day to go before the gas chamber. Some pit bull rescue lady Mom knows had seen him and knew how sweet he was, so when his number came up on the euthanization list, she got on the phone. Mom was too weak to talk so I spoke to the lady, and then Ava and I met her halfway down the thru-way and got the dog."

"I really like him," I announced. I was still squatting down next to him, and by now he'd ventured a few attempts at eye contact, discovered I wasn't taking it as a challenge, and had moved a step closer to me.

"That's good since you're going to have to find him a home. Come on, you're letting the bugs in." She ushered me inside.

Eloise and I sat down at the kitchen table. Candy jumped up onto me, and when Mickey came over to try putting his head in my lap, she growled at him. He looked apologetic and took a few steps back.

"I really like that dog," I repeated, staring at the skinny beast. The big tan spots over his hips made him look like a cow. A skinny cow with an enormous pit bull head.

"What's wrong with you, Alice?"

"What do you mean?"

"You just keep saying that you like that dog."

"What's wrong with that? Look at this dog." I reached for Mickey's enormous head. He looked me directly in the eyes this time as he gently wagged his tail.

"Tell me what happened with Clayton."

"He said he'd had enough of me. He's getting back with his ex-wife."

"I didn't know he had an ex-wife."

"Yeah. He does. But I really don't want to talk about him. Tell me about Mom."

"Still dying," Eloise said, surprising me with what could only be construed as an attempt at levity. "It might just be days now," she added.

"Should I go over and see her?"

"Not now. I was there right before you got back. She's sleeping. In the morning we'll go."

I nodded.

"How's Ava?" I asked.

"Fine," Eloise shrugged, "she was supposed to go to Paris to do some print ad for a perfume company but she canceled in light of Mom's condition."

"That was sweet of her."

"I know. It's weird."

"Yeah." I nodded, understanding all too well. It was discomforting when lovers behaved like people who actually cared.

Eloise and I spent a companionable sisterly evening together. She cooked couscous for us and helped me with evening dog chores before heading off to Ava's. After she left, as the dogs started settling in on various surfaces throughout the house, I went into the living room and lay down on the couch. Candy curled up in a ball at my feet. Mickey, who hadn't let me out of his sight, wedged his body next to mine, put his head on my shoulder, and, within a few seconds, started snoring. I crooked my neck in order to stare at him. He was the most beautiful thing I'd ever seen.

12. ELOISE

Ron was licking my feet and Ava was sitting at the far edge of the bed, sulking. It was evening now and I'd been back and forth from Ava's to Mom's several times but had only seen my mother once. She was having a very bad day, even by the standards of the terminally ill, and had only been conscious for a few minutes. She had asked after Ava in a way that worried me, a way that implied she was wondering about my future, wanting to assure herself that I had found a mate. I tried to make her believe I had. I actually did believe I had. Until about 8 p.m. At which point Ava had started sulking.

"Cut it out, Ron," I said to the dog. This was his new thing. This obsessive licking of a human's hands or feet whenever he felt tension in the air.

Ron momentarily stopped bathing my feet and looked up at me.

"Go do something else," I said. He tilted his head, then went back to licking. I sat up and tucked my feet under me. Ron tried to lick my face.

Ava had her back to me. We had been fighting, ridiculously enough, about the baby's gender. She wanted a girl and had announced that the kidney bean–sized thing living in my belly was in fact female. I had told her I'd prefer a boy, at which she'd had an uncharacteristic fit of pique culminating in even more uncharacteristic sulking. She was sitting at the edge of the bed with her back to me. She was ignoring Ron's shenanigans.

"You're supposed to be nice to me," I ventured.

She spun around so fast I got dizzy.

"I am nothing but nice to you," she said violently.

"What's wrong, Ava? What did I do?"

"You don't want me to really be a part of this."

"A part of what?"

"Of your life. The baby's life. The end of your mother's life."

"What?" I stared at her with my mouth open. "Where are you getting this?"

"It doesn't matter. I just sense it."

"But it's not true, Ava," I said, reaching over to touch her arm.

She pulled her arm away.

"Ava, my love, please, what's this about?" I felt nauseous.

Ron was looking from me to Ava and back but was too concerned to lick now.

Ava's face knotted up and tears came to her eyes.

"I'm frightened of you," she said in a small, weak voice.

"Frightened? Of me? But why?"

"I see how your sister is. So proud of her black heart. Proud of all the hearts she's broken. She's harder than cement. I know you must be the same way and I'm just not seeing it."

"That's crazy, Ava, I'm not like Alice. I never have been. And anyway, even Alice isn't as bomb-proof as she pretends to be. She had her heart broken just yesterday."

"Alice?" Ava looked suspicious.

"Her jailbird. He's getting back with his ex-wife."

"I don't know whether that constitutes heartbreak."

"She loved him. In her own fashion."

"It's that *fashion* that concerns me. The Hunter girls fashion."

"We don't have a genetic defect," I said defensively. As much as I've always thought my sister a heartless slut, I don't want other people thinking of her as such or, worse, accusing me of being the same way.

"There is no Hunter girls fashion," I said, glowering at my girlfriend. "I have been through a fair amount of love affairs but so have you. In fact, probably more than me. You're the one who's a glamorous movie star with people of both genders clamoring at your door just to catch a glimpse of you. If you really want to get into all this, we can, just that I didn't think we ever would. I thought there was a level of trust between us that I hadn't experienced with others. It's part of what made me love you so immediately and so strongly."

Ava was staring at me and she looked shamed. Strands of her long blond hair were falling in her face. I reached over and pushed one of them back. I saw that there were tears in her eyes again.

"You can't *cry* on me," I said, "that's too girly. We can be lesbians, but we can't be pathetic, sniveling women."

"Crying is not pathetic, Eloise."

"Crying is, almost without fail, a ruse. A drama-seeking missile, not authentic emotion."

"Do you really believe that?"

"Of course."

"That explains a lot."

"About my black heart? About the Hunter girls fashion?"

"Yes," she said somberly.

At first I thought she was joking, playing with me. Then, when her face remained bunched and dark, I realized this was no game. She truly believed me to be emotionally defective.

I was torn. I wanted to be levelheaded, adult, functional, but my heart hurt.

"I'm going to my mother's," I said, getting up from the bed.

Ava said nothing. Stayed rooted to her spot at the edge of the bed. Ron looked at me expectantly as I pulled drawers open and threw on jeans and a white T-shirt.

"I'm taking Ron," I announced as I put on my socks.

"Why?"

"I need solace."

She gave me a dirty look.

Ron jubilantly followed me out of the bedroom and downstairs, where I snapped a leash onto his collar, slipped my feet into my sandals, and headed out the door to Mom's Honda that I'd been using.

Ron jumped into the backseat and sat up, alert and excited. I turned on the CD player and put on my beloved recording of Paul Anka's "You Are My Destiny" as performed by an obscure but great band called Ferdinand the Bull. I notched the volume up to nearly ear-splitting and peeled out of the driveway.

It was an inky night and driving through it should have scared me but I felt incapable of fear. I just drove.

By the time I got to Mom's twelve minutes later, I had listened to the song three times, singing along at the top of my lungs. *You are my destiny/You share my reverie.*

But I wasn't sure who I was singing to.

I left Ron in the car and went into Mom's kitchen to see which dogs were loose so Ron didn't have to deal with a full-on assault the moment he walked in. Several dogs barked and swarmed me. I patted heads and shushed and called out to Alice. I got no response, then found her in the living room, lying on the couch with headphones on. She was wearing blue and white striped pajamas and had her hair pulled on top of her head in an uncharacteristic ponytail. Mickey, the new pit bull, was wedged between Alice and the couch cushions with his enormous head resting in the crook of her neck. Alice's eyes were closed and she looked at peace; as I noticed this, I realized I couldn't remember ever seeing my sister at peace. I tiptoed back out of the living room and went to retrieve Ron since only Mickey and three others appeared to be loose.

When I came back in, Alice was standing in the kitchen looking dazed.

"Oh," she said, "where did you come from?"

In that moment it seemed like there were myriad ways to answer that question, but I opted for the straightforward.

"I was at Ava's."

"Do you want some cake?" Alice asked.

"Cake?"

"With white icing. Don't you like that?"

I studied her carefully. She was behaving very strangely. Remembering that I liked cake with white icing? She had never been one to bother remembering those little life details, knowledge of which signified a level of intimacy Alice and I had never really had.

"Yes," I said, "I love cake with white icing. How did you know that?"

"What do you mean?"

"You never remember things like that."

Alice looked confused. She sat down heavily on one of the kitchen chairs. Mickey, who had been standing plastered to her side, tried to climb into her lap.

"No, Mickey." She gently pushed the big spotted dog away. "I'm sorry, Eloise," she said, looking up at me, "I'm sorry."

Just as I'd never seen Alice look at peace, so had I never heard her apologize sincerely. I thought I might start weeping so I turned to the fridge and pulled open the door, nearly yanking it off its hinges in my quest to view this cake with white icing.

"No," Alice said to my back, "there, on the counter."

I glanced over and saw a frumpy white cake. It looked homemade.

"Who made this?"

"Me."

"You're *baking*?"

"If I'm going to hole up here in the woods after Mom is gone, I'd better learn to cook."

It all ripped me apart. Her talking about our mother being gone, the idea that Alice was opening herself up to something as banal as cooking. Everything was shifting, nothing was as it always had been.

I started crying then. I don't remember the exact moment. Whether it was taking the first bite of the homely but delicious cake, or maybe when Alice extracted from me the details of the fight with Ava. But the tears came and Alice wrapped me in her arms and held me for a long, long time.

We were like little kids then. The ocean of differences calm.

It was a strange feeling.

After tending to the dogs, we went into Mom's room together. Joe had called, asking us to bring some things over for her the next day. It hadn't been said out loud, but our mother seemed to want to stay at her lover's. Alice thought it had something to do with the dogs, with not wanting these creatures she had rescued to worry over her decline. I thought it had more to do with Mom wanting to be with Joe. Her last-minute love. Maybe it was neither. Maybe the newfound devotion of her daughters was too much for a sick woman to bear. Maybe we would never know.

Alice found Mom's favorite nightshirt in one of the dresser drawers and I was left to search through the hall closet for the Scrabble game that came with a Lazy Susan. After we'd stockpiled these items, along with face cream and bath oil, we both found ourselves frozen in our mother's bright-green bedroom. She'd been in this house for a long time and it was full of her. Full of pieces of her I had never known and might never come to know.

"She's dying," Alice said after we'd been quiet for several minutes.

"Yes," I replied simply.

Alice sat down heavily on the bed. Mickey immediately jumped up next to her and put the upper half of his body in her lap. She absentmindedly stroked his huge white head. A few seconds into this, Candy appeared, some instinct alerting her that her human was handing out affection to the new interloper. Candy put her delicate front paws on Alice's shoulder and leaned close to lick her ear. My sister, who had repeatedly told me how grossed out she is by licking of any sort, did not protest or move.

"I think I want to sleep in Mom's room tonight. Do you want to sleep in here too?" she asked.

"Yeah," I said, sitting down next to her on the bed, "I do."

Maybe it should have seemed odd. Two adult sisters who barely got along sharing a dying mother's bed with each other and with as many dogs as could fit. Maybe it wasn't odd. It was the natural evolution of everything falling apart.

I'd just gotten to sleep when I heard dogs barking and a light was thrown on. I opened my eyes and saw Alice standing in the bedroom doorway speaking with someone I couldn't see.

I sat up and craned my neck. It was Joe; his face was gray.

"It's time," he said, peering around Alice and seeing that I was awake.

"Time?"

"Your mother's time has come. Sooner than expected."

I didn't know what to say or do and, as Alice and Joe stared, waiting for Joe's words to have their effect on me, I grabbed hold of Ron, who was curled at my feet. I closed my eyes and squeezed the blond mutt.

"Come on, Eloise," Alice said, gently but firmly.

I got up. Took my clothes from the top of the dresser

and went into the bathroom to put them on. Ron followed me.

Alice and I moved around settling the dogs back in. She locked Mickey, Candy, Ron, and Ira in the bedroom with some chew toys since they were the likeliest candidates for anxiety over the humans departing at an unusual time.

We were all three silent as we followed Joe, who lit the way with a flashlight, over to his house.

Though I'd been in and out of Joe's house many times over the last week, I hadn't really noticed it and, in spite of everything, took a moment to marvel at the clean spaciousness of the place. From the outside, it was a somewhat humble-looking blue clapboard house. Inside, though, a tall ceiling soared over a big room holding nothing but a grand piano and a painting of a petulant nude woman.

"It's so lovely in here," I heard myself murmur, at which both Alice and Joe stared at me like I was insane.

Alice and I followed Joe beyond the vast room, down a hallway and into the bedroom, much of it taken over by carts filled with medicine. The hospice nurse, a thin red-headed woman who Joe had summoned a few hours earlier, was sitting on a straight-backed chair off in the far corner. She was reading a paperback and barely looked up when we came in. She was, I suppose, used to the scenes of death and the heartbreak of those left behind.

Mom looked awful. Even twelve hours earlier she had still looked like Kim Hunter, a comely fifty-something woman. Now, her face was hollow and gray. Her eyes were closed and her black hair was plastered to her skull. The nurse had an IV going and its threatening needle protruded from Mom's right hand. There had been days like this before. Days of IVs and oxygen and nurses and doctors. Mom had always bounced back. But she'd never looked like this.

"She was awake about fifteen minutes ago," Joe said.

He had taken a seat at the edge of the bed and was

looking down at Mom. He reached over to push a strand of hair off her clammy forehead. The sorrow in his face was almost unbearable and, in that moment, I felt much worse for him than for myself or Alice. Joe loved my mother like I'd never seen anyone love my mother.

Alice was kneeling at the other side of the bed. She had propped her forearms on the mattress and was staring at Mom, as if willing her awake.

"What happened?" I asked Joe, pulling a chair over so I was near him.

He looked confused.

"I mean, why . . . um . . . why the turn for the worse?" I felt like an idiot as soon as I said it. I'd always thought of cancer as a very slow killer, but I'd actually known several people who'd gone very quickly. "Never mind," I added, though Joe showed no signs of answering me.

I sat watching Joe and Alice stare at Mom. But something was gnawing at me.

"I'll be right back," I said, though neither Joe nor Alice even looked up.

I went through the big piano room and into the kitchen where there was an old-fashioned wall phone. I picked the receiver up, stared at the rotary dial, then slowly dialed Ava's number.

I let it ring twelve times, but nothing. I hung up and tried again. This time, on the sixth ring, her sleepy voice answered: "Yeah?" She sounded incredulous.

"It's me. Mom's dying. I'm at Joe's house. Will you come over?"

There was the slightest pause. Then: "I'll be right there."

I thought terrible things. Terrible because they were irrelevant things having nothing to do with the last moments of my mother's life. I thought about breakfast. I thought about Ava's lingerie. I thought about the time Alice hit the

Pick 6 for 122K and offered to buy me a car, back before I'd fallen in the manhole and struck it rich. I thought about everything except my mother and the many tendernesses and torments that had passed between us.

She was rattling now, that death-rattle sound, descriptions of which I remembered, maybe from Camus's *The Plague*, maybe from some other hideous but beautiful account of death. Her breathing was so labored I just wanted it to stop.

I got up several times. Walked through the piano room, into the kitchen, outside. Sometimes Ava would follow me. Not intruding. Just making sure I was all right.

I was there at the bedside, when, close to dawn, Mom opened her eyes.

Alice had gone to get Ira, the three-legged hound mix Mom had rescued six years earlier and still hadn't found a home for. Though Mom always claimed not to have favorites and not to consider any one of these orphans as her personal dog, it was understood that, in fact, Ira was very much her dog and, as such, had a right to say goodbye.

"Ira," Mom said in a tiny, hoarse voice.

"I thought you'd want to say goodbye," Alice said.

Mom's eyes got glassier. Ira put his lone front paw on the edge of the bed, wedging himself in between Joe and Alice, and gave Mom's shrunken, sweaty face a tentative lick. He intuited, as dogs do, that there was something gravely wrong. He was gentle with her.

"Ira," Mom said again.

This was her last word.

I saw her hand move. Scrabbling at the sheet, reaching for Joe's hand. Her own hand relaxed once it found his. I saw her gripping him fiercely. Then her eyes stared straight ahead.

Light was starting to show at the window.

"She wants us to go swimming," Joe said.

The nurse had closed Mom's eyes so she wouldn't keep staring out at those she'd left behind. Ira was whimpering. Alice was slumped in a chair. Ava was holding me.

"Swimming?" It was Randee, the nurse, who acknowledged that Joe had said something.

"Last night," Joe explained, "Kim told me she'd die by dawn and we should all go swimming. Specifically skinny-dipping."

Alice's head snapped up and she stared at Joe.

"That makes sense," Ava murmured.

"It does?" Alice sqinted at my girlfriend.

"Well," Ava seemed nervous now, "yes, sort of. To me."

"How so?" I asked Ava, turning to look at her tear-streaked face.

Ava had wept more than I had. More than Alice or even Joe.

"She wants us all to be together doing something liberating. Help release ourselves. And, by extension, her. She doesn't want us holding onto her. She has places to go."

"I think that's right." Joe was nodding.

"Where exactly are we supposed to go skinny-dipping?" I asked.

"We could go to the rock star's pool. He's never there," Alice said, referring to the musician who lived down the road. None of us were sure what band he was in, nor what his name was. Alice had seen him once and said he was sexy but I didn't even know what he looked like. Somewhere along the line, though, Mom had been introduced to him, yet she could never remember his particulars. He was just a nameless, loner rock star who had a big house with a huge pool that we could all see from the road.

"I'm sure he has some sort of elaborate security system and/or is home," I said.

"We don't need to break into the rock star's pool. There's a pond on Stoll Road," Joe said. "Her friend Janet's old house. It's been for sale for ages and Janet has long moved out. It has a lovely fresh-water pond. Kim and I spent many an evening there."

We all looked at him.

The pond was discussed at length as Mom lay there, still and gray and, I imagined, stiffening. A consensus was reached. We would go skinny-dipping and we would take all the dogs.

"We're just going to leave Mom here?" I asked no one in particular.

"Yes," Joe replied.

"Aren't there regulations against that kind of thing?" I asked, hoping that there were, hoping that the dead weren't just left to lie there while the living went swimming.

"I'll take care of everything," Randee spoke up.

We all turned to stare at her.

I wondered what taking care of everything might entail. Was there a medical examiner involved when someone died of cancer? Or would she just be moved straight to the funeral home in Kingston? I wanted to know. But not at this moment.

"So we just leave her," I said.

"She would want it that way," Joe said.

Under normal circumstances, I would not trust the opinion of one of my mother's lovers, but Joe was different, and these weren't normal circumstances.

I cast one more glance at my dead mother before we all migrated out of Joe's house and over to Mom's to collect dogs and beach towels.

I thought there was some likelihood of our getting arrested and it causing a big stir, not just on a local level but, due to Ava's presence, at an international level. As we pulled into the driveway of the vacant gray house on Stoll Road, I fantasized about the headline: *Larkin's Free Love Lark*.

Ava and I got out of her Volvo with Ron and Rosemary and Carlos and Lucy in tow.

Alice and Joe emerged from the van, unloading the rest of the dogs, including the infirm and aged ones who usually never went on these sorts of outings as they had trouble navigating anything more than a five-minute walk. But Joe had been insistent that all the dogs come. And we knew it's what Mom would have wanted.

The land was beautiful, a rolling green meadow edged by maple and pine, the house, set into the treeline, a simple but tasteful gray wood box with many windows.

"Are we completely certain no one is home?" I asked Ava.

"I'll find out," she said.

Joe and I watched her stride up to the house and ring a bell, following this up with a loud knock. When, after a few minutes, no one emerged with a shotgun, we decided we were safe.

The pond was at the far edge of the property, by Stoll Road. There was some chance of passing cars looking over and seeing us as the shrubs and trees set against the deer fencing didn't give complete privacy. Not that people in Woodstock would be particularly shocked at nude pond swimming, but some might try joining in.

"Eloise, what are you waiting for?" Alice had, in the space of a few seconds, stripped off her clothing and was standing, pale and skinny and naked near the pond, throwing sticks in for the dogs to chase.

I took my shirt off then cast a glance toward the road where I saw a cyclist laboring up the hill. When the guy reached the top, he sat back down on the saddle, reached for his water bottle, glanced over, and, I think, did a double take.

I waved and took my pants off, embracing the spirit of the moment.

Hi, Mom, I thought, knowing she'd appreciate this.

I wasn't sure if she was in a position to hear me. Though I have some notion that the dead linger and look down on the living, particularly in the weeks immediately following death, there might be some sort of waiting period after the time of physical death.

I saw Ron standing at the edge of the pond, barking at Ava. We didn't know how Ron felt about water. He waded through the creeks on the Rabbit Hole trail just fine, but he'd never been in over his head.

I moved to go help him in, and at that moment, he jumped in and started biting at the water as he paddled over to Ava.

I ran to the edge of the pond and jumped in. It was colder than I'd expected and I swam furiously toward the edge, planning to climb out, but Ava floated up to me and pulled me back down into the water. Then she kissed my forehead.

"This is nice," she said, like we were at some civilized wine-tasting party in Europe.

"Thank you," I said, feeling like her saying that signaled her approving of my loopy family and, by extension, of me.

"Are we okay?" I asked, looking into her big blue eyes, "or are you just being here for me because my mother is dead?"

Ava looked at me long and hard. "Eloise Hunter," she said, "I am in love with you. Every part of you. Including the parts that scare me. I'm sorry I was awful earlier. I don't freak out often, but when I do, I really do."

"Is that a yes?"

"Yes," she said, touching my face.

I believed her. I believed she would try to love me. And that was more than I had believed in years.

There were thirty or so minutes of chaos with dogs and humans mingling in the pond. Now and then, Joe and Alice and Ava and I would look at one another and small, sad smiles would pass between us.

Finally, when we were getting shriveled and cold and

most of the dogs had had enough, we all got out and began drying ourselves off.

The sun had come up. It was a clear, beautiful day.

13. ALICE

I had been trying to get rid of the toothless, one-eyed Chihuahua for four weeks now. This had been one of my dead mother's last wishes, that, first and foremost, I find a home for Carlos, the charismatic but unattractive Chihuahua who'd been rescued from an upstate meth lab nine months earlier. But Carlos, in spite of his diminutive size, was a hard sell to would-be adopters. Even people specifically in the market for Chihuahuas wanted dogs with teeth and two eyes. They didn't care that Carlos was genial and intelligent and played well with others.

I had a new prospect lined up. A man who'd seen Carlos on Petfinder.com and filled out an e-mail application. This prospect was due to stop by in forty-five minutes, but the thought of impending human contact had not yet motivated me to shed my dead father's bathrobe, put on some clothing, and run a brush through my hair.

I had Carlos propped on the kitchen table and was rubbing him with a rag, the way you would a horse, to make his coat shine. Mickey sat, as ever, at my side, carefully studying what I was doing, the way he carefully studied everything I did, everything any of the other dogs did.

I had started examining Carlos's gums when the dogs, a mere six of them now, all ran to the door, some barking, some growling, some just standing wagging their tails.

I put Carlos down, closed my robe, and yanked the door open, expecting either some local political candidate or a solicitous handyman type here to offer his services.

Instead, I found a dark-haired strapping guy standing there looking incredibly earnest.

"Yeah?" I said, squinting at this apparition.

"Hi, I'm Matthew?" He didn't seem convinced of this. "About the Chihuahua?"

"Oh . . ." I said. In the same moment I realized the guy was attractive and that I was wearing a filthy bathrobe and hadn't brushed my hair in days. "Right," I added, "come in."

"I'm sorry, am I early?" he asked politely.

"Yes," I said.

"Oh," he looked dejected, actually hung his head the way a child might, "I have a really bad memory. I wasn't sure what time I said I'd come by."

"It's fine, come on in." I ushered him past the wall of dogs at the door.

Matthew came into the kitchen then squatted down on his haunches and opened his arms. The big dogs made a beeline for him and Mickey, in his enthusiasm, knocked the man backwards. He fell on his ass and started laughing. Meanwhile, poor Carlos stood off to the side, looking peevish, as if he knew this particular human was here to see him and the big dogs had ruined it.

"This," I said, scooping the Chihuahua up, "is Carlos." I deposited him in Matthew's lap.

I never would have pegged this big manly man as a Chihuahua type, but to see him holding the dog, looking at poor Carlos as if he were the most beautiful thing ever, well, it was heartwarming. And my heart hadn't been warmed in several months.

After a few minutes, I excused myself and went up to Mom's bedroom, which I still couldn't think of as my bedroom, to put some clothes on. I found a pair of blue jeans on the floor by the laundry hamper, a white tank top nearby. I held the tank top up to my nose and sniffed. Not too bad. I put it on. I went into the bathroom to look at myself in the mirror and actually gasped audibly, causing Mickey, who had followed me upstairs, to tilt his enormous white head.

"Shit," I said aloud. I looked awful. No sooner had I realized this than I also realized I didn't really care. Sure, the guy was a big attractive slab of a man but I had sworn those off.

I went back into the bedroom where there was a phone by the bed. I dialed Ava's landline, hoping Eloise would pick up. She did.

"Hi, Alice," she said in that soft, tired voice she'd had for a few weeks now as her pregnancy progressed. She still didn't look wildly pregnant but she was weak and weepy and swollen and Ava had cancelled a film in order to stay home tending to her and the four dogs of Mom's they still hadn't found homes for.

"There's a very attractive man in the kitchen," I said without preamble.

"What?"

I explained.

"And why are you telling me this?"

"Because I don't know what to do. I feel stirrings."

"Stirrings?"

"You know, of the old me. I want to pounce on this guy."

"Really?" Eloise, who had spent years lecturing me on what she perceived as my indiscriminate sexual rapaciousness, almost sounded happy about this. She had, for the last few weeks, been nagging me about my depression. About the way I seldom changed out of my dead father's bathrobe and just sat morosely in our dead mother's house trying to find homes for our dead mother's dogs.

"Really," I said. "But I feel disjointed at the prospect of pouncing. I mean, I feel like I'm not my old self. I won't know how to proceed."

"It's just like riding a bike," Eloise assured me. "You'll be fine. Go for it, Alice. You need something to pull you out of your torpor."

"Yes," I said. "Okay."

I started asking her about herself, but she told me to get off the phone and tend to the strapping man in the kitchen.

I found him laying flat on his back, with Carlos on his chest, Candy under his right arm, Lucy licking his face, and Mickey standing near his head. It was a striking vision.

"I guess the dogs like you."

"Oh," he said, sitting up, "you're back." He glanced up. "Wow. You put clothes on."

"Yes. I do actually get dressed sometimes. I've just been a little low. My mother died."

"I'm sorry." He didn't take it further. Didn't ask when or how and I was grateful for that.

We looked at each other. He was now cradling Carlos like a baby.

I started in on the dog questions and learned that Matthew lived alone in a rented cabin where, yes, he was allowed to have pets but, no, he didn't presently have any other pets.

"And what kind of work do you do?"

"Trees."

"Trees?"

"Everything to do with trees. I cut 'em down. I make tables with them. I like trees."

"Right," I said, envisioning reporting to Eloise that the strapping man really liked trees.

What are you doing later? I thought, but for some reason didn't ask.

"Well," he said, gently putting Carlos on the ground and then standing up, "is there anything else?"

Would you like to go upstairs? I thought, but, again, didn't ask.

"I think you're good for Carlos but I want to sleep on it and you should too."

"Okay," he said in his big, soft voice.

He was standing close to me, looking down at me. I

could imagine what he tasted like, what he'd feel like. There were just a few inches between us. I could have moved closer, lifted my face up to his big beautiful mug. He might have been surprised. But he would go with it. One thing would lead to another, and there we'd be, a tangled mess of limbs and sheets and body fluids.

"Okay then," he said, as if he knew what had just gone on inside me.

He turned toward the door. I saw him out. Watched him get into a big blue pick-up truck.

"What the fuck is wrong with you, Alice?" I asked aloud when he'd pulled out of the driveway and I'd gone back into the house.

Mickey looked at me and tilted his head. Candy wagged her abbreviated tail. Carlos let out an excited bark.

As the day progressed, as I wandered through dog chores, gambling chores, and even a few house chores, I thought about Matthew, the tree man. I could see the end before I'd even gotten to the beginning.

I tried calling Eloise again but there was no answer. I thought about calling Ida, Mom's NA pal who seemed to be cultivating a friendship with me. But I didn't have the strength to try explaining my plight to someone who didn't know me. Though it was an absurd thing to do, particularly around post time for the seventh race, when Arthur would be in the middle of the Pick 6 sequence, I dialed his number.

"What?" he yelled into the phone.

"It's Alice," I said with as much force as I could muster.

"I know. Why are you calling me? I'm getting slaughtered out here. Goddamned state-bred turf sprints."

"I don't play the Pick 6 when those unmanageable races are in the sequence," I said loftily.

"Did you just call to tell me how smart you are?"

"No. I need friendship and succor."

"And you're calling *me*?"

"You're my friend, Arthur, admit it."

"Alice, what the fuck is wrong with you?"

"I'm not sure." I was actually relieved to find Arthur back in usual form. Right after Mom died, he had been sweet and sensitive and had gone so far as to leave New York City—which he only ever did to go to Saratoga—and come up here for the memorial service. It had moved me and I suppose that's why I was calling him now.

"Well, it must be bad if you're turning to me for a shoulder to cry on. What is it?"

"I really don't know. Just general malaise, I guess."

"Alice, what the fuck is wrong with you calling me at the track using words like *malaise*? What is this? You've got to get out of the woods. You're falling apart. Just sell your mother's house and come back to the city already. You've made your point. I actually miss you. Now come on."

"You miss me? Really?"

"Jesus, get ahold of yourself, Hunter. I'll start to think you like me or something."

"But I adore you."

"Of course you do. But you don't actually *like* me. Are we done here? I gotta go."

"Yeah," I sighed, "you can go. You *have* made me feel better."

Arthur growled a goodbye and hung up in my ear. And I truly did feel better. Even though I was considering moving permanently into Mom's house in the woods, even though I'd suddenly sprouted a moral compass and couldn't manage to pounce on the tree cutter, even though most of the things in my life were upended, Arthur was the same. A constant. A reminder that I could always go back.

That night, I called Matthew and told him he could have Carlos.

"Oh," he said, so softly, "thank you so much. I'll take great care of him."

"I know."

I thought of innumerable other things to say but kept them to myself. We arranged a time the next day when Matthew would come get his new companion.

I got used to watching the dogs leave. After Carlos, there was a rash of successful adoptions. Harvey went to a racing writer I knew from Kentucky, Lucy went to a marathon runner in nearby Kingston. All but Simba, a sweet, lazy black Lab, had been placed in suitable homes and it was just Mickey, Candy, Simba, and me. It got so the house actually felt empty. But I didn't have the strength to be active in rescue the way Mom had. I could never bring myself to go to the kill shelters, plucking some dogs while leaving the rest to their fates. I had decided that, if and when a dog in need presented itself, I would help, but I wouldn't go out of my way to bring in new orphans. I had enough to do trying to keep up with my work, taking care of the house and Mickey and Candy, and not losing my mind.

One afternoon, there was a knock at the door. Candy went crazy, barking and growling, while Simba and Mickey just stared at the door with their tales wagging gently. I went so far as to run a hand through my hair and make sure my fly was closed before opening the front door.

"Can I borrow a cup of sugar?"

It was Joe. The neighbor. Mom's lover.

"Sugar?" I squinted at him.

"Sugar." He smiled, offering his well-organized and very white teeth. Ira, Mom's three-legged hound who had moved in with Joe the day she died, was faithfully at his side.

"You're really just checking to make sure I haven't gone insane, aren't you? Did Eloise tell you to come over?"

I had been blowing my sister off for more than a week

now. She wanted me to go with her to various prenatal appointments and yoga classes but I kept turning her down in favor of holing up by myself, with just dogs for company.

"I haven't spoken to Eloise in days," Joe protested. "Why, is she questioning your sanity?" He entered the kitchen and looked around, like he'd never seen the place before.

"Eloise has always questioned my sanity. But now more than ever. I told her I'm staying here. Going to sell my father's house in Queens."

"But that's fantastic, Alice," Joe said, his whole face lighting up in a way I hadn't seen since Mom died.

"It is?" Eloise thought my decision to move to the woods so uncharacteristic she'd asked if I wanted Ava to recommend a therapist.

"I'm really glad, Alice."

"Do you miss Mom?" I heard myself ask. Just like that. No warning.

Joe flinched.

"I'm sorry. I didn't mean to be so abrupt."

"No," he said softly, "it's okay. You have no way of knowing just how badly I miss Kimberly."

What had possessed me to ask such a question? Of course he missed her.

"Sometimes I need to censor myself," I said.

"No," Joe replied slowly, "no. That was one of the things your mother most admired about you and Eloise. The way you both just say whatever comes to mind. Which you got from her."

"Yeah," I felt myself smiling, "we did get that from her."

Joe and I fell silent. I made coffee and offered him some of the wretched banana bread I'd baked earlier. The only person I'd found so far who'd eat anything I cooked was Mom's NA friend Ida. She was obviously trying really hard to win my friendship.

Joe knew better than to eat anything I'd cooked.

"No thanks," he said as politely as possible.

"Mickey loves it," I said. "Jumped up on the counter last time I made it and devoured the entire loaf, including the plastic it was wrapped in."

"I don't know how to put this, Alice, but if a pit bull who was just a few months ago dying of starvation on the streets is your arbiter of culinary success, well . . ."

"You're lucky my domestic ambitions and accompanying expectations of appreciation are so minimal or I might punch you."

Joe smiled. I smiled.

Eventually, he actually borrowed a cup of sugar, then pecked me on each cheek and left.

Outside, dusk had come.

It was time to feed the dogs.

Also available from Akashic Books

INFINITY BLUES poetry by Ryan Adams
286 pages, trade paperback original, $15.95 (hardcover, $24.95)

"Ryan Adams, one of America's most consistently interesting singer/songwriters, has written a passionate, arresting, and entertaining book of verse. Fans are going to love it, and newcomers will be pleased and startled by his intensity and originality. The images are vivid and the voice is honest and powerful."
—Stephen King, author of *Duma Key*

"*Infinity Blues* is Ryan Adams at his personal, unforgettable best. Strong and beautiful and funny and pure. Like all his work, it's soul poetry of the highest order."
—Cameron Crowe, filmmaker

BROOKLYN NOIR
edited by Tim McLoughlin
350 pages, trade paperback original, $15.95
*Winner of Shamus Award, Anthony Award, Robert L. Fish Memorial Award; finalist for Edgar Award, Pushcart Prize.

Brand new stories by: Maggie Estep, Pete Hamill, Arthur Nersesian, Ellen Miller, Nelson George, Sidney Offit, Ken Bruen, and others.

"*Brooklyn Noir* is such a stunningly perfect combination that you can't believe you haven't read an anthology like this before. But trust me—you haven't. Story after story is a revelation, filled with the requisite sense of place, but also the perfect twists that crime stories demand. The writing is flat-out superb, filled with lines that will sing in your head for a long time to come."
—Laura Lippman, winner of the Edgar, Agatha, and Shamus awards

QUEENS NOIR
edited by Robert Knightly
342 pages, trade paperback original, $15.95

Brand new stories by: Maggie Estep, Denis Hamill, Alan Gordon, Tori Carrington, Joseph Guglielmelli, Kim Sykes, and others.

"Keen Queensian eyes will find that no mistakes were made in capturing the borough, from its subway lines to its edgy sensibility."
—*Queens Times Ledger*

RUINS a novel by Achy Obejas
300 pages, trade paperback original, $15.95
*A Barnes & Noble Discover Great New Writers selection

"Daring, tough, and deeply compassionate, Achy Obejas's *Ruins* is a breathtaker. Obejas writes like an angel, which is to say: gloriously . . . one of Cuba's most important writers."
—Junot Díaz, Winner of the Pulitzer Prize for Fiction

THE AGE OF DREAMING
a novel by Nina Revoyr
320 pages, trade paperback original, $15.95
*Selected by the *Advocate* as one of the Best Books of 2008

"*The Age of Dreaming* elegantly entwines an ersatz version of film star Sessue Hayakawa's life with the unsolved murder of 1920s film director William Desmond Taylor. The result hums with the excitement of Hollywood's pioneer era . . . Reminiscent of Paul Auster's *The Book of Illusions* . . . [with] a surprising, genuinely moving conclusion."
—*San Francisco Chronicle*

THE SACRIFICIAL CIRCUMCISION OF THE BRONX
a novel by Arthur Nersesian
300 pages, hardcover, $22.95

"Arthur Nersesian's fresh take on the saga of legendary urban planner Robert Moses unfolds as a double narrative, each interlocking half as compelling as the other. This riveting, intricately plotted novel carries the reader through various worlds—some real, others fantastic—to a breathtaking finale."
—Kate Christensen, author of *The Great Man*